To Jessica and Olivia
For cheering Naomi on from the beginning

PIECES

ALSO BY MICHELLE D. ARGYLE

PIECES

THE BREAKAWAY BOOK 2

MICHELLE D. ARGYLE

MDA
BOOKS

Summary: "Naomi Jensen runs away with her former kidnapper while also trying to heal from the emotional scars of Stockholm syndrome."

Edited by Diane Dalton

Cover design and typesetting by Melissa Williams Design

I

April

"WHO IS THAT WOMAN YOU KEEP DRAWING?"

Naomi looked up from her sketchpad and smiled. On Wednesday mornings, Finn was the waiter at the Java Lounge café. He had surfer hair—thick, wavy brown locks swept across his forehead. It fell into his face whenever he looked down. Naomi wondered how he kept from running into the tables. Somehow, he never did.

"Well?" Finn asked, leaning closer to look at her drawing.

She slid her arm over the entire picture. She and Finn always talked when he brought out her order, but he had never asked her about her drawings before. It was new territory for their casual friendship. "She's a character from a novel."

"Oh?" He leaned even closer, the carafe in his hands tipping dangerously close to her sketchpad. "Which novel? Is it one you're writing?"

She inched the sketchpad away from him. A smirk crossed her face. "You know I don't write. It's a scene from a favorite book, that's all."

The smell of the coffee in the carafe was stronger than the regular smell of cinnamon rolls, flaky pastries, and whipped cream drifting through the Java Lounge in the mornings. The coffee was straight black. It reminded Naomi of waking up in the mornings at the house where she had been held captive for a year. She squeezed her eyes shut, trying to will the memory away. It was over. Over. But she could never get the house out of her head. Their house. Eric's house. She didn't know what to call it, even two years after her escape. They had made coffee every morning, so coffee would always remind her of them. She decided from now on she would call it *the house* and leave it at that.

Finn tried to peek at the sketch. She decided it wouldn't hurt to show it to him, and lifted her arm from the paper, allowing him a good view. It was the beginning outlines of a woman walking into the ocean.

"You're really good," he said in a voice filled with awe. He straightened, but stayed rooted to his spot. "Why are you choosing film instead of art as your major?"

She laughed. "You don't think film is a form of art?"

"Of course it is! I'm just looking at your sketch. It's so good."

She looked at the sketch, beaming. The reason she came to the Java Lounge was because it was a place where people left her alone. That was, until she met Finn. She liked the way he was genuinely interested in speaking with her, but she was surprised at how great it felt when he complimented her art.

"Thanks," she said after an awkward pause. "Film seems more practical, that's all. It combines a lot of different art mediums I love."

He nodded slowly, as if he had to chew on her words for a bit. He had a dimple in his left cheek that made him look lopsided in an endearing sort of way, and a wicked-looking yin and yang tattoo on his left bicep. It was partially hidden by his T-shirt sleeve, but the longer Naomi looked at the tattoo, the more she realized Finn's skin was the sweet color of caramel.

"Did you apply to any art or film schools?" he asked. "There's one in California—USC. It's supposed to be really great. I have a few friends going there."

She tried not to shudder at the mention of California. Jesse was in California, in federal prison. She would wait for him to get out—that was her promise to herself. Five years was his total sentence. It was a short amount of time for what he had actually done, thanks to his plea bargain and obvious desire to change. The others hadn't been so cooperative. Eric, Evelyn, and Steve had received much longer sentences, between fifteen and twenty-five years. Naomi had no trouble thinking of them as kidnappers and thieves, but Jesse was different. He had set her free. The first two years of his sentence had been torture for her, but that didn't mean she couldn't get through the rest.

Finn was watching her, waiting for an answer to his question.

Her mouth dropping open a little, she leaned away. "No, I was thinking about Berkeley at one point, but Harvard just . . . happened. The program here isn't bad." Her voice was beginning to sound edgy and defensive. She shut her mouth before she said anything stupid.

Finn shrugged. "Well, Harvard is great no matter what you do." He looked at the sketch again. "So why is she walking into the ocean?"

She frowned. "I know it looks like she's trying to drown herself, but I keep trying to fix it so she doesn't look like that. In the book, she dies."

Finn was quiet. His blue eyes were focused on the sketch and Naomi wondered what kind of judgments were forming in his head.

"So you want to change the end of the book?" he asked.

"I want to draw her happier, that's all. I haven't managed it so far, but I'll get there."

He nodded, looking confused, until a man called out to him a few tables down. He was lifting his coffee cup for a refill.

"Be right back," Finn said, and hurried off.

Sorry he was gone, Naomi picked up her pencil to begin drawing again. She felt a hot blush creep up her cheeks as she noticed her racing pulse. Finn always made her feel this way when he talked to her. Falling for him was not what she had planned when she had decided to open herself up to a harmless friendship. She needed to get through the next three years without attaching her heart to anyone. She wanted Jesse and nobody else. But perhaps a friend wasn't so bad . . . as long as she kept her distance.

When Finn returned, she looked up to see his expression set firmly with determination.

"So, we've been friends for a while," he said, swallowing. "I mean, you know, every Wednesday when you come in. I mean . . ." He winced and started over. "If you aren't busy some night, would you want to get together for a drink or something?" He held up his free hand. "Just as friends if you want."

She opened her mouth. She really enjoyed his company, but he didn't know about Jesse. She wasn't sure how to respond.

"I can't drink yet, legally," she said, and inwardly cringed at using the dumbest excuse she could possibly think of to get out of a date, even if he wasn't going to call it a date. "I don't turn twenty-one until May."

"Beginning or end?"

"Beginning."

"That's in two weeks. Close enough. We can meet at my place so nobody asks for ID. I live off-campus."

She laughed. "You think I'm going to fall for that?"

Pulling a sarcastic expression, he replied, "Are you really that staunch about the legal age limit?"

"I didn't used to be." She looked away and rolled her pencil back and forth across her drawing. This was why she usually avoided talking to people. She should have known her friendly conversations with Finn would eventually lead to her past. Everything stemmed back to the kidnapping, to the one thing she couldn't mention. Ever. It was as if the center of her life was that single year of being held captive, a force as strong as gravity, constantly pulling her back to the memories, the emotions, the house, the smells, the food. Even now, the coffee from the carafe, the way Finn stood over her like Jesse always had, waiting for her to give in, made her palms sweat. He was the kind of guy she might have been drawn to if Jesse had never happened. Her counselor's words repeated in her head. *Don't be afraid to let your past and present come together to create something new. Don't be afraid . . .*

But she didn't want her past and present to come together. She didn't want to date Finn, even if he did have gorgeous eyes and skin and a wicked tattoo. Oh, hell, who was she kidding?

"I'm sorry," she said with an apologetic glance at him. "I can't date anyone right now."

Finn shrugged. Naomi expected disappointment to fill his eyes, but he seemed fine. In fact, he seemed pleased. He was probably the kind of guy who loved the chase. "All right, as long as we can still be friends."

"Of course!" The last thing she wanted to do was lose him. The truth was he was her only friend outside of Jesse. The only other person she could possibly consider a friend was her housemate, and that was pushing the definition. Becca was studying law. Since she was rarely home, they hardly ever had meaningful conversations.

"Good thing, then." Finn gave her a warm smile and left to refill somebody else's coffee cup.

Naomi picked up her pencil and continued drawing. After a moment, she snuck a glance at Finn. He was a nice guy. He didn't steal jewelry. He didn't kidnap people. He turned around, catching her gaze. A smile spread across his face as he passed by. When he was gone, her shoulders slumped. He really was great, but at the same time, it was sad how low she had set the bar for "nice guy".

II

May

CLASSES WERE ENDING SOON. NAOMI SPENT AS MUCH time as she could at the library, studying for exams. She skipped going to the café two Wednesdays in a row, knowing if she saw Finn again she would give in to meeting him for a drink or a movie or hanging out. Something other than their happy conversations while she ate her almond cake and drank her iced tea. On the third Wednesday, her birthday, she woke up and stared at the clock. Eight-thirty. Sunlight filtered through the half-closed blinds, falling across her nightstand where her phone sat covered in a thin layer of dust from the past few days. She hardly ever took the phone with her. She never called anyone and nobody called her, except for her mother.

"How are your classes, honey? Are you meeting nice people? Have you met with your counselor this month?"

As much as she had grown to love her mother recently, their relationship still felt awkward, a child learning how to walk, always falling and skinning its knee. The awkwardness wasn't a problem as far as Naomi was concerned. At least she knew her mother loved her now. At least they could talk to each other.

She picked up her phone and brushed off the dust as she thought about the dimple in Finn's cheek. Then she thought about Jesse and his red hair and all his freckles. He was so not her type, but her heart beat faster every time she thought about him. She wanted him to hold her. She wanted to belong to him. He was strong and knew what he wanted—to change for the better. He had turned himself in after setting her free, and that was no small matter. She didn't know anything about Finn. Compared to Jesse, he was probably boring.

But even boring sounded good right now. It was her birthday and nobody cared. Jesse cared, of course, but there was nothing he could do sitting in a cell. He wasn't even allowed to send her a card or letter. Her mother might call her later. Becca might bring home a cupcake or something, if she remembered. Last year they had stayed up all night watching old 1980's sitcoms and eating French silk pie from the Java

Lounge. That was because Naomi had told Becca it was her birthday. This year, she didn't feel like reminding anyone.

She remembered her birthday with her kidnappers. Jesse had given her an iPod. That was the same night Eric and Evelyn's father had died in prison of a heart attack. That was the night she had started falling in love with Jesse. She recounted the kidnapping events to her counselor, a woman named Stacy Richards, every third Friday of the month. When she talked about the memories, they sounded ridiculous.

"Your situation was not normal," Stacy said the last time they had met. "Most kidnap victims are physically abused. These people wanted to . . . adopt you, in a way."

"They wanted to keep my mouth shut," Naomi answered, annoyed that Stacy was confused. She wasn't supposed to be confused. She was her counselor. She was supposed to know everything.

"Oh, I understand that, Naomi. In fact, I think it's excellent progress that you answered my comment in such a way. It shows you're understanding the situation for what it was."

But no matter how much Naomi spilled her fears and thoughts to Stacy, it never felt real. So many counseling sessions over two years. Everyone wanted to fix her, but she wasn't sure she was even broken.

She brushed off the last of the dust from her phone and stared at the date glowing on the screen. Her birthday. Twenty-one. She was no longer in the awkward teen years and no longer in the limbo age of twenty. A serious adult now. Adults felt alive and important, and whether Jesse was here or not, she needed to feel alive, to share her feelings with someone outside of Stacy. She needed a friend. Someone. Anyone. Her life had become—or maybe it always had been—pathetic and lonely. The only time she had ever felt otherwise was with Jesse, and all he was at the moment was a memory.

Swinging her legs over the side of the bed, she looked at her backpack stuffed with books and papers. To hell with all of it. Her class started in an hour, but for the first time in two years she didn't want to go sit in a classroom. She wanted to go to the café to see Finn.

* * *

"Good morning," Finn said after she sat down and pulled out her sketchbook. Her heart pounding, she looked up and stammered, "Almond cake and—"

"Iced tea, of course," he finished for her. Today he wore a faded blue T-shirt and a pair of jeans ripped on the left knee. Somehow, this worked with his personality and the surfer hair. She had asked him at one point if he surfed, and he had laughed. "Only once, but the water was freezing, even with a wetsuit. Not sure I'm a fan."

He was smiling at her. "Anything else you want to order?"

She kept her attention on his eyes, avoiding the coffee carafe in his hands. She wouldn't let her memories ruin what she wanted right now. She suddenly wondered if her two-week absence had lessened Finn's attraction to her, but as quickly as she asked herself the question, she noticed a sparkle in his eyes that put her both at ease and on edge. What a fine line this was. She valued his friendship, but keeping it on the friend level was going to be difficult.

"No," she said, trying to smile.

She looked at her phone sitting next to her sketchpad. If her mother called about her birthday, she didn't want to miss it. She wasn't sure if that was incredibly sentimental or incredibly naïve for someone turning twenty-one.

"Wait," she said, reaching out her hand before Finn turned to leave. "I think I want something else."

His half-smile widened as he looked down at her hand receding into her lap. "Oh?"

She could do this. She could. She was strong now, like Stacy was always telling her. She could keep everything in line.

"It's my birthday today."

Finn's smile widened even more, a grin deepening his dimple. With a nod, he urged her to go on.

She swallowed. "And I'm going to get chocolate cake instead of almond cake . . . and I . . . I'll take you up on your offer." He opened his mouth to speak, but she cut him off. "Drinks are fine, if that's what you want to do, but don't go getting any ideas I want to date you or anything, because I already have a boyfriend. This is just as friends, like you said before."

His smile fell, but not so far as to make him appear dejected. Perhaps a little shocked.

"A boyfriend? Have you had a boyfriend the whole time I've known you?"

He didn't sound upset. He shouldn't, she realized. She could tell he wasn't implying it was wrong for her not to have told him. He was simply surprised. "Yes, I have," she said, picking at a fingernail, "but he doesn't live here, and I never get to see him, so it's complicated."

That was putting it lightly.

"I see."

She knew he didn't really see, but who cared?

"So, tonight, then?" she asked. "Are you free?"

"I am." He glanced at his watch. "How about nine? I'll pick you up."

This was it. She was doing something, and it didn't involve Jesse. He would want her to be happy and make friends.

"That sounds great." Ripping a piece of paper from her sketchpad, she wrote down her address and phone number and handed it to him.

* * *

She tried on eight different outfits before deciding on a boring pair of jeans and a tight black shirt with a scoop neck. It was a safe outfit. It didn't scream 'sleep with me!' She hoped it whispered *'hey, let's hang out.'*

She looked at herself in the mirror and remembered the bedroom in the house, the smell of Evelyn's rain-scented fabric softener on the sheets. She remembered curling up next to Jesse in the evenings. He had been sleeping with her for a few nights before he decided to help her escape. Being with him in her room was her fondest memory. She knew it sounded terrible when she admitted to Stacy, "I loved sleeping with my kidnapper. I know that makes me sound like a freak. Maybe I am a freak." But Stacy hadn't treated her like a freak. She had said she understood the whole falling in love thing and that what had happened to her over the course of a year justified her decisions at the time. Naomi wasn't sure if that was true or if Stacy said crazy stuff like that to get her to talk.

"Are you *going out*?"

Becca stood in the doorway, her jaw dropping open as she watched Naomi fasten half her hair up with some bobby pins.

"Yes, but it's not a date."

"But you never go out. Ever."

"Yeah, well, I am now."

"Uh-huh. Well, you look hot. Does he know it's 'not a date'?" She made air quotes with her fingers to emphasize Naomi's own words.

"I don't look hot." She turned sideways, checking out her profile. Maybe her jeans were a little form-fitting, sexy and tight over her butt and thighs. And her shirt hugged her too, but what else was she supposed to wear? Sweat pants and an extra-large T-shirt?

"Do I?" she asked. "Really?"

"Yes, you do."

"Well, crap. He's just a guy—a friend. We're hanging out. It's my birthday."

Becca clapped a hand to her forehead. "I forgot it was your birthday! I'm sorry." She had pale skin and short black hair Naomi was sure she dyed. Her lips were deep red. She was going to make an intimidating lawyer someday, like a day-walking vampire ready to take anyone down.

"I didn't expect you to remember. I found something to do tonight, so don't worry about it."

"If you say so, but happy birthday, anyway."

"Thanks."

A knock on the door sent Becca into a frenzy. "Is that him? He's coming to pick you up? That means it's a date, I hope you know. What's his name?"

"Finn."

"Got it." She spun around and raced downstairs, her footsteps pattering like a scurrying mouse.

Looking at herself again, Naomi decided to stick with her outfit. Finn was waiting by the door when she walked down the stairs. He was wearing the same clothes as earlier. That was a good sign, but now she realized she shouldn't have changed.

"This is a nice place," he said, looking around. "Like, super-nice."

Naomi shrugged. She had forgotten how lucky she was to have rich parents who paid for her to rent an entire house, and a nice one at that. Becca's parents weren't bad off, either. A lot of the time she forgot what lengths people would go to in order to get money so they could live comfortably. That was what her kidnappers had done. It had all been about money and comfort in the end.

She thought about Jesse in a small cell with cinder-block walls. A hard bed. Crappy food. At least he would have time to read. He loved to read. But she had heard horror stories of prison and how awful inmates were to each other. And here she was, living in her fancy house, going to Harvard, and now heading out on a date with a guy she knew wanted to be more than friends. Her world seemed so shallow all of a sudden.

"You ready to go?" Finn asked.

She nodded. "Drinks, right?"

"Yeah, there's a great club downtown, if you're okay with that."

"Sure."

"Have fun," Becca said as Naomi grabbed her purse and gave her an angry glare.

"Do not say date!" she whispered.

Becca grinned, and Naomi turned her back and followed Finn out the door.

* * *

Maybe it was a date, but Naomi decided it didn't matter. She wanted to have fun for the first time in forever. Finn took her to a small nightclub that smelled like vanilla and cinnamon. For some reason it put her at ease, and she settled into a chair at a table near the bar. The music was loud but not annoying. Finn was across from her, and in the dim light he looked hotter than usual. His skin seemed darker, his hair messy in a way that made him appear more confident, somehow.

She had to stop thinking of him as hot.

"So, you've mentioned before you're from California," he said, leaning forward. "What part? I have some family out there."

"South of San Francisco."

"What city?"

She pursed her lips together. She wasn't giving him that information. She refused. The last time she had told someone her hometown, they had put two-and-two together and figured out she was "that Naomi girl who was kidnapped by jewelry thieves a few years ago." It had been a nation-wide story during the trial. It was the last thing she wanted to talk about right now.

"Nowhere special," she muttered, and looked up as the bartender motioned to Finn their drinks were ready. He stood up to get them. Maybe this was a bad idea. If he found out she was *the* Naomi Jensen, the one who confessed to falling in love with her kidnapper, he would know exactly who her boyfriend was. He would think she was insane, and their friendship would be over.

"And here is your first drink of the evening," Finn said with a sly smile as he set her piña colada in front of her.

"The first, huh?" She took a sip and closed her eyes. It was sweet and cold with a sharp tang that lingered after she swallowed. It had been a long time since she'd had alcohol—the last time had been with Brad over three years ago. He had always shoved beers in her hand to loosen her up. He had thought he was so cool, drinking underage. That very fact was what had kept her from drinking for so long. She didn't want it to become a crutch.

"Good?" Finn asked.

"Yeah, but one is all I need tonight, thanks." She sipped some more, probably faster than she should, and remembered punching Brad in the face the first time she saw him after her escape. It had felt good, but it was far from a decent payback for all the crap and abuse he had put her through. At least now she would be able to spot an abusive relationship if she landed in one again. Finn didn't seem like he would force her into anything. Maybe that was why he was so appealing. She liked someone in control, but they had to be tender about it and their intentions had to be on the right track. That was Jesse once he had decided to change. And, from what she could sense so far, maybe Finn too.

"So?" Finn asked. "What city? Why's it a big secret?"

"No reason." She looked behind her shoulder and nodded toward the crowd beyond the tables. "Do you want to . . .?"

His eyes lit up. "You sure that's okay with your boyfriend?"

She let out a heavy sigh. "You must think I'm the most boring person ever. I want to prove you wrong, that's all."

"Then let's go." He stood and took her hand, pulling her from the chair and into the crowd. "You're not boring—I've never thought you were boring," he said loudly over the music as he watched her start to dance. People moved all around them, but everyone kept their space.

Finn moved a little. He seemed to be waiting to feel her groove and how she wanted to dance. She felt her cheeks blush hot as she let the music pound into her. It had been a long time since she had let go like this. Stacy's voice filled her head, her mother's voice, and finally her own voice. *Forget Jesse. Forget him. Just for a minute.*

Moving her body to the beat of the music, she slid her hands up her thighs and waist, feeling the tight denim against her skin. She focused on Finn and motioned for him to join her. He inched up against her body and loosely wrapped an arm around her, matching her moves, his body fluid and strong, not too aggressive, and after a few minutes she was lost in the music and dancing and Finn's eyes. He smelled like the Java Lounge, like cinnamon rolls and cookies. She put an arm around his neck, inching her fingers up to his hairline. There was a thin layer of cool sweat on his skin, and it made her smile. Why had she denied herself this sort of thing for so long? She liked to dance, to feel connected to someone as they moved with her. She had gone to a few clubs with Brad in high school. That was where she had learned how to dance. Brad had taught her, and as she moved in ways she remembered doing years ago, all the memories came back—Brad forcing her onto his bed, Brad hitting her face, Brad walking with her down the beach to a smoky bonfire, Brad jealous of her flirting with that guy . . . whatever his name was . . . Damien. He wore glasses and had hair that fell across his forehead, like Finn's.

She stopped dancing.

"What's the matter?" Finn stopped and looked down into her eyes.

Blinking, she realized how warm she was. Brad had been her first and only boyfriend before she was kidnapped. Damien had been the second guy she had even considered dating, but it had never happened. Jesse had been the third guy in her life, and the most intense. Now there was Finn. She didn't even know his last name. In fact, she didn't know much of anything about him, except that he was nice and smelled like a bakery and danced better than Brad ever did.

She shook her head and started dancing again, but her beat was off. "Nothing."

"It's something," he replied, but didn't push her to answer as he started moving with her once more. She was surprised at how quickly he got her back into the beat of the music. The song changed, and again he kept her on track, focusing on her.

"What's your last name?" she asked once the third song started and sweat began trickling down her back. "I can't believe we're on a date and I don't even know your last name."

He smiled and tightened his hold on her for the first time. "I thought you said this wasn't a date."

"It sure feels like it is, whether I like it or not."

"And do you like it?"

She tried to wet her lips, but her mouth was dry. Her shimmery lip gloss was long gone. She was nervous and feeling sick and excited and angry all at the same time. "Just tell me your last name."

He leaned closer and said in a thick Italian accent, "Giachetti."

Naomi had to force herself to keep dancing. "You're Italian?"

"Only a quarter, but yeah."

Of course she would find herself attracted to an Italian. Two of her kidnappers were Italian. Evelyn cooked the best Italian food she would probably ever eat. Their whole plan was to take her to Italy.

"Naomi, are you okay?"

Snapping out of her daze, she nodded and slowed her dancing. All around her, bodies were moving, faces smiling, couples kissing. The smell of sweat and alcohol was overpowering the vanilla and cinnamon. She took her hand off Finn's neck. "Can we, um, can we—"

"Sit back down? Sure." He led her to the table, where she sipped at her drink as if it might save her life. The sweetness wasn't appealing anymore. It made her wince.

"Do you want to leave?" Finn asked. He hadn't even touched his drink yet. Instead, he leaned across the table, looking concerned. "Is it the drink?"

She could see in his eyes that he also wanted to ask, *is it me*?

She pushed her glass away. "Can we maybe go somewhere else?"

"Sure." He stood and helped her up, wrapping an arm around her as they left. She wasn't sure she wanted his arm around her, but it helped her feel safer from her own thoughts. From herself.

III

FINN'S CAR WAS OLD, BUT IT WAS CLEAN AND HAD leather seats. Naomi wanted it to swallow her up. She wanted to go home, but was too afraid to tell Finn that. He shut her door once she was seated, and then walked around to the driver's side. Once he was in, she fastened her seat belt and stared straight ahead. The parking lot was full of cars, the moonlight reflecting off so many colors and glass, like some sort of frozen carnival.

"Did I do something wrong?" Finn asked, not making any sort of move to start the car.

She turned to look at him. "No, no, it's me. It's all me. I'm sorry."

"Don't apologize. Do you want to talk about it?"

She shook her head. "I don't spend time in places like that. I guess it was too much all of a sudden."

He nodded. "I understand, but you're a great dancer." He closed his eyes. "I mean, really great. I wouldn't have guessed that about you."

Looking back to the moonlight and the cars, she shrugged. "Sorry."

"Why are you sorry?" She jumped when he touched her arm, and he backed away, looking surprised. "I wanted to tell you I'm okay if you want to go somewhere else. We can go to my place, or we can drive around. I know a great spot you might like where we can just talk. I promise I'll take you home anytime you want."

He seemed to know exactly what to say to make her feel better. She nodded. The night was still young, and she had to admit going home so soon to lie in bed and feel sorry for herself was sounding less and less appealing. "All right."

As he drove, she kept glancing at his hands. He wore a high school class ring with the letters NEHS. She guessed the emerald stone set in the center was his birthstone.

"Is your birthday in May too?" she asked.

He smiled. "It was yesterday. I turned twenty-two."

"Oh, well, happy late birthday. I'm sorry I didn't know." She picked at a small tear on the seat. "Did you do anything fun?"

"If you count playing basketball with my roommates, sure." He laughed. "I prefer what I'm doing tonight, honestly."

"Oh, you mean hanging out with an insecure girl who won't even tell you her hometown?"

Clamping her mouth closed, she cursed herself for drawing attention to what she had tried so hard to avoid earlier. She didn't know what it was about Finn that made her want to open up, but it was refreshingly annoying. She snuck a glance at his reaction. He seemed unaffected.

"Well," he said after a moment, "I wouldn't have asked you to hang out with me if I didn't like the way you are. If you don't want to tell me your hometown, I don't mind."

She lowered her attention to the tear in the leather seat. She had already made it larger, and took her hand away.

Finn turned the car into a dark lot, gravel crunching beneath the tires before he parked and turned off the engine. "We're here."

Naomi looked ahead at what appeared to be train tracks. "Um, where is 'here'?"

"A spot I visit when I need to think."

"Train tracks?"

"Yeah, come on." He got out of the car.

Too impatient to wait for him to walk around and open her door, she stepped out and looked around. From the glow of the streetlights, she could see the tracks stretch into the distance and then disappear into the night. Russian olive trees made crooked shadows. She wasn't sure she believed Finn wanted to "just talk" here, but the spot seemed peaceful enough, and the road wasn't far away. Cars drove by occasionally.

Finn motioned for her to follow him toward the tracks, and as she stepped onto the ties, she slipped. Finn grabbed her hand.

"There's a spot where I like to sit and watch the river down past the trees," he said, steadying her and then leading her up the tracks. "We can't see the river in the dark, of course, but we can hear it, and that's even better."

Naomi smiled. She liked the way he still held her hand, squeezing her fingers. It made her heart skip a beat. His Italian last name no longer mattered. Nothing seemed to matter for the longest space of time as they walked away from the car and the streetlights. Soon all that lit their path was moonlight.

Naomi knew she should be frightened of Finn leading her somewhere dark and isolated. She had no idea where the tracks led, but she had been through many worse things than walking into the dark with a guy.

"Here," Finn said, and helped Naomi sit on the edge of the tracks. He sat next to her, but didn't take her hand again. He leaned forward, bringing his knees to his chest. "This is where you can hear the river the best."

It was so dark that nothing distracted from the sounds surrounding them. First, Naomi heard crickets, loud and harsh, and then the rustle of the trees. There was the faint hum of traffic in the distance and then the river, barely a trickle until it grew louder as the other noises faded away. Soon, all she could hear was the rush of water and Finn's breaths in rhythm with her own. She closed her eyes, expecting Finn to make a move at any moment. Why else would he have brought her here? In so many ways, she wished he would, no matter where it led. She wanted a hot rush of emotion. It didn't matter if it was fear or excitement or passion, or even guilt. Anything was better than the dull ache she had felt for so long after the trial, after all those hours of testifying, convincing herself she was a victim and they were the criminals, hating herself for the words her mother said she had to say, for her own guilt in driving the final wedge into their dreams and shattering them, for the shame on their faces, for the pain in her own heart. After it was all over, she wanted to *feel*. She was not broken. She didn't need to be fixed. She was like the river, a hidden sound in a sea of noise—something nobody could understand because they would not take the time to sit down in the dark and listen.

And then there was Finn, who was not making any moves to touch her or fix her or judge her. He sat quietly, resting his chin on his knees.

"Isn't it great to get away from everything?" he asked, almost as if she wasn't there. "I know my life isn't complicated or loud or anything, but sometimes I have to get away."

"Yeah," she said, resting her chin in her hands. "So, I haven't asked you yet. Is Finn short for something?"

He laughed. "Finnegan, but only my mom is allowed to call me that."

"Right." She smiled at him, but felt her heart sink at the mention of his mother. Her mother hadn't called her yet today. It didn't surprise her, of course. She felt her back pocket where she had put her phone. It was set to vibrate instead of ring.

"So, you're at Harvard, right?" she asked. "You've never told me your major."

He was quiet. She looked sideways at him, raising an eyebrow as she wondered if she had asked the wrong question.

"I'm not in school yet," he answered. "I want to be, but it's . . . complicated right now."

"Oh." The trembling in his voice warned her not to press the subject. She decided to take it in another direction. "Well, when you get in, what do you want to study?"

He raised his hands as if forming a large shape in the air. "I love to build stuff. I'm thinking architecture."

Naomi clenched her jaw. Why? Why? Why? Jesse was an architect. It was as if the universe was conspiring against her, throwing in random things to keep reminding her of the past.

Finn turned to her. "Are you all right?"

"You must think I'm insane," she said, scrambling to her feet. "I'm sorry, Finn. I'm sorry I keep reacting like I'm crazy all of a sudden. I've tried so long to keep away from things that remind me of what happened . . . and him. It's always him. He never leaves. Everywhere I go, he's there. And I want him there, but I can't be with him, and that makes the memory of him unbearable. Anyway, I'm sorry."

She turned away. She wanted to run down the tracks and disappear, but that wouldn't get her anywhere.

"Are you talking about your boyfriend?"

"Yeah."

She expected Finn to jump into a list of questions, but he didn't say anything. He didn't even stand up when she started backing away. Her shoes crunched on the gravel between the wood tracks.

"I think everyone has something," Finn said in a relaxed voice, as if she wasn't panicking right in front of him. "My mom has cancer and might die any day. My dad left us when I was five, and when I finally got to see him again, it turns out he's married with eight kids. I don't mean anything to him. So it's always something, isn't it?"

He looked up at Naomi, his face barely visible in the moonlight. The shape of his body, the memory of his warmth pressed against hers on the dance floor, made her knees weak.

"The reason I started talking to you at the Lounge was because you seem alone," he said, "like me. You want to be alone, but you don't really want to be alone, do you? There aren't a lot of people like us around here. You think you're hiding things, but you're more real than most of the people I see every day." He shrugged and looked toward the trees. "So, yeah, that's why I brought you here. I knew you'd understand this place. I knew you'd probably open up and let me talk to you more than we do at the café."

Naomi stood still, the sound of the river loud in her ears. Maybe everything that reminded her of the kidnapping and Jesse was a coincidence and she needed to chill the heck out, like Finn. She couldn't imagine what it might be like to be so understanding about everything.

Taking a deep breath, she walked back to her spot and sat down. "Thanks," she said, wetting her lips. "I don't know why, exactly, but thanks."

He turned to her and smiled. Even though she couldn't see his eyes very well, she knew he was looking right at her. It was as if he was looking *into* her, as if he saw her like nobody else but Jesse had ever seen her.

"Whatever it is you're dealing with, you'll get through it," he said, and then paused for a moment, leaning forward as if he wanted to kiss her. It was something she had expected a few minutes ago, but now it made her breathing uneven—excitement, maybe—but the memory of kissing Jesse was too strong.

Leaning closer anyway, she led Finn into the kiss. She needed to kiss someone, to connect, to feel alive. She needed to kiss Finn. Now. He could never replace Jesse, but that didn't matter.

The river seemed to rush around them, loud and constant and forever, and he took hold of her more passionately than she expected, his lips pressing against hers, warm and reassuring. She had underestimated how much he wanted her. Squeezing her eyes shut, she realized she was not imagining he was Jesse. He was Finn and he was kissing her and Jesse was thousands of miles away.

She jumped when her phone started buzzing. It was so quiet outside that even the vibration was loud. Finn pulled away, chuckling as he caught his breath. "What a time for a phone call."

"Sorry, nobody ever calls me except my mom. I need to answer it." Slipping the phone from her pocket, she looked at the glowing screen and saw the name *Karen Jensen* flashing at her. She wasn't sure she wanted to talk to her mom in front of Finn, but it was probably just a birthday wish. She put the phone to her ear and turned a little bit away from Finn. "Hi, Mom."

Her mother's voice, so much like her own, said, "Hi, sweetie. Happy birthday."

"Thanks."

"Been a good day?"

She glanced at Finn and smiled. "So far, yeah."

"Your father says happy birthday too. You should have a card in the mail. Have you checked yet?"

"No, not yet."

Silence filled the air. Naomi doubted her mother could hear the river or Finn breathing beside her. All of a sudden she wanted him to hold her and kiss her again. Her skin turned hot.

"So, there's something . . ." Her mother paused, and Naomi stiffened at the change in her tone. There was hesitance and worry, the same tone she always used when they talked about anything Jesse-related.

"Just say it, Mom."

"I shouldn't tell you this. I don't think you should know, but his father has been pestering me for over two months. He wants you to know, even though you are not allowed—and I repeat, *you are not allowed, by law*—to see him yet. There might be something down the road we can work out, but right now his parole clearly states he cannot see you because of the circumstances of your previous relationship."

It was just like her mother to sound like a law book. Naomi's tongue was a wad of tissue paper in her mouth. The river faded away. Goosebumps popped up on her arms. "He's out? It's only been two years."

"He's on parole. The plea bargain specifically stated good behavior allowed him the possibility of parole. If you attempt to see him or vice versa, if he breaks curfew, if he fails at his job, if he doesn't check in, if he does anything wrong, he's back in for longer, do you understand? I know the semester is almost over and you want to come home for the summer, so I'm telling you this now so there are no questions about what you can and cannot do when you get here."

"I've got it, Mom." She glanced at Finn. Kissing him felt like the biggest mistake she could have ever made, no matter how good it had been. Now she was going to feel torn—exactly what she had wanted to avoid. "I'll think of him as still in prison. This doesn't change anything."

But the truth was it changed everything.

IV

FINN DIDN'T ASK ABOUT THE PHONE CALL OR NAOMI'S mention of prison. When she finished, he helped her up and they walked back to the car and drove home. He parked in her driveway and kept his hands on the steering wheel.

"Naomi, I have to apologize for kissing you," he said in a tight voice. "That was stupid of me. You're with someone. I'm not making things easier, and I feel like a—"

"Don't worry about it."

He stared at his hands on the wheel. "You don't have to explain anything, of course, but whatever's going on, I hope you know I'm here for you if you need or want anything."

Naomi picked up her purse from the floor and grabbed the door handle. Her mind was filled with Jesse, of flying home and not being able to see him. She turned to Finn, her hope for building a harmless friendship sinking. "I don't want to sound rude, but it's not anything you can help with." She thought of his kiss and how nice it had been for about ten seconds. She wanted to feel it all over again, except there was Jesse now. There was always Jesse, and she had been a fool to try to ignore him.

"All right." He let go of the steering wheel, as if he wanted to reach for her. She stared at the class ring on his finger and wondered how many girls he had kissed and how many times his heart had been broken.

"Thanks for a great night," she said, forcing a smile. "It was nice of you to take me out."

He swallowed and returned his hand to the steering wheel. "Anytime."

She grabbed the door handle.

"Wait!" He leaned over and touched her shoulder. The feel of his hand on her made her warm all the way through. "I want to make sure you have my number in case you need anything."

"Oh, right," she replied, as if it was the most natural thing for him to say. She slipped her phone from her pocket and poised her thumb over the keypad. "What is it?"

He gave her the number, and she shakily punched the buttons. Then she typed in *F-i-n-n G-i-a-c-h-e-t-t-i*.

"There," he said with a relieved sigh. "I can't lose you completely, right?" She was reaching for the handle again and turned to look at him one last time. "Unless," he said after clearing his throat and looking away, "you don't want to see me again?"

She smiled and pushed back the guilt tearing through her. "I promise we'll get together again next semester. Goodbye, Finn, and thanks." She let herself out of the car and rushed inside as fast as she could, her eyes filling with tears.

* * *

By the time the semester ended and she had taken all of her exams, Naomi couldn't keep her mind off Jesse. The memory of Finn's kiss was nothing compared to being with Jesse, and the possibility of failing her classes because she couldn't focus on schoolwork and studying seemed unimportant. All she could do was count down the days until she drove to the airport to fly home. She avoided the Java Lounge even though her mouth watered for a slice of almond cake. She missed Finn, but if she saw him, she knew she would end up telling him about Jesse. Maybe she could tell him later.

When the day arrived to leave, she packed her bags, shut off the utilities since Becca was already gone for the next few months, and locked the front door. Her parents would keep up the payments so the landlord wouldn't rent the house out during the summer, and for that she was glad. She could leave a lot of her things here.

The flight was long and tedious. She sat next to a man who smelled like leather and kept leaning over to look out her window. She turned on her iPod and cranked up the volume. The song was one of Jesse's favorites, from a band that had been popular a few years back. There were so many reasons she wanted to see him again. The last time she had seen him was in the courtroom on the day of his sentencing. He had chosen to be there, she kept reminding herself, he had turned himself in. Even so, she had still felt like the entire situation was her fault. He had agreed to a plea bargain and told the judge everything—how he had been the one to pick her up in the parking lot and put her in the car when Eric wanted to shoot her instead, how he had contemplated letting her go and kept talking himself out of it, how he had tried to get her to like him so she wouldn't want to escape. That was the worst part— knowing most of his motivations were selfish and not driven by his affections for her. In fact, he admitted he hadn't fallen in love with her until the last few months of her captivity, so all those times he had seemed to want her earlier on . . . she didn't want to think about his motivations then. He had changed. That was what mattered. That was why she couldn't let go of him now, and one of the reasons why the judge had given him a significantly lesser sentence. He had hurt Evelyn and stolen jewelry, but Eric and Steve had blackmailed him, so how bad was he, truly? He had never hurt her during her captivity, not once. He had protected her, been there for her when she had nothing left. And now he had changed. She doubted many people were capable of that kind of transformation. Even her mother, who had improved a lot since the kidnapping, hadn't altered so completely. Jesse was strong and had a kind heart, and he loved her like nobody had ever loved her.

* * *

As soon as she spotted her mother, she smiled. It was good to be home. The air was warmer here, and more familiar. No matter how long she lived away from home, she would never love the California ocean air any less.

"It's so good to have you back," her mother said as Naomi fell into her arms. She smelled like her shampoo, a flowery scent Naomi had never noticed until after the kidnapping. Of course, there were a lot of things she had never noticed about her mother until after the kidnapping. Her life, it seemed, would always be split into *before* and *after*.

"Are you hungry?" her mother asked, tucking her hair behind her ears. Naomi was surprised it was down, sleek and blonde. She always had it up. "Let's get your bags and then grab some lunch. Your father said he'd meet us wherever we like."

"Sure."

Despite knowing better, Naomi kept looking around for Jesse, as if she might spot him somewhere. Her mother looked at her sideways.

"You're not going to see him. He's in Berkeley with his father. That's two hours away, and I doubt he's allowed to leave town."

"I know, Mom, I know."

They found her luggage on the baggage claim carousel and headed out to the car. Naomi had flown into the local airport, so home was close by. She didn't want to go out for lunch. Her bedroom sounded like a better place to wallow. Once they were settled in the car, she pulled out her iPod and started pushing the ear buds into her ears. Her mother cleared her throat.

"We're ten minutes away from lunch and I haven't seen you in five months. Do you think we can talk for a minute?"

Naomi put the iPod away and dumped her purse on the floor. She knew her relationship with her mother was juvenile, but they had a lot of lost time to make up for. In a lot of ways, it was as if she was fifteen again, only this time with a mother who was concerned about her. It made her happy and frustrated at the same time—happy that her mother saw her and cared, but frustrated because she wanted to scream, "I'm an adult, so treat me like one!" But she knew it would get her nowhere, and she didn't feel like an adult, so she wasn't quite sure how to act like one. It was easier to turn on her iPod and ignore everything, but that was clearly not going to fly today.

"So, tell me about your classes," her mother said, touching Naomi's arm. "How were your exams?"

Naomi clenched her fists as she thought about how awful it had been to get through that last week of school. She had studied. Kind of. She knew she had probably failed most of the tests.

"They were hard," she muttered, backing away from her mother's tender touch. "I'll register for my next classes as soon as I get back."

"You're still wanting to do film?"

"Yes, I think so. I need to get my Bachelor's before I start the actual program, so I guess we'll see." She remembered Finn's mention of USC and the cinematography program there. The thought was like a dust bunny floating along the edges of her mind, skipping about in the breeze of everything else.

Her mother smiled as she pulled her phone from her purse and opened it to find a number. "Will you call your father?" she asked, handing the phone to Naomi.

"Tell him we'll be at Carter's. It's not far from his office."

Naomi took the phone and pushed the call button. It wasn't often she went out to eat with her parents, but it had become tradition every time she came home from another semester.

"This is Jason," her father answered.

"Hi, Dad."

"Naomi, you're home!" His voice was polished and confident. It always soothed her, somehow.

"Yeah, Mom says she wants you to meet us at Carter's for lunch."

"Mmm, sounds great. I'll be there in a little bit, okay? Order me the garlic shrimp linguini. They usually have it on the menu."

"Sure thing." Naomi winced at the mention of shellfish and said goodbye as her mother pulled into the parking lot of an upscale restaurant. Naomi would have preferred a cheap hamburger joint, but she couldn't envision her parents in such a place. Her mother was dressed in her usual office clothes, and her father would be in a suit and tie.

"Going back to what you said before," her mother said, meeting Naomi's eyes, "whatever you choose to do at Harvard, I'm proud of you."

Naomi opened the door and grabbed her purse off the floor. "Thanks, Mom."

"I mean it." She gave Naomi a beaming smile and wrapped an arm around her as a greeter opened the door for them. "You're going to add beautiful things to the world."

Naomi took a deep breath and scrunched her nose at the smell of fish and garlic. She hated fish, but she had never told her mother that. She had told Evelyn, but only because Evelyn had thought to ask her. It was always an odd sensation when she realized her kidnappers knew more about her than her own parents did.

V

June

JUNE STRETCHED OUT BEFORE NAOMI AS AN OCEAN OF nothingness. Several times she thought of calling or texting Finn to see how he was doing. She missed talking with him. She missed her regular Wednesday breakfast of almond cake and iced tea. The local café didn't serve almond cake. Every time the craving swept over her, she picked up her phone and scrolled to Finn's number, but couldn't bring herself to hit *call*.

Thinking back on last summer, she remembered it as tolerable. Aside from helping her parents with the Naomi's Hope foundation—a project she was proud her parents had started to help fund searches for missing children—she had spent a lot of time on the beach or going for long walks. She tried to dive back into the same things as soon as she was home.

One thing she hadn't done yet was borrow her mother's Mercedes SUV and drive along the coast. Last summer, she had taken the SUV every few days and stopped to take pictures of water or rocks or a beautiful sunset. Other times, she drove into San Francisco and went shopping or asked permission to film a street performer. Summers were declared free from counselors, so it was her time to relax and see if she had truly made progress during the year. This summer seemed to be moving backward. As June slipped into July and she thought more and more of Jesse, it was as if the few months after he had helped her escape were happening all over again. All she wanted to do was curl up on her bed and sleep forever. So she did, but only for a week instead of forever. On the sixth day, her mother came upstairs and opened the door without knocking.

"This has gone on long enough, Naomi."

She rolled over in bed, an arm over her eyes as if she was sick and couldn't look at anything. "What has gone on long enough?"

A heavy sigh. "You know what I mean. It's been over two years. You've had time to recover past this stage, and knowing Jesse is out on parole changes absolutely nothing. Moping about it isn't going to get you anywhere."

She was wrong. It changed everything. "I'm not moping."

"What do you call hibernating in your room for a solid week?"

"I call it nothing. I spent last month shopping with you and helping with the foundation. And I just finished an entire semester of school. I'm tired."

There was a pause and Naomi imagined her mother putting her hands on her hips and glaring. "You haven't helped much with anything. Anytime I'm with you, you're moping. Last summer you were at least trying to be happy. Now you're acting like a sulky five-year-old."

That was it. Naomi moved her arm from her face and sat up, her eyes narrowing. "And how would you know how I acted when I was five years old? You were never around." She lowered her voice as it started shaking. "You didn't even care."

It was the first time she had ever confronted her mother directly about how she had been raised by nannies, and she could see the dagger hit its mark. Her mother winced, faltering for a moment until she regained her composure. Naomi looked away, ashamed of her outburst.

"Yes," she admitted, "but that has changed. I care now."

"Yelling at me to grow up is not caring."

Her mother's shoulders fell. She looked up at the ceiling and took a deep breath. "I'm sorry. This . . . this parenting thing is new to me." Walking into the room, she sat on the end of the bed. "I don't know what to do for you, Naomi." She pinched the bridge of her nose. "I don't know."

Naomi sat up a little more, realizing it was one in the afternoon and she was still in her pajamas. She had to admit it was pathetic. She couldn't blame her mother for being concerned. "I'm twenty-one, Mom. You shouldn't feel like you have to parent me now."

Sliding her hand from her nose, her mother turned with tears glittering in her eyes. She was so beautiful. Naomi knew she was forty-seven, but her age didn't show in her luminous complexion and silky blonde hair. Even though she was working from home today, she was dressed in her usual attorney clothes—a cream pencil skirt with a white silk blouse. Naomi knew her closet was filled with such outfits. She always wore creams and whites, as if she was outwardly projecting how innocent and pure she was. The ironic thing, Naomi realized, was she was far from pure. She had made huge mistakes, and they both knew it. Still, in so many ways, Naomi envied her happiness and success.

"I want to parent you," her mother said, blinking back her tears. "I'm your mother, and you deserve to have me be there for you, even as an adult." With a gentle hand, she cupped Naomi's face. "Please let me try now that I have that chance, even if it's awkward."

Naomi reached up to touch her mother's hand. For a long moment, they looked at each other. Naomi wondered what it was like to have a daughter, to feel that need to control another person's life like her mother so obviously wanted to control hers. Or maybe it wasn't control her mother craved. Maybe it was something else. Before she could let that sink in too far, Naomi softly nudged her mother's hand away. "I'll stop moping," she said in a confident tone.

Her mother looked at the ceiling. "That's not what I want. I want you to be—"

"Happy?" Naomi interrupted, her confidence slipping away. "Of course that's what you want. That's what everybody wants for me. Even my kidnappers wanted that, but it was because they thought I wouldn't try to escape if I was happy with them. Why do you want me to be happy, Mom? So you don't have to worry about me? So you can focus on other things instead?"

Naomi knew the words would sting her mother, but she didn't mean them in such a way. She was truly curious.

Her mother focused on the ceiling, her jaw tightening. "I suppose it's not all about happiness," she said. "I suppose it's impossible for you to understand what I want for you and why I want it." She looked away from the ceiling and stood up from the bed. With hardness in her expression Naomi had never seen before, she said, "I know you're an adult now. I know you can make your own decisions, but you're not living completely by your own means. I've sacrificed so many things for you—things you can't even imagine—so you can have a comfortable life and pursue anything you want." She took a deep breath. "Even if I don't approve of those things. I almost lost you because of those sacrifices. I'll admit a lot of it was selfish, but after you were gone, I remembered my initial motivations. I remembered . . ." She pursed her lips and turned away.

"Remembered what?" Naomi leaned forward. She had never seen her mother open up like this.

"Nothing. I can't talk about it right now, not when you think I don't care."

"I know you care, Mom. I—"

She waved her hand. "Forget it. Go back to sleep. Your summers are supposed to be free of pestering and counselors."

Before Naomi could protest, her mother walked out of the room and softly shut the door behind her. Naomi scolded herself for being such a brat, but she didn't know how to fix it. Everything seemed broken and distant, and it was all her own fault.

Picking up her phone on the nightstand, she stared at the screen. With a trembling finger, she scrolled to the name James Sullivan. Jesse's father was so much like him. It comforted her to know James had given her a standing invitation to visit him anytime. Now that Jesse was on parole and apparently living with him, maybe that invitation was closed. She had visited him once last summer. He was an English professor at Berkeley, and they had talked about books and art and spoke little of Jesse. Maybe if she showed up at his door . . .

No, no she couldn't.

Either way, she had to get out of the house. She had to do something besides moping, as her mother put it.

* * *

It was almost too easy to get the keys to her mother's SUV. All Naomi had to do was put on a comfortable outfit, pack all of her camera equipment, and slip on a pair of sunglasses. She found her mother in her office, her attention fixed on the computer screen in front of her. "I'm going to take pictures," she said, shifting her feet. "Can I take one of the cars?"

Her mother looked up and smiled. "Decided to come out of your cave, huh?"

"Yeah, you were right. I need to stop moping."

Nodding, her mother wheeled back from her desk and stretched out her arms. "You want the Mercedes?"

"Yeah, if that's okay?"

"Of course it's okay. Jason and I haven't driven it for months now, so it'll be good for you to take it out." She tilted her head and her eyes narrowed. "Where are you going?"

"Up the coast." She adjusted the backpack on her shoulders and leaned against the doorway, wishing she had driven her own car back from Harvard instead of flying home.

With a glance at her watch, her mother frowned. "How far up the coast? It's two-thirty."

"I don't know. I might go shopping if I get as far as San Francisco. I can stop for dinner somewhere."

Her mother's frown deepened. "That's getting pretty far from the coast."

Naomi knew what was going through her mind. That far north was dangerously close to Berkeley. "Maybe I'll just go to Santa Cruz. I have my phone. You can call me. Come on, Mom, you were telling me I need to get out. So, I'm getting out."

An uncomfortable silence stretched between them. Her mother looked her up and down, checked her watch again, and then wheeled her chair closer to the desk once more. "All right, you can have the Mercedes for the day, but please be back by ten or we'll worry. Your father doesn't like it when we don't know where you are or when you'll be back." She paused. "I don't, either."

"I promise I'll be safe." She narrowed her eyes. "How the heck do you two deal with me gone all year at school?"

"That's different, I guess. You're in your own house near campus, and you're so busy with schoolwork you probably don't go out much. Right?"

"You make it sound like my life is pretty lame there." She looked away. "But yeah, you're right."

Her mother leaned forward. Naomi could see her fighting to say something, but then she bit her lip and steadied her hands on the desk. "Call if you need anything, okay?"

"Okay. I'll be fine, Mom. I'll be in the car most of the time, and I can drive safely. I did this all last summer, remember?"

"Yes, I know."

But Jesse wasn't on parole last summer, Naomi reminded herself before turning to leave. She didn't know if she was going to go as far as San Francisco, but her heart beat faster at the thought of being able to do such a thing—even if it was against the law for him to see her. Somehow that made her want to see him more.

VI

ONCE SHE WAS ON THE COASTAL HIGHWAY, NAOMI
cranked up the stereo and rolled down her window to
let the wind blow through her hair. Sometimes she
wondered what it would have been like if Jesse had
never helped her escape. She could be in Italy with him
and the others. She might have learned to live a normal
life there, forgotten she was held captive as they took
her on trips through Europe and spent the money they
had stolen. No jobs. No school. She wondered what it
would have been like and how she could still think it
might have been a good thing, or how it would have
been possible. A different identity, maybe? Knowing
Jesse and his connections, that was probably how they
would have accomplished it. They were criminals. They
were insane thinking they could live the rest of their
lives like a vacation. Despite everything, she yearned to
see them again. In so many ways, they were victims too,
especially Evelyn. At least she would be out in fifteen

years if she didn't do anything stupid. That wasn't too much of her life to lose.

Naomi's iPod switched to a song that made her take her foot off the gas. It was the same song she and Finn had danced to at the club. Its pounding bass thumped through the car and the muscles in her body ached, as if they wanted her to stop the car and get out so she could move like she had on the dance floor.

No.

No more Finn.

It was all Jesse now. The kiss had been a mistake, and she would tell Jesse she was sorry.

She glanced at her camera equipment in the backseat, her resolve breaking. She had no intention of stopping to take pictures. She was on autopilot, heading straight for Berkeley.

* * *

Two hours later, she was rubbing the tops of her aching thighs with one hand. She wasn't used to sitting in a car for so long, even with the cruise control engaged. She was in Berkeley now, and after stopping to fill up the car, she drove to James's apartment. It was a clean, quiet street. James's building was yellow.

Naomi imagined what it might be like to see Jesse again. Frightening. Surreal. From what she understood, it wasn't illegal for *her* to seek him out, but she still wanted to be careful. Maybe she was wrong. Getting him in trouble wasn't her intention. She only wanted to see him, even if it was from afar. Her mother had hinted he would have a job, so if she waited long enough, she might see him coming or going. Then she would . . . well, she wasn't sure.

Parking the Mercedes across the street, she undid her seatbelt and stared at the third-floor apartment where James lived. What now? She tapped her fingers against the steering wheel as her stomach started to growl. She hadn't eaten lunch, and now it was five o'clock. If she had been thinking clearly, she would have stopped for something to eat earlier, or at least brought something to snack on. When it came to Jesse, she didn't think clearly.

Maybe there was something in the glove box. She leaned over and popped it open. There were insurance papers, a pen, some napkins, and a box of Good & Plenty. That was surprising. She had no idea who liked them—her father or her mother, since they both used this car. She tore open the box and dumped some of the candies into her mouth, her mind stuck on the fact that she had no idea what kind of candy her parents liked. One of them liked licorice, apparently. Or maybe neither of them did since the candy hadn't been opened. It was stale now, but it still tasted good. She chewed it, letting the gritty sugar coat her mouth as she watched James's apartment like she was some sort of stalker. For a moment, she considered leaving, but as soon as she saw Jesse, it all faded away.

She almost didn't recognize him behind the wheel of his father's green pickup truck. His hair was longer than she remembered. For a moment, her head spun. She dropped the box in her hands and it fell to the floor, spilling the pink and white candies everywhere. He was parking almost directly across the street from her now. As stupid as it was, she hadn't planned this far. Now he was getting out of the truck.

She had long since rolled up her window and turned on the air conditioning, so it wasn't as if she could yell to him. Instead, she opened her door as fast as she could and tripped over her feet as she stumbled out onto the road. She shut the door and the sound made Jesse stop and look up. His mouth dropped open.

"Naomi?"

"I heard you were on parole." She brushed a sweaty hand across her forehead. "I . . . I—"

"I'm not allowed to see you," he interrupted, taking a step back. His hand lingered on the open truck door. "I'll be sent back to prison if I attempt to contact you or see you. I'm not even sure I can see you after my parole is over. It might be a long time." He looked at the ground. "I have a hearing next week. I'll find out more then."

Even from across the street, Naomi could see the muscle in his jaw tightening with anger. She knew it wasn't aimed at her. "You aren't attempting," she said. "I've taken the initiative, so it's not your fault."

"Yes, but if my parole officer finds out about this, he won't be happy. I was lucky enough to be released to my father. If you're found here, I'll be in more trouble than you can imagine." His face was stiff, his body tense. Naomi realized what a mistake she had made, but there he was, right in front of her. It was too much. She took a step forward, relieved the road was quiet with no traffic at the moment. Jesse glanced down the street, then back to her. His expression softened as she walked toward him. Each step was heavy, as if she didn't believe she would ever reach him.

"Naomi," he said when she was halfway across the road, "I have an impeccable record so far. It's why I was put on parole so early. If I . . ." His voice trailed off as she stepped closer. The need in his eyes was apparent now. He was lonely and tired and desperate for her—that much she could see as he rushed forward and took her into his arms before she could reach him on her own. He kissed her hard on the mouth, his lips as steady and passionate as she remembered. The kiss blossomed around her, his breaths deeper as he squeezed her so tightly she almost ran out of breath.

He pulled out of the kiss. "I missed you."

"I know," she whispered. "I missed you too. I need you. I couldn't stay away. I'm sorry." Burying her face in his shoulder, she let herself melt against him despite the sharp, bitter smell of grease and dust on his skin. Being in his arms felt so good she thought she might start crying with joy.

He rubbed her back and kissed the side of her head. "Naomi, I know you want to stay with me, but I have to . . . I have to get you back in your car. You have to leave."

She pulled away and nodded. Her nose was starting to run. He always made her cry. Nobody had seen her cry as much as he had. It should have been embarrassing, but a part of her felt more attached to him because of it. He knew her weakest spots and how to patch them up when she couldn't do it herself. He knew her better than anyone.

Guiding her back to the Mercedes, he kept an arm around her. She sensed he didn't want to let her go, but one of the reasons she loved him was because of his desire to do the right thing. It was why he had gone to prison, and sometimes she wondered if it was all for her, or if none of it was.

He peeked into the backseat. "You told your mother you were taking pictures, didn't you?"

Blushing, she opened the door. "Yes."

"And you drove straight here without stopping to eat."

She looked up. "How did you—"

"Why else would you be eating licorice right now?" he asked, laughing. "You do realize I hate licorice, right?"

"You do?" It was something she hadn't known about him, but then again, she hadn't known him that long in the grand scheme of things. Not that it mattered.

He leaned forward and licked his lips. "Yes, I do, but I'll kiss you again anyway. I'd kiss you forever, even if you tasted like licorice every time."

"How brave of you," she replied with a laugh. He kissed her again, not as passionately this time, but enough to make her breathless once more. She wrapped her arms around him as she leaned halfway into the car through the open door. Jesse kept her steady, and she ran her hands down his arms, noticing he was more toned than before.

"Jesse," she said between kisses. "Where are you working?"

He stopped kissing her and smiled. "At a construction site. I wear a hardhat all day." He looked down at her hands on his biceps. "I also worked out in prison."

She frowned. "You're qualified for better work than construction. Why—"

"Because I took what I could get, Naomi. It doesn't look so great to would-be employers when they see a two-year, jobless gap on my resume. And I have to report that I'm on parole. It might be a long time before I can get back into architecture with a good firm. I could try freelancing or starting my own company, but that would take more money than I have—to do it right, anyway."

Money. It always came back to that. She looked away. "I didn't mean it's bad you're working construction. I meant—"

He put a finger to her lips and leaned in to kiss her forehead. "You don't need to worry about any of this. Things will work out. They will always work out for you and me."

The intensity in his voice put her on edge for a moment, but she pushed it aside as he kissed her again. She forgot his fumbled words and worried looks. She forgot about the Mercedes and the licorice and prison and being kidnapped. There was only Jesse, his strong arms around her, the way he ignored the taste of licorice in her mouth, the way he held her so tightly she knew he would sacrifice anything for her.

"Jesse!"

He ripped away from her, backing up so fast she stumbled into the open Mercedes and scraped her ankle on the gravel. She cried out, looking down to see blood beading across her torn skin. Jesse was back by his truck now, his eyes widening as he looked at her ankle and then turned to his father marching down the walkway from the apartment complex. The two looked so alike, it was uncanny. Naomi blinked and steadied herself as James walked around the front of the truck, his attention darting from her to Jesse.

"Explain yourself," he growled at Jesse. It was the first time Naomi had ever seen him angry. He was usually so calm.

Jesse shut the truck's door and faced his father. "It's nothing. I was helping Naomi back into the car so she could leave. I told her she couldn't be here. We were kissing goodbye and that's it."

Naomi raised an eyebrow. More like making out goodbye.

"Damn straight she can't be here." James whirled around to face her, but the distance from across the street undermined the threat in his eyes.

"Naomi, I understand why you would want to come here, but when I told your mother about Jesse and asked her to inform you he was on parole, it was so you'd understand not to come here anymore. Surely, your mother informed you Jesse is not allowed to see you. Do you want him back in prison?" He turned to Jesse. "Did you have anything to do with this?"

"No, Dad."

The anger on Jesse's face startled Naomi. It was aimed at his father, fire swirling in his eyes. Naomi had never seen such an expression on him, even when she had seen him angry with Eric. She took a step back, almost losing her balance as she tried to make sense of what she was seeing. Then, as quickly as it came, the anger dissolved and Jesse's countenance relaxed.

"I'm sorry about coming," she said in cracked voice.

James held out his cell phone. "Your mother is on the line. She called to tell me you might show up."

With her voice stuck in her throat, Naomi walked across the street. Her body felt stiff and foreign. Her ankle throbbed. So, her mother didn't trust her. She had let her take off knowing she would come straight here. Something dark boiled inside Naomi's chest as she looked at Jesse and took James's phone. She placed it to her ear.

"Mom?"

There was silence for a moment.

"You need to come home right now. I told you not to see him."

"I wasn't planning to," Naomi grumbled, turning away. "It just happened."

Wow, that sounded stupid. She cringed.

"Don't give me that crap, Naomi. Get your ass home. Right now. If you're not home in two hours, I'm coming to find you."

Shocked, Naomi opened her mouth to retort, but the line went dead and she realized her mother had hung up. She lowered the phone from her ear and stared down at it as if she expected her mother to call back and apologize. She had never heard her say the word "ass" or talk in such a rude way, especially to her. It was as if the universe was shifting into another dimension. A bad one.

Looking up at James, she gave him his phone. A part of her wanted to scream at him for treating her and Jesse as if they were children and couldn't make their own decisions and mistakes, but at the thought of how James might react, her anger boiled down to a simmer. Everything was surreal all of a sudden. She wanted nothing more than to get back in the car and drive until she could shake the feeling.

"I'm sorry," she apologized to James. "I didn't mean to cause any trouble."

James let out a sigh. "I don't want to lose Jesse again when he's making such a huge recovery. His parole adamantly states he's not allowed to be in contact with you until he has served his time. Parole doesn't mean he's free, and even when he's released, there will be restrictions for him."

She glanced at Jesse, catching a glimpse of his eyes. He looked like he wanted to sweep her up into his arms again, but he knew better than to try.

"I understand, Mr. Sullivan. Goodbye." She finally looked fully into Jesse's eyes. "I'm sorry." She walked back to the Mercedes. Climbing in, she stepped all over the candies she had spilled. She started the car and drove away, trying her hardest not to look in the rearview mirror.

VII

NAOMI WENT STRAIGHT TO HER ROOM WHEN SHE arrived home. Her mother rushed out of her office and followed her up the stairs.

Unsure if slamming the door would be too childish, Naomi left it open and turned around to face her mother. She was still dressed in her skirt and blouse, but she looked much more tired than she had before. It was seven-thirty. She had probably been worrying for the past five hours.

"Why did you let me go?" Naomi asked as she folded her arms.

Her mother folded her arms too, but kept her expression calm. "Because I wanted to see if you would go to him. I want to trust you. I'm trying."

Naomi looked away, guilt sweeping through her. She hadn't realized her mother's trust in her was on such thin ice. "I haven't seen him for so long," she explained. "I wanted to see him, that's all. See him, not talk to him. Then he got out of the truck and I couldn't help myself. He was so close. I love him. I couldn't help it."

Her mother's expression faltered for a moment, jumping to annoyance and disbelief before she plastered it back to stone. "Love is not an excuse to put his future in danger, as well as yours. Seeing him too soon isn't good for your recovery. How many times have your counselors told you that?"

"About five-billion," Naomi snapped, unfolding her arms. "Everyone seems to think enough time will make me fall out of love with him, that I'll come to my senses and realize he's a criminal and unsafe, even if he's served his time and changed. But he's a person too, Mom, like you and me. He's made mistakes and he's trying to change. He deserves a second chance." She folded her arms again, calming herself down. When she looked into her mother's eyes, they were glassy. "I feel things for him I've never felt for anyone else. How can I change that? How can I just . . . stop . . . loving someone?"

Her mother thought for a moment as her shoulders relaxed. "I've never meant to imply you can't be with him. I'm saying now is not the right time, and betraying my trust like you've done today is going to tear us apart if it keeps happening. Do you want that? After everything people have done to you?"

Naomi took a step back. "So if we tear apart, it's all my fault?"

Her jaw flexed. "No, that's not what I'm saying."

"Did you tell Dad about this?"

"I told him as soon as he got home, yes."

"And what does he think?"

Her mother blinked. "He told me to let you make your own mistakes. He's always been more lenient than me, but I know what your kind of thinking is going to lead to, and it's not pretty." She stepped forward and wrapped her arms around Naomi, pulling her into an awkward hug. "I want to protect you. I lost you once and I don't want to go through that again."

Naomi kept her arms stiffly folded, keeping the hug uncomfortable for a few seconds before relaxing. "Nobody is going to kidnap me again, Mom."

"I know, but there are other ways to lose you."

Naomi didn't answer. Her stomach growled, and her mother let her go and backed into the hall. "Mindy has dinner ready. Want to come downstairs and eat?"

She shrugged. "I guess so."

When they were all seated, Naomi looked at her parents and remembered her life without them when she was held captive. She had thought then that they didn't love her—and perhaps they hadn't. But they did now. Her father kept smiling at her as he talked to her about her classes and how he wanted her to come visit his office in the next week.

"I want you to see the business side of things. Do you think you'd be interested in going that route?"

She picked at the green beans on her plate. Mindy always put slivered almonds on them, and Naomi lined up the pale cream-colored fragments with her fork. Then she pushed her mashed potatoes away from the beans and started shaping them into a square. Separate pieces. She didn't like things touching. "I want to do film, Dad."

"I know you do, but film comprises a lot of things. Directing, cinematography, editing, all of that. And if you do any of it freelance or decide to go into the production end of things, you'll want those business skills. I want to show you around. You don't have to like anything." He laughed, and Naomi looked up at his clean-shaven face and sparkling blue eyes. He was always charming, she realized. She wondered why she hadn't inherited more of his outgoing personality. "I'm not trying to convert you!" he said, holding up his hands. "Or if you think it would be too boring, you could come with me to see the German office. You're mother's always too busy."

She smiled at his obvious desire to share a part of his career with her. "That's fine. I can come see the office here." Maybe it would keep her mind off Jesse.

She went back to poking at the almonds and her phone made a dinging sound. Text message. She dug it out of her pocket and hid it beneath the lip of the table so her parents couldn't see. Nobody ever sent her text messages.

Incoming text from unknown number.

She pressed the button to receive the message.

Hi, Naomi, it's Jesse. Got your number from my dad's phone and I'm texting from a friend's phone so this isn't traced. I trust him. Won't be calling or texting you outside of this, but wanted to tell you thank you for coming to see me. I know you feel like you're in trouble, but it was good to see you.

She stared at the message for a long time. She could feel her parents' attention on her downturned head. Then the phone dinged again and another message came through. She pressed the button.

Sorry, phone only lets me send so many characters. When parole is over, I want to see you. Also, odd question . . . do you have a passport? If you don't, maybe think about getting one soon. Don't tell anyone about these texts, and don't text me back. Shouldn't be contacting you, but had to say I love you.

A passport? Of course she had a passport. Because of her father's German office, her parents had always made sure she had a current one in case she wanted to visit. Yeah, right.

At the thought of Jesse asking her if she had one, she held her breath.

"Naomi," her mother said in a cautious voice. "What's the matter?"

She looked up. "Nothing. Just a text."

"Oh, from whom?" Her mother chewed her food slowly, leaning forward as her fork dangled from her hand.

The phone dinged again. Naomi nearly jumped out of her chair. "Nobody," she said, looking down at the screen.

Incoming text from Finn Giachetti.

Unbelievable. She never received texts, and now three in a row. She looked up at her mother. "It's from a guy at college."

"Oh?" Her mother stopped chewing. "You were dating someone there?"

"No, he's a friend."

Looking down again, she pressed the button to receive the message.

How's your summer going? I got a promotion at Java, so next time you come in you'll have to ask for the assistant manager.

Her pulse quickened as she read his words. She hadn't realized how much she had missed his friendship. Smiling, she looked up to see her parents exchanging a knowing look. Of course they tacked on extra meaning to the word "friend." She remembered his kiss, the way he had made her feel like herself again. She hit reply on the phone and typed, *That's great! Can't wait to see you in a few weeks. Have you done anything fun over the summer?*

"I'm happy you're making friends there," her mother said.

"Why? So I'll forget about Jesse?"

"No, that's not what I said."

Her phone dinged with Finn's reply.

I'm kind of bored, honestly . . . especially on Wednesdays. I'm excited for you to get back!

She squeezed the phone, wishing she had the courage to call him and talk to him. Her thoughts and emotions for Jesse pushed through everything else.

She returned with, *I miss our Wednesday talks. First thing I'm doing when I get back is coming in for some almond cake.*

Pursing her lips together, she turned off her phone and set it by her plate. She picked up her fork and stabbed a green bean. She noticed her parents didn't separate their food into neat piles like she did. It was as if she was afraid letting her food touch might explode the universe. Maybe something was wrong with her. Maybe she needed a counselor during the summer and not just the school year.

"Naomi?" her mother asked.

Setting down her fork, Naomi stood from the table and grabbed her phone. "I'm going for a walk."

Her mother swallowed what was probably a long lecture on friends and college and branching out, and looked at her husband before they both nodded. Sighs escaped their mouths as Naomi gave them a weak smile and left the table. In many ways, she knew she had always been mature beyond her years—logical and practical, levelheaded—but around her parents, all of that fell away and she was left acting like a sulky child. Maybe it was as much their fault as hers. She needed to get away to figure it out.

As soon as she was outside, she kicked off her sandals and left them on the deck. The sandy trails leading down to the beach were warm and dry, and the tall grasses tickled her arms as she passed by them. If she stayed long enough, she could watch the sunset, but part of her didn't care. She had no plans except to get away from her parents. No matter how grateful she was to be with them, they were suffocating her. As long as she lived under their roof, whether it was this house in California or the one they paid for in Massachusetts, she would never feel truly free.

Once she reached the end of the trails, she kept walking until her feet sank into wet sand. It was one of her favorite things to do—connect with the ocean in whatever way she could. As seawater rolled over her toes, she closed her eyes and let it lick its way up to her ankles. Then the wave receded and she looked down at the leftover bubbles, watching as they popped and left behind thin, sticky foam. The sunlight was rich orange now, filtering through some higher clouds along the horizon. It made the sand a warm brown, and for a moment she wanted to sit down and let the water splash over her entire body.

She looked back at the house and decided to walk on. She needed to be farther away from them. Today had snapped something inside her. College had been a temporary fix for making her feel independent, but in the end, she was at their mercy. Always. Even when she was held captive, she had felt that same sort of dependency, only on another family who was now in prison. Her parents' money paid for everything. Her clothes, her phone, her car at college, even the pens and notebooks she bought for her classes. That was why she needed Harvard and a degree, so she could live on her own one day. Her father's words frightened her. *And if you do any of it freelance or decide to go into the production end of things, you'll want those business skills.*

Of course, if she ended up with Jesse, he would take care of her. She wondered how she might adjust to a different lifestyle then, and if it even mattered as long as they had each other.

Watching her footprints fill with water, she kept walking up the beach. There were jellyfish scattered across the sand, shiny and transparent. There were smooth rocks, some shells. She bent to pick one up and ran her thumb over the surface as she imagined what it would be like to work every day for a paycheck. It was what her parents lived for, what they loved the most, it seemed. Her mother rarely traveled, and her father left for Germany three times a year for business. They adored their careers as much as each other—and her too, supposedly. For the second time, she turned and looked back at the house. She thought she saw them watching her from the glass doors leading out to the deck. She looked away and threw the shell into the waves, back to its home.

VIII

July

THE NAOMI'S HOPE FOUNDATION WAS SOMETHING Naomi had to get used to. The first time her mother took her to the building downtown, she found it hard to look at the sign with her name on it. Weird. It was even weirder talking to parents and boyfriends and girlfriends and wives and children who had all lost hope of finding their loved ones again. Many of them, when they found out she was *the* Naomi Jensen, looked at her with confident expressions, as if she could single-handedly bring back the person they couldn't find. She had been found and saved. She represented hope and grace and whatever else they needed to go on.

Today, as Naomi walked into the building with her mother, she braced herself for the pressure that came with comforting others on the brink of despair. Everyone who worked in the center was a volunteer. Some of them were private investigators gathering needed information. There were also financial advisors, sponsors who helped pay for continuing searches, and some were like her, victims who had a happy ending and were there for moral support. Mostly, she helped organize paperwork, which was what she hoped for today. She didn't feel like talking to anyone.

"Thanks for coming today," her mother said as Naomi walked beside her into the main lobby. "I always appreciate it."

"No problem, Mom. I know what this means to you. I want to help."

Naomi headed straight for the office once they were inside. She turned on the computer and looked at the calendar on the desk. There was nothing special coming up, and today seemed calm enough with few people in the lobby. She could see them through the blinds on the door's window. There were two sets of parents she recognized from last summer. Her mother hugged each of them as she said hello. Both couples had lost older children in their teens—considered runaways, if she remembered correctly. She guessed everyone had thought she was a runaway at first. How easy it was to misjudge the facts.

She looked away from the window and pulled out a list of things that needed to be done on the computer. An hour later, her mother came in with an exhausted expression. She sat across the room on a tattered sofa next to a water cooler.

"Next week is training week for parents and schools. Do you think you can help out with that too?"

Naomi nodded. "Yeah, I don't see why not."

"Good, because I had four volunteers cancel on me." She glanced at the door she had closed behind her, and then leaned forward and put her head in her hands. "Sometimes I wonder what I'm doing, Naomi. This seemed like a good idea at the time, when you were missing. It was therapeutic. I was doing good in the community, helping parents, teaching everyone about safety and caution and the importance of being there for loved ones. But it's . . . it's so much sometimes. Most of them will never be found. There are so few happy endings." She looked up, her eyes bloodshot. "Happy endings like yours."

Trying not to wince, Naomi looked away. Her ending was far from happy yet, at least the way she saw it. She focused on a pad of paper where her mother had doodled a picture of a zebra. The stripes were haphazard, as if she had been busy talking on the phone when she was coloring them in. Still, it was a good sketch. Naomi hadn't known her could mother could draw. "There's a lot you don't see," she said, thinking about how to respond. "Like when we do the trainings, maybe we have prevented something from happening. You never know."

Her mother sighed. "Yes, yes, you're right."

Staring at the zebra again, Naomi asked, "Did you start the foundation to find me?" When she looked up after a few moments of silence, her mother's bottom lip was trembling.

"I never thought I'd find you," she answered. She stood and pulled a paper cup from the dispenser by the water cooler. "I started all of this to make myself feel better. There, now you know. It wasn't some noble feat like everyone thinks. Still, when I organize and show up to our annual awareness walk, I feel good about what your father and I have started. I feel good about putting a lot of money toward something so charitable. I feel good seeing you here, helping, especially when you sit down to talk to someone who is hurting so much." She held the paper cup in her hands, her back to the cooler as Naomi looked up at her. "Because I know *you* are hurting, and yet you still talk to them. You must feel obligated because your name is a part of this. I'm sorry if you do. I'm sorry—"

"Mom, don't." Naomi stood and walked across the room. She noticed the crumpled paper cup in her mother's hand. She wanted to take it from her and throw it away, but it was as if a wall of insecurity was stacked up between them and she couldn't step forward any farther.

"Don't what?" her mother asked. "Feel sorry? Naomi, you don't understand what I mean when I say that."

Naomi opened her mouth to say she was sorry too, but the door opened and her father walked in carrying a box. He smiled at both of them.

"I had the flyers printed for the Petersen boy." He took a deep breath. "This is the third set. I don't even think the last set has been taken down yet."

"No, they want those ones"—her mother nodded to the box in his arms—"sent to Arizona. That's where he was last spotted, and they have a church there willing to distribute them." She waved her hand at the desk. "Put the box over there. We'll get them ready to go out today."

Her father nodded and then looked at Naomi, the smile spreading across his face so genuine she couldn't help but smile back. He crossed the room and kissed her on the cheek. "Hi, sweetie."

"Hi, Dad." For a moment, she felt happy. Then she looked back at the crumpled cup in her mother's hand.

IX

August

HER FLIGHT BACK TO MASSACHUSETTS COULDN'T come fast enough. She had been in such a rush to get home once the semester was over, and now all she wanted to do was return to her old habits and schedule of being alone. No judging from her mother. No more stressful foundation and sad people. No more knowing Jesse was only two hours away.

She and Finn had texted back and forth over the past few weeks, but she was still worried a phone call might seem too awkward—at least on her end. She wanted to see him face-to-face and tell him how she felt about staying friends. She kept asking herself if it was possible to stay friends with a guy and not fall for him when he was as hot and nice as Finn. She had known from the very beginning what might happen if she allowed her relationship with him to go anywhere beyond friendly café chit-chat, but how could she possibly call it all off? She would have to be as open with him as she could about what she felt for Jesse.

Now at the airport, her mother pulled up to the unloading bay and popped the trunk as Naomi unfastened her seatbelt.

"Do you want me to help you get your bags checked in?"

Naomi laughed. "No, Mom, I think I can manage. I've done it how many times now?"

Her mother shrugged. "A few, I guess." She leaned forward, as if to give Naomi a hug. "I'll just—"

"You can help me get them out of the trunk." Naomi opened her door and walked around to the rear of the car.

Her mother walked around a moment later, her face solemn. "I'm going to miss you, sweetheart."

Naomi paused, her hand wrapped around the handle of her largest bag. Evelyn had always called her sweetheart. She wasn't sure if it was a comfort or a burden to have her mother use the same term now.

Pulling on the bag, she thought about that day on the beach when she threw the shell into the waves, how smothered she had felt. Even now, she felt strangled as her mother helped her hoist the heavy bag out of the trunk. She wasn't sure she should keep coming home for summer break, unless Jesse stayed in Berkeley, of course, and there was a possibility of seeing him. He hadn't texted her since the two he had sent, and she hadn't dared try to see him again. She was sure he would let her know when he was released.

She looked down at her purse hanging on her shoulder and thought about the passport tucked in her wallet. This was the first time she would be traveling with it. She had found it buried in her desk at home, squished between some art projects. She knew it wouldn't be an easy choice to use it, if that time ever came.

"I'll miss you too, Mom." She set her bag down and hugged her mother, making sure to hold on a little longer than normal before letting go.

"Promise me you'll let me know if you need anything," her mother said, cupping Naomi's face in her hands as if she were ten years old and boarding her first flight. "I remember how intense everything is as you get into the higher classes, even at the undergraduate level."

"Yes, Mom, I will. I promise."

"I'll make sure your account gets steady installments." She raised an eyebrow. "Although you spent very little last semester. You know it's there to use, right?"

Naomi almost laughed. The money had added up over the past two years. She could buy a brand new car off the lot and shop every night for a year before it even started to dwindle. She shrugged and then realized the money meant everything to her parents. They worked hard to earn it, and to be able to give it to their daughter was obviously a big deal. "I appreciate it," she said in earnest. "I'll try to spend more. Or something."

Her mother laughed. "You don't have to spend it right away. I'm making sure you want me to keep sending you more."

"I can always save it, yes." For a moment, panic seized her as she thought about what might happen if she didn't have that money, even though she didn't spend much of it at the moment. Perhaps, subconsciously, that was why she didn't spend it.

"That's good," her mother answered. "I spoke with your father about setting up a portfolio for you. When you come home next summer, we'll get you in some classes so you can start learning how to invest."

"Great, Mom." They stared at each other in awkward silence until Naomi turned to grab her other bag and secured it to the top of the rolling luggage already out. "Bye. I love you. Tell Dad I love him too."

"I will. He's sorry he couldn't come see you off. Big meeting this morning."

"I understand."

After another hug, Naomi rolled her luggage onto the main walkway and entered the airport. When she looked back, her mother was answering a call on her cell phone. Some things never changed.

* * *

Becca was home when Naomi walked through the door. The house smelled like salt and limes.

"What are you making?" Naomi called out, shutting the door with her foot.

Becca poked her head out from the kitchen. "Welcome home!" She looked over her shoulder. "It's a new recipe I'm trying—margarita chicken. I hope it turns out. Derek hates chicken if it's too dry, and I can never get it just right."

Naomi licked her lips. "That sounds good. If you want, I can show you how to cook it moist."

"You can?" Becca's eyes widened as she wiped her hands on her apron. "How?"

"Let me get my bags to my room and I'll show you."

A few minutes later, she was in the kitchen placing raw chicken breasts between two pieces of plastic wrap. She opened a drawer and pulled out a meat pounder she hadn't used in a long time. "The trick is to get it all the same thickness," she explained, and whacked the center of one of the chicken breasts with the pounder.

Becca jumped. "Guess if you're pissed off at someone, that's a great way to let it out without killing them."

"Hah, yeah." Naomi continued to pound the four chicken breasts to get them a quarter-inch thick.

Folding her arms, Becca rested her hip against the counter and watched. "So where did you learn all this?" she asked over the *whack! whack! whack!* of Naomi's pounding. "I swear, every time you cook it's like some amazing gourmet thing. Did your mom teach you or something?"

Naomi stopped pounding. "My mom can chop vegetables, and that's about it. I think she barely learned how to use the coffee maker, like, two years ago. She relies on the housekeeper most of the time. Or my dad. He likes to cook, but he never has time to show me anything. I'm pretty sure I know more than him."

"Okay, so who taught you?" Becca leaned forward, waiting for an explanation. She hadn't dyed her hair in a while, and her dark brown roots were starting to show against the raven black. Naomi noticed she wasn't wearing her usual red lipstick.

"How's Derek?" Naomi asked, wishing she hadn't offered to help. In the two years she had lived with Becca, she had somehow managed to avoid telling her about the kidnapping.

"He's fine." Becca pinched her lips together. It was the face she usually pulled when Naomi got evasive about her past. Naomi knew Becca was only trying to get to know her better, but her approach was a little too courtroom. She always felt like she was being examined on the witness stand. Why she kept avoiding the subject, she wasn't sure. This time it felt wrong. If she was going to keep living with Becca—her only friend outside of Finn and Jesse—she had to tell her the truth. She whacked each piece of chicken a few more times and then set the pounder in the sink as her mind filled with memories from the house.

"A lady I knew a few years ago taught me how to cook," she said while peeling away the top layer of plastic wrap. "She was Italian and she made the most delicious things. I used to hate mushrooms, and now I love them. Her food was that good." She smiled. "Although I still hate seafood. She couldn't seem to push that on me while I was there."

"While you were where?"

Naomi spotted the bowl of marinade Becca had prepared. She set it by the chicken and carefully dropped each piece into the mixture. "I know this is going to sound insane," she said, "but haven't you ever put together my name and hometown and a big story about a kidnapping a few years ago? I thought you'd put two-and-two together pretty fast, being in law school and all. It was a major case. I got national coverage."

Becca took a step back. "The CEO story? That big software company?"

After washing her hands, Naomi reached for the box of plastic wrap so she could cover the marinade. "Yeah, that one."

"You were kidnapped? That CEO's daughter is *you*?"

"Yeah."

"And you never told me?"

Naomi carried the marinade to the fridge and set it on the top shelf. Most of the shelves were empty, but Becca had bought Coke. Naomi grabbed a can and opened the lid. "I thought you'd figure it out," she said with a shrug.

"No, not really. I remember the parents . . . I mean your parents, and some hype about them neglecting you or something." She tugged on a piece of her hair. "And some controversy over one of the kidnappers and . . . you." Her face blanched. "You were in love with him and he went to prison."

"Yeah, crazy, huh?"

"Are you still in love with him?"

Naomi took a sip of Coke and stared at the kitchen floor. It was wood, and she noticed a fine layer of dust along the edges near the cabinets. "Yeah, I am. He's out on parole and I went to see him. I wasn't supposed to because he's not released yet and he's not supposed to have any contact with his . . ." she made quotation marks with her fingers ". . . victim."

"Oh, wow." Becca looked around for a moment and then walked to the table and pulled out a chair. She sat down and stared at Naomi as if she were a complete stranger.

Naomi swallowed another sip of Coke. "I don't understand why everyone acts this way when they find out. This is why I didn't tell you about it in the first place. Just because I was kidnapped doesn't mean you have to treat me differently."

"But he's a *criminal* and you're in *love* with him. So that's why you never go out on dates. What about that guy you went out with on your birthday?"

"Finn?" She laughed, trying to make it sound natural. It came out shaky. "Oh, he's just a friend and it wasn't a date." She turned away, afraid she was blushing. There was no way she was going to tell Becca about the kiss.

"Huh, well, this is incredible, Naomi. I had no idea. So the whole cooking thing, you learned all that while you were captive? What kidnappers teach their hostage how to cook?"

"I wasn't a hostage. They wanted to keep me. Forever."

Silence.

Naomi turned around to see Becca's mouth hanging open. "And no, Evelyn didn't teach me everything about cooking. She taught me a few things, enough for me to start learning on my own once I was . . . once it was all over and I was back home. And I've learned a lot here too." She clapped her hands together. "So, for the chicken, when it's finished marinating, put it in a skillet on medium-high to sear it until it's golden. Then flip it and do the same on the other side. Then get your thermometer and—"

Becca raised her hands as if surrendering. "Holy shit, Naomi, I don't care about the chicken. You were kidnapped. Don't you want to talk about it?"

She shouldn't have told her.

"No, I don't want to talk about it. I told you so you would know, and that's it. And if you ever tell Finn, I will kill you."

"He doesn't know?"

"He knows I have a boyfriend, but that's all."

"A boyfriend in prison."

"He's on parole now, not in prison. And he might have done bad things in the past, but he's different now. He's changed." She set her Coke can on the counter and walked out of the kitchen.

"Wait! I was going to tell you to join us for dinner!" Becca called out. "Derek'll be here in an hour. You can invite Finn."

Naomi didn't look back. She went upstairs and slipped into her bedroom, shutting the door before she stretched out on her stomach across the bed. It was stupid to get angry with Becca for judging Jesse, but she couldn't help it. Her heart felt like it was on fire anytime someone assumed he was some terrible criminal and she was stupid to love him. Maybe he had been an awful person. Maybe he still was and she couldn't see it. She hoped she hadn't lost that much of her sanity, but as she looked around at her piles of unfinished art projects and the stacks of history, art, and language books on her shelf from previous semesters, she wondered how sane she truly was. Other students lived on campus and got drunk at parties. Other students dated and graduated and got married and led normal lives. She wanted to marry an ex-con and pretend being kidnapped had been a normal thing she could forget about. Burying her face in her quilt again, she held back her tears and waited for the pain to ebb away into nothingness. It usually didn't take long.

＊ ＊ ＊

The next few days were filled with settling back in and registering for classes. Every semester, Naomi sat in her bedroom with her laptop and registered online, but this time when she tried, an error message popped up that said she needed to visit the campus registrar in person. A little buzz started in her head. As she drove to campus and found a parking spot, the buzzing grew louder.

Failure, it hissed. *You. Screwed. Up.*

Her heart was pounding by the time she reached the building and stood in line. She knew what they were going to tell her, and she didn't want to hear it. Maybe she was wrong. Maybe she was overreacting. She readjusted her backpack on her shoulders and looked down at her sweating palms. She wasn't wrong.

"I-I can't seem to register online and it said I needed to come here," she told the lady at the window.

"All right. Let's look up a few things."

Naomi gave the woman her student ID. As she waited, she looked at all the lines around her. There were so many people she didn't know, so many she didn't even want to know. When she looked back on her life, that part of herself hadn't changed because of her kidnapping. She had been a loner in high school, and she was a loner now.

The lady at the window looked up from her computer. "You're welcome to register," she said with a smile, "but you'll need to do it with an advisor here." She looked at the monitor and squinted. "It looks like they might want to speak with you about your GPA and your scholarship."

Annoyed at the unnecessary step to be told to go see her advisor, Naomi nodded and left. It was after one o'clock before she could get in to see her advisor in another building.

"Naomi, hello!"

Kate Ramirez was one of the only people Naomi had voluntarily told about her kidnapping. It seemed necessary for the person guiding the future of her education to understand the problems of her past. Kate urged her to sit down and pulled up Naomi's file.

"I'm surprised you remember me," Naomi said with a nervous laugh. "You must see hundreds of students a year."

Kate winked at her before turning her attention back to the monitor. She was young, probably in her late twenties, with black hair like Becca's, only it wasn't dyed. She had thick bangs cut straight across her forehead. Naomi focused on her silky yellow shirt with little bows tying off the sleeves.

"Of course I remember you," Kate said with a laugh. "You're an exceptional student, and you're unique."

Naomi wasn't sure if she should be offended. The way Kate said "unique" clearly meant, *like I'd forget someone with such an interesting past.* Because it wasn't her exceptional abilities as a student that set her apart. Harvard was full of exceptional students.

"So," Naomi said slowly, leaning forward, her chair creaking. "It's my grades, isn't it? I've lost my scholarship?" A bitter taste entered her mouth.

Kate stopped scrolling down the screen and turned to face Naomi. "Well, yes." She winced and shook her head. "You were doing great, and then you turned off. Your professors noted a lack of coursework submitted and you graded poorly on every exam." She folded her arms. "Did something happen? A death in the family? An accident of some sort?"

"No, and it's not the scholarship I'm worried about—I have money in my account to cover tuition, if I need." She looked down at her hands and started scratching at a spot on her wrist. Her mother might kill her if she drained her account for tuition. It was a lot of money, and she wouldn't have much left to pay for anything else during the semester.

Kate raised an eyebrow, making it disappear behind her bangs. "This is a renewable scholarship,

Naomi, and it's merit-based. Winning it was a huge accomplishment, and I would hate to see you lose it. If you write an appeal letter, you may be able to get it back. It appears they've put the scholarship on probation for a short period of time." She swept a hand across her bangs, feathering them a little. "And this isn't only about tuition money. If you want to get anywhere in this institution, you must keep your grades at a certain level. You know all of this."

The disappointment in Kate's expression made Naomi look away. She could hear muffled voices from the office next door. She shifted in her chair. "I've never . . . I've never had bad grades before," she said, her cheeks burning. "I don't know what to do."

The smallest hint of a smile played on Kate's lips. "You wouldn't be the first student I've heard say that. It isn't the end of the world, but I'm afraid to say you've lost your scholarship for the time being—unless you appeal—and you must retake the courses you failed, whether you care about the scholarship or not. I would say you could take makeup exams, but there were also assignments you didn't turn in, as well as some attendance issues."

Naomi felt queasy. "So I failed them? Completely?"

Kate scrunched her nose. "Did you look up your grades when they were posted?"

"No, I was . . ."

Distracted. Obsessed. Too busy worrying about Jesse.

Kate sniffed and looked at her monitor. "You failed your art history class. Your final was a large portion of your grade. You passed the rest, but not with satisfactory grades. I suggest retaking the courses."

Naomi held her breath and gripped the edge of her chair. "That will put me behind, and I have to pay for them again, right?"

Kate nodded. "Of course, but with no scholarship this time. This is why when you came in your freshman year I told you how important it was to keep up your grades." Her arms were still folded, and her stern expression hardened for a moment before melting into pity. "As I said before, the funding institution may make an exception if something in your personal life took precedence over your grades. Is that what happened?"

Naomi realized this was the second time Kate had asked the question. Scratching at the spot on her wrist again, she mumbled, "I don't think what happened would count as a convincing appeal."

"Does this have to do with your kidnapping?"

Naomi looked up. "Um, kind of. I found out Jesse . . . you know, the guy who—"

Kate smiled. "Yes, I know who you're talking about."

"I found out he's on parole. My mother told me right before the end of the semester, and I couldn't think of anything else but him. My world turned upside down. I didn't expect him to get out so soon." She rubbed her hands on her knees. "I know it sounds stupid. I know I can't get back my scholarship just because I fell in love with someone."

Kate frowned. "You might be surprised, Naomi. I can e-mail you the paperwork for an appeal. Think about what you can do to convince them you were having a hard time. You see a counselor for the kidnapping, don't you?"

"Yeah."

"Get her to write up a statement for you. Do whatever you can to get the money back."

Naomi nodded and stood from her chair. She wanted to be home.

"And if you want to retake your courses, I can get you signed up," Kate said, leaning forward as if to grab Naomi and sit her back down. Instead, she looked at her outstretched arm and lowered it. "Don't take this too hard. This is just a hiccup and you'll get over it easily."

Looking down at Kate, Naomi held her breath. Retaking courses for an entire semester wasn't a hiccup. Jesse wasn't a hiccup. Things were far from resolved with him. She wondered if her mother would pay for the rest of her schooling if she was unable to get another scholarship or win back the one she had lost. She didn't want to find out. She wanted everything to go away or at least get back to normal, even if that meant Jesse was back in prison for three more years. She couldn't do both. And, she realized as she looked over at Kate's computer and the screen showing grades and notes and everything relating to her academic life, maybe she didn't want to do both.

"Can I talk to my parents and come back?" she asked.

"Of course, but classes fill up fast, so don't take too long. And fill out that appeal paperwork as soon as you get it."

"Thank you for your help." She turned to leave, but stopped when Kate cleared her throat.

"Naomi, good luck. I still think you're an exceptional student."

Naomi smiled and thanked her one more time, then left. When she was outside, she pulled out her phone and scrolled to her mother's number. Her hand trembled as she poised her finger over the call button. She couldn't. Not yet. Her mother was so proud she was at Harvard, following in her footsteps, even if it wasn't for a law degree. This would ruin everything. She remembered her mother's bloodshot eyes that day in the office, the crushed cup.

She scrolled past her mother's name on the phone and kept looking through the list. The list wasn't long, but one name screamed louder than the others. Finn Giachetti.

X

WHEN SHE ANSWERED THE KNOCK ON HER DOOR, Naomi found Finn standing on her front porch with a cup of iced tea and a Styrofoam box she guessed contained a slice of almond cake.

"I'm sure you could order this somewhere else," he said with a lopsided smile as he held them out to her, "but nobody makes the combo quite like Java, and you said you wanted to order some when you got back."

She couldn't keep the smile off her face as her mouth started to water. "Finn, I invited you over for dinner. That didn't mean you had to bring something."

He rolled his eyes. "No, I invited myself over for dinner against your protests, so that *does* mean I had to bring something. Now, enjoy." He pushed the cup and box at her. She took both. "And here's a straw."

She balanced it on top of the cup and stepped aside to let him in.

"What can I help with?" he asked, rubbing his hands together as he entered the kitchen. "You clearly said this isn't a date, so I'm going to help."

Naomi was still standing by the door. She pushed it closed with her foot and followed Finn into the kitchen. He was wearing the ripped jeans again. In fact, she was sure they were the exact same pair he always wore. She smiled at his black Jimi Hendrix shirt.

"It's pretty much done—just spaghetti. Nothing special."

He walked to the oven and peeked inside. She had put in a loaf of French bread earlier. "Did you make that?" he asked, looking over his shoulder.

"I haven't mastered baking yet," she said, shrugging. "I bought the loaf at the store, but I made a garlic spread to put in the middle. It's warming up in there."

"Still, it looks great. And the sauce?" He lifted the lid off the stockpot and peeked inside. "Did you make this from *scratch*?"

Chuckling, Naomi walked to the counter and set down her almond cake and iced tea. "Yeah, I did. Why are you so fascinated?"

He returned the lid on the pot and turned around. "I don't know. My mom doesn't cook much—she never cooked when I was growing up—so, yeah, this all smells amazing. I'm used to eating at Java or boiling ramen noodles." He put on a wicked smile. "I knew it was a good idea to invite myself over. Maybe I'll do it more often."

Naomi grabbed the straw on top of her iced tea and began tearing off the end of the wrapper. "Finn, about us hanging out, I called you because I'm . . . well, I have a problem and I don't think anyone will understand except you. I don't think my housemate Becca would understand what I've done since she's never dropped below a 4.0 GPA. She tends to judge people who slack off." She finished unwrapping the straw and shoved it through the hole on the cup lid. "And my mom will kill me when she finds out. I'm not sure what I'm going to do and I . . ." She picked up the tea and took a long gulp. The heavenly taste kept her tears at bay for the moment. There was no way she was going to cry in front of Finn.

He waited for her to finish. She took another sip of the drink and continued.

"And I have things I need to tell you because you seem to understand me on a level not many people do. Well, two people. You and Jesse."

Finn nodded.

"Jesse is my boyfriend."

"I thought as much."

She looked down at her feet and noticed her nail polish was almost worn off. She always painted her toenails red—the same red Evelyn had used on her nails. When she looked up at Finn, he was peeking into the uncovered pot on the back burner.

"Noodles," he said, smiling as steam rose up around his face.

Naomi rushed forward. "I need to check them." She snatched a spaghetti spoon and leaned past Finn so she could reach the pot. He didn't move as she twirled the spoon and caught some noodles.

"Want me to get out of the way?" he asked, grinning down at her.

With the spoon still poised over the pot, she looked up at him and realized he was close enough for her elbow to brush against him. He smelled like almond cake. She asked herself for the hundredth time why she had let him come over for dinner.

"No, I'm good," she said, backing away with the spoon raised in the air. She looked at the dangling noodles dripping hot water onto the floor. The ends were beginning to turn white, which meant they were done. She lifted the spoon above her mouth and took a bite. "Perfect," she mumbled, chewing. As soon as she noticed Finn watching her with a huge grin on his face, she turned away. "Can you drain the pot in the sink? There's a colander already in there."

"Sure."

Fumbling her way around the kitchen, she let Finn help her set the table and dish up the food. When they were both seated, she put her hands on her knees and took a deep breath. No matter what happened, she wouldn't screw up. She wasn't going to hide anymore. She was going to tell Finn the truth, trusting he would understand and be there for her when nobody else could be. She hoped confiding in him would show him how highly she thought of him. His eyes were on her. He unfolded his napkin and set it on his lap. She let out her breath and picked up her fork. "Let's eat."

He smiled. "Excellent." After his first bite, he leaned forward and licked his lips. "Amazing, Naomi. It's better than a restaurant."

She laughed. "Thanks. Maybe I should teach you some cooking skills if you like it so much."

"I'd love that."

They kept eating. Naomi knew the spaghetti was nowhere near as good as Evelyn's, but she kept trying to perfect it. It reminded her of the first time she had eaten it—not a good memory, but food seemed to be one of the things from her captivity she held on to with warm feelings. Perhaps her memory of how the spaghetti tasted was over-enhanced, but she was certain she would get it right someday. She watched Finn as he polished off one plate of spaghetti and dished up another.

"I hope you don't mind," he said, glancing at her as a sly grin crossed his face.

"Not at all. There's nobody but us." Resting her chin in her palm, she smiled at him. "So tell me about your promotion."

"Oh, that!" He swallowed. "I've been there for about a year now, so when the assistant manager left, I applied for the position. I didn't think I'd get it." He looked down at his clothes. "I mean, I was just a waiter, and I don't always present myself as super professional. Plus, there was no way I was going to cut my hair. But they didn't seem to care about any of that. The last assistant manager was so clean and polished all the time. I thought that's what they wanted."

"You didn't think you'd get it? Seriously?" She leaned back in her chair. "You're so open with people, even if you think you're a quiet person. You seem like a natural leader. And look, you even got me to open up and go out somewhere on my birthday. Do you have any idea how huge that is for me?"

He swallowed another bite of food as a frown spread across his face. "Actually, Naomi, I hope this doesn't freak you out, but after the semester ended and you were gone, I tried to look you up online to see if I could find you on Facebook."

She stopped breathing for a moment. It didn't freak her out that he had tried to find her, but she knew typing in her name would pull up hundreds of links about her. All those news articles and TV clips—most of them she had never watched, and didn't want to. She closed her eyes. "I'm not on any social networks. I deleted everything I could after I . . . I . . . that's what I was going to tell you. I—"

"Yeah, I found out about what happened to you."

She opened her eyes. "So now you know who Jesse is. Now you're going to think I'm some sort of—"

His change of expression cut her off. He looked concerned.

"I have no idea what you're going through," he said, setting down his fork. "I understand now what you meant by the train tracks when you said you couldn't be with him. I thought you meant he was going to university somewhere else, in another state or something. But he's in—"

"He was in prison. He's on parole now."

"Right, but I take it you're still not allowed to see him."

"No."

"And that's hard for you."

She nodded. Finn seemed to be waiting for her to speak. It was his patience with her that opened her up, she realized.

"Finn," she said in as strong a voice as she could, "this is hard for me because . . ." She glanced at his yin and yang tattoo and thought about how she felt so light and dark at the same time. She looked up into his eyes.

111

"It's hard for me because I like you more than anyone I've met in a long time, but Jesse, he's . . . I don't even know how to explain it. He's different, and I've loved him for so long, and it's not fair to you because I know you're interested in me, and I'm in love with someone who kidnapped me, and you probably think he's some big creep." She looked down at her lap. "But he's not, and I'm sorry. I'm sorry if you feel like I've led you on, but now you know where I'm coming from."

Rubbing her knees again, she tried to lift her focus to Finn, but could only get as far as her plate of spaghetti. "I need a friend right now who can try to understand where I'm at," she continued. "You make me feel comfortable with myself, so that's why I called you." Before Finn could say anything, she forced herself to look at him. "And I kissed you because I think you're hot and you're nice and you listen to me. At that point, I thought Jesse wouldn't get out of prison for three more years. I was lonely and I like you and I wasn't thinking. I'm sorry."

Her hands were shaking now and she steadied them against her knees. "There, I said it. Now you know."

Finn lifted his napkin from his lap and set it on the table. He rested his hand near his water glass and ran a finger along the base. "I don't know why you think you've led me on," he said, smiling gently. "You told me you have a boyfriend, and I've already told you I was sorry for the kiss, so we're on even ground. There's nothing to worry about. I hope you understand I'm not expecting anything outside of friendship." His smile widened. "Although I'll be disappointed if I can't come over and eat all the time."

His honesty settled her down. The trembling in her hands subsided. "Friends with benefits, huh?" she asked with a smirk.

"Sure, even if the benefits are food, I'll take it."

She laughed.

Later, after Finn had helped clean up the dishes, they went outside to take a walk to the nearest park. The sun would set soon. Naomi liked the way it fell across the sidewalk in golden patches. The smell of freshly-cut grass hung in the air.

"There's one thing," Finn said as they walked side-by-side. He kept his hands shoved into his pockets. His hair fell across his forehead as he looked at the ground. "You said your housemate wouldn't understand because of her GPA, and your mom will kill you when she finds out. What does that have to do with your kidnapping?"

"Oh." Everything rushed back to her as she realized how easily she had forgotten about the scholarship and her grades. She told Finn about what had happened earlier that day when she tried to register and that she had called him right after she left her advisor's office.

"I've never had bad grades before," she said, finishing the story. "I feel like a huge failure, and you're the only one I can talk to about it. I don't know if I should use the money I have to pay for my tuition and register while I can, or if I should call and ask my parents what they think I should do. They'll be so disappointed." The very thought made her mouth go dry.

They had reached the park by this point. Finn guided her to a bench and sat down. She sat next to him and watched a lady walking three Pekingese a few yards away. They trotted in front of their owner, constantly looking back as if seeking approval.

"I know you don't want to," Finn said, leaning forward, "but I think you should call your parents. They're going to find out eventually, and the longer you take to tell them, the worse it's going to look."

Naomi wrinkled her nose. "Yeah, you're right. Of course you're right." She tapped the bench with her fingernails, her thoughts slipping along the figures in her bank account. She could use that money and postpone telling her parents. Her mother wouldn't check the account for weeks. Maybe. But who was she kidding? "You're too nice, Finn," she said, still tapping.

"Too nice, huh?"

The lady with the dogs was getting closer. "I don't mean it in a bad way, honestly."

He raised an eyebrow.

She sighed, knowing she had to explain further. "See, I had this boyfriend in high school. His name was Brad. His mother wasn't rich, but he acted like he was. He dressed in all these stupid name-brand clothes, and he wore expensive cologne. We'd always go to these parties on the beach where everyone would get drunk, and then he'd take me to his house and he'd, well, he was a jerk and he was abusive. I'm over all of that now, but the way you are, how different you are from him, it makes me happy. I used to think every guy was like Brad. I didn't know any different, but then I met Jesse, and now you." She stopped and watched the lady pass them, her dogs yipping at her and Finn.

"Hush, now!" the lady hissed at them, yanking on their hot-pink leashes.

"Yeah," Finn said, chuckling. "I'm not an abusive preppy wanna-be."

"No, that's not what I meant." Naomi leaned forward, bending in half as she pressed her forehead to her knees. She squeezed her eyes shut and gripped the edge of the bench. She wanted to fold in on herself and disappear, but that wouldn't solve anything. That much she knew. She breathed slowly, knowing she had to make Finn understand.

"What I mean," she continued, "is that it's pathetic how I never knew any different. It's pathetic that I think about Jesse and I would die to be with him, but I'm still wondering if he *is* abusive in some way. I think that's my biggest fear—that he won't be what I think he is because I'm blinded by what happened to me. He's changed for the better. I know he has, but I'm still scared. Then I think of you and how happy I feel when I'm with you. I feel like myself. I'm like that around Jesse too, but I also know him better, been with him longer. I know he has issues and I don't know how things are going to be with him, but he means so much to me."

She let go of the bench and sat up. Her face was hot from all the blood running to her head. She was dizzy until Finn turned to her and pulled her into his arms. He held her tightly, saying nothing. She relaxed against him.

"So what I'm trying to say," she said, resting her cheek on his shoulder, "is that you're nice and I'm not used to that. Sorry it took so many words."

He laughed. "And you hope my niceness lasts," he finished for her.

"Yes."

"Even when Jesse is free."

"Yes."

"And even when you leave to be with him."

116

She tried to pull away, but Finn kept a tight hold on her and said, "No, no, I didn't mean that in a bad way. Don't get upset. I'm making sure we're on the same page. You love Jesse, right?"

She opened her mouth, but no words would come. She knew what Finn was trying to do. He knew she was attracted to him. She had told him as much earlier. If she could tell him she loved Jesse while he was holding her, she would know it was true. But was it? She remembered stumbling out of her mother's SUV as soon as Jesse drove up. She pictured his face, the way he had kissed her and told her he hated the taste of licorice, but kissed her anyway. He had been there for her in a time of her life when she was most vulnerable, most frightened, and most alone.

"I don't know," she whispered.

This time, when she tried to pull away from Finn, he let her go. She looked at the dimple in his left cheek and the way he trimmed his sideburns a little longer than most men his age. The truth was, all the little things she loved about Jesse were getting smaller in her mind, especially now as she looked at Finn. So she focused on a spot over his shoulder, at a tall tree shading the path winding through the park. She thought about Jesse's freckles, the small spattering of them across the bridge of his nose, the deep red of his hair. He wasn't her type, by any means, but it didn't matter. It was obvious she was physically attracted to Finn as much as she was to Jesse, but there was something deeper about Jesse that made her latch on to him stronger than it had with anyone, even Finn. It likely had to do with the circumstances of their meeting, the amount of time they had shared in so intimate a space, the fact that he had rescued her. There were other things too—his courage to change, the way he read to her from books in such passionate, heart-melting tones, how tangible his love had become for her.

Finally, she looked at Finn. "I do love him. I guess a lot of people might say the *why* and *how* of my love for him is wrong, but I can't make it go away."

Picking at a piece of paint peeling from the bench, Finn said, "I can understand that." He pulled off the strip of paint and tossed it onto the ground. "So we're on the same page, then? You want to be with Jesse, and this thing between us is just a friendship?"

Naomi nodded, her stomach flipping upside down. "Yeah."

"I'm cool with that." Finn smiled, but it looked forced. He stood from the bench and held out his hand to help Naomi to her feet. "I'll walk you home."

Naomi took his hand and didn't let go until he pulled away and pushed both of his hands into his pockets.

XI

"YOU DO REALIZE WE'RE NOT MADE OF MONEY," HER mother said over the phone once Naomi called her and told her about the scholarship. "No matter how much you think your father and I make. Do you have any idea how expensive tuition is at Harvard? It's not just another penny in the jar. We can afford it, yes, but it will eat into other things—the foundation, for one. We don't have sponsors with bottomless pockets."

It was the first time Naomi had ever heard her mother talk about money in such a way. "I know, Mom. I'll pay for it myself, then."

"With what?"

"The money you've put in my account."

There was a long pause. "That would maybe pay for one semester. Then what are you going to do?"

"I don't know. Get a job. Apply for a loan."

Another pause. Naomi imagined her mother dying of sarcastic laughter on the other end.

"Mom, I know a job wouldn't cover it all, but if I was trying, you could at least help me. You won't stop my rent payments or anything, right?" Her throat swelled as she pressed the phone tightly to her ear. She had never once in her life had to worry about money. "Mom, I'm so sorry. I'm so, so sorry."

There was silence for a moment, and then her mother sniffed. "We're not going to cut you off, sweetheart. Of course we'll keep paying your rent. I'm just . . . I'm disappointed. You've always kept up your grades. Even when you came home once you were released from the hospital, you did what it took to get your GED. You were a mess and you still graduated with a 4.0." She stopped, and Naomi imagined her putting a hand to her forehead. "I don't understand why finding out about Jesse's parole would have kept you from passing your classes with flying colors, like you always do."

Naomi wanted to finish the thought for her and say, "Like you always did, huh, Mom?" but she kept her mouth shut.

Silence.

Relaxing her hand on the phone, Naomi stopped pacing her bedroom and sat down at her desk. She ran her finger along the edge of her laptop. "Mom, I—"

"I'll call the school today and get your tuition paid," she interrupted. "You focus on getting your grades back up this semester."

"Yes, Mom."

"I love you, Naomi, but if you can't do what it takes at Harvard, we'll have to figure out something else—as long as you're relying on us, anyway. We can afford to pay for you to go there, but not if you can't earn it."

"I understand." Again, she thought of USC, but shoved it away. For some terrible reason she couldn't pinpoint, the thought of studying film somewhere else—anywhere, for that matter—made her want to hurl, but she was too far in to go back now.

"Go register for your classes and please focus on school. Do you understand?"

"Yes."

Naomi imagined her mother shaking a finger at her, as if she was a toddler being scolded. But this *was* a scolding, one that stung her to the core. She was getting tired of her mother's displeasure, even if she deserved it. She had to end the conversation.

"I love you, Mom. I gotta go."

A long pause. "All right. Please call me if you need anything . . . *anything* . . . okay? You aren't alone."

"I know."

But she felt alone. She ended the phone call and set her phone on the desk.

* * *

For three weeks, Finn came over almost every night for dinner. Naomi started teaching him a few basics. "So you don't have to survive off ramen noodles," she said, laughing as she showed him how to cook a hamburger. The next night she showed him how to make baked potatoes, and the night after that, lasagna. Dinner food, breakfast food, it didn't matter. The list went on and on. When they sat down to eat scrambled eggs with some toast and sliced strawberries, Naomi took a bite and let out a heavy sigh. The eggs were missing something and she had no idea what it was.

"I can never get them right. Not like he did."

Finn looked up from shoveling the eggs into his mouth. "Like who did? Jesse?"

"No. Eric."

"Oh." He finished chewing and swallowed. "It's interesting how much you care. I've never seen anything like it."

She took a long drink of orange juice and then poked at a strawberry with her fork. "Well, I lived with them for almost an entire year. I was never allowed to go anywhere except the backyard, so you can imagine how close I'd get to them, especially when I could see they cared for me. I didn't think anyone else ever had. My parents were never there for me back home, and Brad was a jerk. My counselor keeps saying people won't understand. I know she's right, but thanks for not thinking I'm crazy." She jabbed the strawberry with her fork and put it in her mouth. "Or maybe you do think I'm crazy."

"No, I don't. You feed me, are you kidding?" His smile was warm and sincere. She knew he cared more about her than just for the food she made.

"Well, tomorrow I'll teach you how to make one of my favorite pasta dishes."

"Sounds good to me." He looked up and moved his hand across the table, closer to her. "And I don't think you're crazy. I think it's impressive how deeply you feel for people."

She looked at his hand and moved hers on top. Touching him made her lips twitch into a smile. She knew she should avoid getting closer to him, but she couldn't help it. She curled her fingers around his hand, squeezing.

"Thank you, Finn."

He was still for a moment, and then slipped his hand out from under hers.

∗ ∗ ∗

That night, they went to the train tracks and listened to the river again. Naomi rested her head on Finn's shoulder and thought about what she would do when Jesse was free. It was getting more difficult to keep her feelings from slipping into a soft, sweet affection for Finn. Then she realized she had already let them get that way, as if being around him was a security blanket—a way for her to keep warm when the chill all around her was too much. Finn put his arm around her and then quickly removed it. He started talking about how he grew up in New York with his mother and how she was diagnosed with cancer when he graduated from high school.

"She refuses to get chemo," he explained, "and I support her decision. She wants to live her life until it's over without all the pain and expense of medical treatments. So far, she's been fine, living a lot longer than the doctors predicted. She takes care of herself, but she can't work anymore because it's too stressful." He paused. The chirping crickets seemed louder. "So, when she said it was her dream I go to Harvard like she did, I told her I'd try."

Surprised to hear his mother had gone to Harvard too, Naomi almost moved her head from his shoulder.

She stayed as still as she could as she asked, "But you haven't?"

"Not yet. My grades weren't the best in high school. I'm afraid if I don't get in, it will hit my mom hard. She can't have that sort of shock when stress can make things so much worse."

Naomi stiffened a little as she let that sink in. "So, you're waiting until she's . . . gone . . . or something?"

Finn shifted. "It sounds so bad when you say it that way."

"Well?" She lifted her head and tried to look him in the eyes, but he kept his focus on the ground. "Finn?"

"She thinks I was accepted and I'm taking classes right now," he said, kicking at some rocks. "That's why I can't move back home. This is such a big deal to her. I'm not sure how I'm going to get accepted."

"You go see a guidance counselor and ask. I can't believe you've lied to her. You told me to call my parents about the scholarship thing. They've paid my tuition and now I'm back in classes. I even filled out the appeal paperwork to try to get the scholarship back, even though I doubt they'll consider it. Still, I tried. Everything is working out because you pushed me a little to do the right thing. Lying to your mother isn't the right thing. If she found out, that would hurt her more than knowing you didn't get in." She folded her arms. It was much easier to deal with other people's issues than her own. How easy it was to spit out opinions and advice like a ticket dispenser.

Finn kept kicking at the rocks. "I know, I know. She was so happy when I moved here. She misses me, but she loves that I'm following in her footsteps. I'm her only child, and Dad left her so long ago. I'm all she has to put her hopes on."

"Then don't disappoint her in something far bigger than what school you're going to. There are other universities. Harvard isn't everything."

She couldn't believe she had just said that, because it had been everything to her not so long ago. Now, she wasn't so sure.

"I know."

Leaning forward, Naomi tried to look into Finn's face. The moon was bright. She could see the rigid set of his jaw and the frown on his lips.

"Finn, I understand the pressure thing. My mom went to Harvard too. She's a lawyer. Do you have any idea how that makes me feel? How much I know that no matter what I do, I will never measure up to her? Coming here has been the closest I can get."

His silence was thick, but she knew he was processing what she had said. "That's some heavy pressure, yeah," he said. "At least you're doing something about it. I've been avoiding so much crap lately. I was thinking about moving home and telling my mom the truth, but then you started coming into Java and we got to be friends, and then we went out that one night, and then I was made assistant manager, and I've kept putting it off. Now I see you all the time and I don't want to leave. I want to try to apply again. I want to make my mom proud and be as strong as I always try to believe I am."

"Crap, Finn, I'm sorry. I didn't know I was a part of your decision to stay here."

"No, it's a good thing. I told you—now I want to try harder. I'll apply again and see what I can get, even if I'm put on a wait list."

"Good, because you're smart and you shouldn't be wasting your time working in a café when you could be working in a café *and* working toward designing buildings." She nudged his shoulder. "Right?"

"Yeah."

"Jesse is an architect," she said, surprised it came out so quickly. "He graduated high school early and got his degree in college by the time he was twenty."

Finn let out a puff of air. "Damn."

"Yeah, I know. But he screwed up in other parts of his life, and sometimes I wonder if it's because he was trying too hard to get ahead and impress his dad, who wanted him to teach English instead. I'm saying it's okay to take things slower. Figure out what you want."

He turned to her, his attention finally on her. She chewed on her bottom lip as the desire to kiss him again swept through her. No. Wrong, wrong, wrong. Only friends. She wanted Jesse. It was always Jesse . . . or was it? The more she looked at Finn, the more she questioned her decision. In the dark, everything felt off-kilter and blurry. Finn was so immediate. She wondered what it said about her that she wanted him all of a sudden. She leaned closer, wanting another kiss.

"Is this what you want?" he asked, backing away. "Harvard? Film? Everything you're going after? Even Jesse?"

"I-I think so," she stuttered a little too quickly, trying to recover from the obvious rejection. "I mean, I'm in so deep now, with everything. How could I possible change it?"

He looked at her with longing in his eyes. "It's never too late to go back. Is it?"

"Go back where?"

"I don't know. Never mind."

"No, Finn, what did you mean by that?"

"Nothing." He stood and offered her his hand. "It's late and you said you have homework to finish."

She took his hand, wondering if he meant to ask if she thought it was too late to go back to *him*. It was tempting. "Yeah."

The ride home was quiet. Finn parked in the driveway and stared at her front porch. "So, are we still on for tomorrow?"

"Sure. Bring the ingredients I texted you about earlier."

"All right."

She opened the door and put one foot out, then paused. Doing her homework sounded like a terrible idea. All she wanted was to be around Finn. Finn. Finn. More and more Finn. "Do you want to come in? We can share a piece of almond cake."

His smile was nervous. She noticed his knuckles were white around the steering wheel. "Um, I don't know if that's the best idea."

"Please?"

Finn shook his head. "Naomi, don't. I can see what's happening, so don't."

"What's happening?"

It was obvious she was an open book. She felt like an idiot with one foot out of the car and the other still in, the whole position awkward and much too similar to how she felt inside her head, divided and vulnerable. She started to pull her other foot back into the car.

"Come on, Naomi. I can read all the signs—you want me. And I'd be an idiot not to admit I want you." He took a deep breath. "You have no idea how much. But you've told me you love Jesse. I've felt that you do."

129

"I do love Jesse, but I'm confused. The more I see you, the more I—"

"Maybe we shouldn't hang out anymore." He focused on his hands. The muscles in his arms flexed.

"Why?" she asked, panicking a little. She didn't like the idea of losing the only close friend she had around.

"It's getting too complicated," he answered. "It isn't fair to Jesse. I don't even know the guy, but I'm not going to be the cause of taking you away from him if he deserves a chance with you. He means a lot to you. Don't screw it up just because we're both lonely and attracted to each other. Remember that conversation we had about lying? Cheating on him is the same damn thing."

Gritting her teeth, Naomi kept her foot hanging out of the car. "I don't know what to say."

He laughed. "I'm not saying we can't see each other. I don't want to lose your friendship, but I don't think it's a great idea to hang out as much as we have been— as long as you're in love with him the way you are. We might do something we'll regret, and I don't want some guy who's been in prison coming after me because I stole his girl." He laughed again, but it sounded nervous.

"Oh, so that's it?" she asked, smiling. "You're afraid of Jesse?"

"I might be." His hands relaxed on the steering wheel. "I think it's best if I don't come over tomorrow. Later, I hope?"

"Yeah, later is good." Naomi stepped out of the car and bent down to say goodbye. "Just friends," she mumbled.

Finn forced a smile. "Just friends. Bye, Naomi."

"Bye." She closed the door and stepped away from the car. When she went inside, Becca and Derek were in the living room watching a movie. Becca looked up, her face aglow in blue light from the television. "Out with Finn?" she asked, a tone of teasing in her voice.

"Yeah."

"When are you going to ask him to stay the night, Naomi? Seriously. You're always together. It's about time you two—"

"We're friends, Becca. That's it."

Naomi thought she heard Derek snort. She ignored him.

"Right," Becca said. "Friends. Well, that's how it starts."

Naomi gave her a glare, but she doubted it was visible as the light on the television dimmed. "And remember *you-know-who*," she hissed.

More blue light. Becca wrinkled her nose. "Oh, right. You don't talk about him, so I keep forgetting about him as an option."

"Yeah," Naomi mumbled, "me too." Tossing her purse onto a nearby table, she went upstairs to finish her homework, but when she looked at it on her desk, she turned away.

XII

October

"Naomi, can you stay for a minute?"

Stopping in her tracks, Naomi watched the rest of the class file out the door. She turned around to face her professor. He was young and thin, with a mop of tight brown curls on top of his head. The artsy type. Every girl who sat on the front row was believed to have a crush on him. Naomi always sat on the second row.

"Yes, Professor Carlisle?"

He smiled, but it was sticky. She thought about all the assignments she had slacked off on lately and knew something unpleasant was coming.

"I know this class isn't that interesting to you," Carlisle said, folding his arms, "but several other professors have spoken highly of you from their courses in the past, and I was looking forward to working with you." His dark eyebrows furrowed. "I have to say I'm disappointed. What can I do to help?"

She opened her mouth, but couldn't think of anything to say that wouldn't sound stupid. *Please help me get back my passion for school. I don't freaking care anymore. And I miss Finn. And Jesse. And what the hell am I going to do if I can't get my butt in gear and finish this semester with high grades? My mom will kill me.*

She closed her mouth.

Carlisle shifted his feet, his eyebrows furrowing even more. "Your advisor spoke with me before the semester started," he said. "She informed me about your situation in the past and how it affects you now. She said you might have a hard time and to help you out. I can't help you if you don't communicate with me."

Naomi looked up. "She told you about my kidnapping?"

"Yes. Most of the staff knows. It's not classified information. I'm sorry if that makes you uncomfortable, but we have many students here who come from prominent families in society. They have to deal with being in the public eye, just as you have. It might not be for the same reasons, but it's still difficult. You aren't alone."

"No, it's not that." She looked at the floor and ground her teeth together. None of it was any of his business. "I don't know." Focusing on Carlisle's shoes, she noticed one of his shoelaces was broken. For some reason, that made her look up. He was frowning.

"Well, I'll tell you what. I can let a few things slide if you're willing to give this a better shot. I want to help you succeed. I've seen your drive to succeed while you're here in class—when you're engaged with other students in discussion—but your assignments are lacking. It's as if you can't concentrate at home. Have you tried doing your homework here on campus instead?"

"Not this semester, no." Mostly, she wanted to be home every possible second in case Finn decided to stop by.

"I suggest trying that, if you can, and if you feel like you can't keep up, you should withdraw from the class so it doesn't harm your GPA."

"Okay." She straightened her shoulders, determined to do better so she wouldn't have to suffer through another conversation like this.

Carlisle softened his expression. "We have staff to help you with problems outside of academic issues, as well. I can recommend someone if you like."

"I have a counselor off campus," she said, her mouth growing dry as she realized she had to go see Stacy again tomorrow.

"Okay, that's great. Well, let me know if—"

Naomi's phone beeped and cut him short. She gave him a weak smile and dug the phone out of her back pocket. She never left the house without it now. "Sorry," she said, her hands shaking as she glanced at the screen.

Incoming text from unknown number.

Well, it wasn't Finn.

Her hope plummeted to the floor. Then it soared. She looked up at Carlisle, suddenly dizzy. "Um, I need to go."

"All right. See you on Tuesday."

"Bye."

As soon as she was out in the hallway, she pressed the button on her phone to look at the message.

Hi, Naomi. So, do you have a passport?

It had to be Jesse.

She typed, *Yes, I do. Um, hi?*

As she waited for his reply, she walked down the hallway, bumping into several people as she stared at the screen, waiting. She was pushing open the main exit when the phone beeped again.

Hi. I miss you so much. Guess what?

She typed back, *What?*

My parole is over.

Her head felt like it was floating off her body, instantly weightless. For the longest time, she had dreaded this moment. She had thought her new obsession over Finn would ruin everything with Jesse and she would have to tell him she had met someone else. She hadn't wanted to live through awkwardness and guilt, but this was all different than she had imagined. Why didn't he *call* her? She needed to hear his voice. The very thought of him connected to her now, typing to her, was surreal.

She typed, *Wow, so fast? How?*

A long pause.

Last of the paperwork is going through, he sent.

The sun beat down on her head as she walked to the parking lot. Her feet felt light, as if they weren't there at all.

She typed, *When can I see you? Can you call me?*

Yes. When is good for you?

Anytime.

Okay. I have something huge to ask you about your passport.

My passport? What about my passport? Tell me!

There was another long pause in his response time. She reached her car and got inside, fastening her seatbelt as she started the engine. Jesse still hadn't responded by the time she drove onto the main road and headed home. Finn was supposed to come over tonight—the first time in two weeks. She would have to cancel.

Her phone beeped and she picked it up off the passenger seat.

Italy.

Italy? She almost dropped the phone. When she looked back up at the road, another car was heading straight for her. She was in the other lane. Cursing, she let the phone drop and swerved back into the correct lane, barely missing the other car. It honked long and hard as it passed by her. She gripped her steering wheel so hard her hands hurt. Adrenaline raced through her, making her vision fuzzy for a moment. She had to pull over and stop the car. Finding the first parking lot she could, she pulled into a stall and stared straight ahead. She was at the Java Lounge. Crap.

Her phone beeped again. She picked it up off the floor.

Are you there?

Yes, sorry, I was driving. As she waited for him to respond, she leaned back in her seat and took long, deep breaths.

Oh, sorry. Do I need to let you go?

No, I'm stopped now.

Do you want me to call you now? I just got home, so I can call if you want. You okay?

Call me.

She gripped the phone and waited for it to ring. At least she had seen him a few months ago and the initial shock of talking to him for the first time in years was over. Still, she was so nervous she thought she might pass out. Or maybe that was the leftover adrenaline from almost hitting another car head-on.

The phone rang and she answered before the ringtone could finish.

Her voice shook as she said in a scratchy voice, "Hello?"

"Hi, Naomi." He sounded different over the phone, his voice deeper. It struck her as funny that she had never spoken to him over a phone before.

"So, Italy? What do you mean by Italy?" she asked, wanting to get that answered right away.

Jesse took a breath so loud she could hear it on the other end. "Well, I've been toying around with the idea of going to Italy. With you."

"Like a vacation?"

"No, like moving there."

She stared at the Java Lounge sign. It was a tacky glowing purple, but somehow it worked with the design of the building and the atmosphere. Move to Italy. Who up and moved to Italy? She had no idea how to respond to that.

"I have school," she said, pronouncing the words as if they were an obvious fact he shouldn't have missed.

"I know, and I don't want to take you away from that if it's what you want to do, but I was thinking about a few problems that might arise when we're together. Italy is far enough away that, well, it would be a good place for us to start over."

The purple sign started to blur. "Problems? Like what?"

"They wouldn't be permanent, but I know you, Naomi, and I don't think you'd deal with it very well. I want to protect you from things like that."

"Things like what?"

Jesse didn't answer right away, but it was beginning to play out in her head. If her relationship with Jesse went as far as she had dreamed, she would marry him. And if she thought Professor Carlisle knowing about her past had been awkward, she couldn't imagine what it would be like to deal with everyone judging her for marrying her kidnapper. The stories. The rumors. The looks.

"Never mind, I think I know what you mean," she finally said. "Maybe we can find a small town to live in and everything will die down. Nobody will care for long."

"Do you believe that? Do you really believe we can live a normal life together here? How has it been these past few years for you? Have people forgotten?"

She shut her eyes. "Kind of, but I try to avoid it as much as possible. It's still—"

"We'll be defined by it, Naomi. You don't have the personality to deal with that kind of shit for very long. It would tear you apart."

She knew he was right. She couldn't even deal with her classes right now.

"Italy would be perfect for us."

She remembered the picture of Evelyn's house in Italy. The olive trees. The blue sky. "Why Italy?" she asked.

"Several reasons. First, because you wanted to go so much when the others planned it, and second . . . I found a job there."

She straightened. "A job? Architecture?"

"Yes," he answered, his breathing a little faster as he continued. "It's amazing—what I've always wanted. In *Rome*."

She grinned. "That's great."

"It is, but it's a little complicated. I already have a flight booked out there in two days so I can visit the company, figure out work visa crap, residency, and find a place to live. And there have been issues with my criminal record, of course. It's taking forever to get through everything."

"So, you did get the job?"

"Not yet, but I'm one of the top choices. They want to meet me. There's a lot of paperwork to get through before anything can be decided. I'm still working the construction job here, but they're letting me take some time off."

Naomi closed her eyes, excited by the possibilities opening up for Jesse and for her. It was becoming clearer why Jesse wanted her to choose Italy.

"If I get the job, Naomi, it pays really well." There was a strain in his voice, almost a pleading tone that tugged something inside her. She leaned forward and held on to the steering wheel with her other hand as he continued. "I've been thinking about this for so long. When I saw you back in July, I could tell you still want to be with me. Could you . . . are you willing to do this?"

The car felt as if it might be filling up with water. She took a few gulps of air and blinked hard. "Jesse, this is huge. I can't back out of some stuff. I lost my scholarship and my parents are covering my tuition. I can't disappoint them. I think my mom would freak out if I told her I was moving to Italy with you. If I quit school, she might—"

"You can't tell your parents any of this," he interrupted, his voice rough.

Naomi sat up straight. "What? Why?"

"Because you know they'll try to stop you. No matter what you end up deciding, promise me you won't tell them. Not yet."

She took another deep breath. "Okay, fine."

"Promise me."

"I promise." She let out a sigh, unsure of everything. The car seemed to fade around her. The purple sign wavered. "You wouldn't go without me, would you?" she asked. "If I decide I can't go?"

"I . . . I don't know."

"You wouldn't wait for me? We could live here at school together and you could find another job in Italy when I'm finished."

"Naomi, there are only so many work visas granted every year. I was lucky enough to get one because I've had my eye on Italy for so long and planned it all right. There's so much tied up in this," he said, his voice faltering. "I don't know if I can give it all up to wait . . ."

There was a long pause. Naomi wished she could see Jesse and his reactions. This was too much. She looked from the purple sign down to the plate glass window of the café and caught a glimpse of Finn talking with the cashier at the front. Looking at him now, she realized he and Jesse were two weights on a scale and that her feelings for Jesse far outweighed those for Finn. She was attracted to Finn. She admired him. She wanted his friendship, but she wondered how deeply all of that went. If Finn asked her to quit school and move to Italy with him, she wouldn't do it. Not at this point in their relationship. Jesse had done so much for her. Nothing could replace that.

"Naomi? Do you understand what I'm saying? I can't guarantee I'll find another position like this. Moving to Italy will help us avoid what we'd have to deal with here."

She thought about Jesse moving in with her at Harvard, if he would ever agree to such a thing. She thought about how her friendship with Finn would fall apart, about how awkward it would be telling people who Jesse was and how she had met him. Maybe she could own it and not give a crap what other people thought. Maybe she could lie. Or be vague about everything. Who was she kidding? People would know and news would spread. The extra stress would keep her from excelling in school.

"Naomi?"

"I'm sorry, I'm just thinking. This is all so fast. I want to see you. Can you come out here?"

"Yes, probably when I get back from Italy."

"How long will that be?" She watched Finn laughing with the female cashier. She had blonde hair with peacock-blue streaks through it.

"A few weeks. Do you have a webcam? We can talk that way until then. I want to see you too."

"Yeah, I've got it on my laptop, but I'm not home yet."

"Then tonight?"

"Yeah."

"It's great to hear your voice, Naomi. I miss you."

"I miss you too."

"This number I'm calling from is mine, if you want to program it into your phone. Why don't you call me in a few hours when you're ready?"

"Okay."

She expected him to say goodbye, but he held on, waiting.

"Naomi, are you okay?"

She nodded, as if he could see her. "I'm great, really. I've waited for this forever. I guess it doesn't seem real now."

"Try to take it easy, okay? I love you."

"I love you too. I'll call you in a bit."

She hung up and kept looking at the café window. Finn was gone, but she knew she had to go in and tell him not to come over tonight. Grabbing her purse with trembling hands, she stepped out of the car and walked into the café. The cashier looked up and smiled.

"Is Finn here?" Naomi asked.

"Sure, I'll get him."

"Thanks."

Naomi walked to a table and sat down. Sitting in the familiar environment triggered her desire for iced tea and cake. She looked up as Finn came to her table and sat down.

"Hey, what's up?" he asked, his smile big enough to make it clear how happy he was to see her. "We still on for tonight?"

She shook her head and grabbed the nearest object she could—a saltshaker. Turning it around and around, she stared at the holes on the top. "Something's come up. We'll have to reschedule."

"All right. When is good?"

"I-I don't know." She looked up and stopped spinning the shaker. "He's free, Finn."

His smile fell and he leaned back in the chair. She looked at his nametag and felt heavy all of a sudden. *Finn Giachetti. Assistant Manager.* She wondered how it must feel to earn money and know it came from her own efforts. Jesse wanted the job in Italy so he could be independent and happy. Finn wanted to make his mother proud and prove to himself he could succeed. But what did *she* want? It had been months since she had pulled out her sketchpad or sat down at her computer to work on a film or a photograph. When she looked at Finn's nametag something withered inside her. Maybe it was determination. Maybe it was hope.

146

"I expected you to look a lot happier," Finn said, interrupting her thoughts. "I'm confused. How can he be off parole so fast? Is that normal?"

Her focus drifted to his face. "He got a shorter sentence for his plea bargain, so I guess his parole was shorter too. I don't know." She paused, trying to decide how much she wanted to tell Finn. "He wants me to move to Italy with him."

"Italy?" Finn's eyes widened. Naomi thought she noticed a spark of panic in them, but couldn't be sure. "How is that possible? Even if he's off parole—"

"I don't know, but I had to tell you. I thought—"

Finn put up his hands, defending himself. "Listen, if this has anything to do with me, relax. We've talked about it already and you know I'm fine with whatever you choose. I want you to be happy, Naomi. We're friends. We've never been lovers. You don't owe me anything. I'll always be your friend no matter what."

She pushed the saltshaker away and felt her shoulders drop a little. "Thanks, Finn. I guess I was worried about that, but mostly I'm worried about making the right decision. I don't have to go to Italy." She looked up and forced a weak smile. "I guess I want your advice. You always give such good advice."

He lowered his hands. "That's a huge decision. I don't know." He searched her face and leaned forward to take her hand. When he squeezed, she relaxed at his touch. "I guess all I can think of is to tell you to listen to your heart and be careful. I trust you when you say Jesse is some amazing guy who can make you happy, but remember why you fell in love with him. Remember what it is *you* want first. He can't make you happy if you don't know what you want. The same goes for him. Remember what you said when you told me to figure out what I want? The same goes for you too."

She looked down at Finn's hand holding hers. "You should be a counselor or something," she said, laughing.

"Maybe I'll go to some smaller university and pursue that, then." He grinned and let go of her hand. "All I know is I'm going to miss learning how to make that pasta dish tonight. I already bought the cream and thyme. I was waiting to get the mushrooms until tonight."

Her mouth watered at the thought of the dish. Evelyn had taught her how to make it and it was one of her favorites.

"I'm sorry. The cream and thyme should keep for a little bit. You can get the mushrooms later. We'll make it soon," she said. "I'll let you know."

Finn's smile turned lopsided. "I have a feeling you're going to drop off the face of the planet."

"You have my number. Call me or text me."

"And Jesse is okay with that? You hanging out with me still?"

"Um, I don't know. I can ask."

"All right." The skepticism in his voice was thick and Naomi knew she had to leave. She needed to be alone. To drive somewhere. Anywhere. And think. She grabbed her purse and stood.

"I gotta go. See you later, Finn."

"See ya." When she was back in her car, she looked up and saw him still sitting at the table, his chin resting in his palm as he pushed the saltshaker in circles.

XIII

NAOMI STARTED UP HER COMPUTER AS SHE SAT AT HER desk with a bowl of ramen noodles. She winced as she chewed, knowing Finn would laugh if he saw what she was eating. The noodles were quick and easy and she was craving sodium. She sent Jesse a text message. *I'm ready. You online?*

Two minutes went by. *Yes, what's your e-mail address?*

Wow, she was considering living with this man, running away with him to Italy, and he didn't even know her e-mail address. She had seen his address a few times when he had helped her download music into her iPod at the house, but she couldn't remember it. She set down her fork and texted him her address. Five minutes later, she received an e-mail from *swiftsully128* inviting her to video chat with him. She clicked the link, and it took her to a window where she clicked the call button. As it rang, she snatched her bowl of noodles and shoveled a bunch into her mouth. Of course, just as she was chewing, Jesse answered. He smiled and waved to her.

"Catch you at a bad time?" he asked, laughing as she chewed and swallowed.

"You answered too fast!"

"What are you eating?"

She blushed. "Ramen noodles. I don't eat them very much, but I'm out of leftovers. I usually cook. You know, because of Evelyn."

His smile widened. "I'm happy to hear that. She made the best food."

"Yeah, I still make that mushroom pasta dish. Remember that one?"

Jesse's eyes grew dreamy at the mention of the dish. "The one with the shiitakes and that thyme-cream sauce?"

"Yeah."

"Damn, I miss that one. The food in prison was awful. Dad cooks, but it's not the same as Evelyn's food." He leaned forward. Naomi noticed he had cut his dark red hair since she had seen him last. It looked nice. Clean. He had shaved too. He wore a button-down shirt that looked like it was new, the top buttons undone. All of this made her warm inside. She had kept her hair down and put on a lacy camisole she thought he might like.

"So," she said, swirling the noodles in her bowl, "this whole Italy thing. How soon, do you think?"

His eyes lit up. "Have you decided already?"

"No, I just want a time frame."

He nodded. "Well, tell me about school. How badly do you want to finish?"

She looked at the stack of books on her desk—the same ones from last semester since she was taking the same courses and the books hadn't changed. The only new class was the one with Professor Carlisle. She was regretting signing up for that one.

"Honestly," she said after a heavy sigh, "I don't like school right now. I've always liked school. It used to be my life."

"Well, it's Harvard. I imagine it's challenging." He leaned back and let out a low whistle. "But Harvard, Naomi . . . that's great. I feel like a jerk asking you to leave."

"It's not your fault, but to answer your question, I don't know if I want to finish. I feel so obligated." She rubbed at a spot on her forehead and proceeded to tell him about her scholarship and her mother and the conversation with her professor. She went on and on about her classes and how art wasn't what it used to be to her. As she talked, she pulled out one of her sketchpads and flipped through the pages, hating every single sketch. To her, they all sucked. Jesse listened.

She tossed aside her sketchpad and picked up her bowl of noodles again. When she took a bite, they were cold. "I guess I'm seeing how hard all of this can get," she said, wrapping up her story. "I don't know how my mom got through law school here. My housemate is in that program. She wants to slit her wrists half the time."

Jesse smiled. "Your mom is intense. Period."

"I know." Naomi thought about the moment Jesse had met her mother during the trial. There had been a lot of poorly concealed glaring on her mother's end.

"So, you feel obligated," Jesse said, picking up a glass he had set on a nearby table. He was sitting in a room she didn't recognize—not his father's apartment, which was stuffed with books. There were no books anywhere around Jesse. "You're also losing interest in your major. Can I ask why? Are the classes too hard? Not specific enough yet?"

She forced down the rest of the noodles and pulled up her hair, holding it off her neck as she thought about his question. It was hot in her room. "It doesn't help that I have to take all the same classes again."

"Right, but you can get through that."

She gave him a crooked smile. "Are you trying to talk me into staying?"

"I want you to make the best decision for you." His green eyes sparkled as he took another drink. "I'll admit

I want to be selfish and talk you into Italy. I've been looking at places we can rent." He set down his drink.

"This isn't helping, Jesse."

He rolled his eyes. "I know, I know. But I want you to know it's all possible."

She nodded, letting it sink in. Possible. It seemed anything was possible when it came to Jesse. "Am I going to need to learn Italian if I decide to go there?"

He laughed. "If we're living there, I assume you would want to learn Italian."

"I guess so. I can't decide yet," she muttered.

"You don't have to."

She stared at Jesse's face, surprised she still remembered the pattern of his freckles and the way he tilted his head when he was waiting for a response.

"I want to hold you," she said, unsatisfied with the video. It didn't give her warmth and smell and touch. "That's all I can think about right now."

He frowned and looked at his watch. "I can come in a few weeks. Promise. I should let you go so you can get some homework done."

"Ugh, homework. I have to write chapter responses. I haven't read the chapters yet. I did all of that last semester, but I can't use the same assignment I turned in before. My professor told me everything has to be new."

"I'm sorry." He stuck out his bottom lip in a puppy-dog pout, and she laughed.

"Don't make fun." She let her playful smile fall into a frown as a million questions entered her mind. "What was it like?" she asked, leaning forward. "Prison, I mean."

Jesse looked surprised at her question. He leaned back from the camera and looked away. "Some days I thought it would never end, and some days I regretted turning myself in. Most men there are scum. Lots of prejudice and ignorance." He shrugged and looked up. "I kept out of it as much as I could, but they don't like it when you're a loner like me. Makes it easier for them to pick on you."

She shut her eyes and thought about Evelyn in her prison cell. And Eric. He was probably the type to let prison wear him down so much he cracked and lost it, just as his father had.

"Thank you," she whispered, opening her eyes to see Jesse watching her with a solemn expression.

"For what?"

"For letting me go and turning yourself in—for going through all that."

"I had to." He stared down at the drink in his hand. "I've tried to erase what I did, but it will never be enough, Naomi. Never."

She blinked, trying to process if what he said was true. He had already done so much for her.

"Naomi, are you okay? You look tired. It's late there."

"Yeah." She rubbed her eyes. "I think my homework will have to wait until tomorrow."

He nodded. "Get some rest, okay?"

"Okay."

She didn't want to end the call, but she knew she had to. She said goodbye. When she was staring at a blank screen, she remembered something she had thought was gone forever. She remembered a series of dreams from her time in captivity. They were filled with dragons and there was a prince who kept trying to save her. He had never succeeded.

* * *

Stacy's office always smelled like the ocean. It was one of the reasons Naomi liked to go. Once, she had asked Stacy how she made it smell so good.

"It's called Sandy Shores," Stacy explained with a half-smile. "It's scented wax." She waved her hand toward a ceramic pot on a bookshelf. A light inside the pot melted wax on a ceramic tray above. Naomi had never noticed it before.

Today, when she entered Stacy's office it smelled like a pine forest. Naomi stopped in her tracks as Stacy held open the door.

"Are you doing all right today?" Stacy asked.

"Sure." After staring at Stacy's manicured fingernails, painted a deep aquamarine color, Naomi swallowed and looked up. Stacy was one of those women who looked a lot younger than she was. Naomi guessed she was fifty, but she appeared thirty-five. She reminded her of her mother, with blonde hair always twisted into a bun or pulled into a low, sleek ponytail. The difference was Stacy didn't wear professional clothes. Half the time she was dressed in yoga pants and a fitted T-shirt. Naomi didn't care, and obviously Stacy didn't either. Smiling, she motioned Naomi into the office, where Naomi settled into her regular seat on the sofa. Stacy sat in a big armchair across from her and asked, "Is there anything you want to focus on today?"

Naomi leaned against two soft pillows and slipped off her sandals so she could bring her knees to her chest. She always assumed the same closed position when she talked to Stacy about the house and her captivity. This time, however, the ritual felt off balance without the scent of the Sandy Shores wax permeating the air. Instead of the beach, she found herself imagining she was in a forest. She shivered.

Stacy's eyebrows rose. She was sitting Indian-style on her chair. "You can begin when you're ready."

Naomi closed her eyes and took four deep breaths as she let her mind slip back into the bedroom at the house. There was tan carpet, an oak dresser, and a handmade quilt on the bed—alternating patches of faded blues and greens. There was a deadbolt on the door, and in her mind it was always locked. She sat on the bed and ran her hand over the soft, worn folds of the quilt, counting to ten in her mind. It wasn't real. No matter how many times she went there, it wasn't real anymore. The problem was it felt real, and that was all that mattered. The door was locked and they were holding her captive. She didn't want to stay there. She knew what they had done was wrong. She would stand her ground. She wouldn't feel guilty when they went to prison.

"Play it out," Stacy's soothing voice said. "One thing at a time."

Nodding, Naomi kept her eyes closed. The locks on the door tumbled open and Eric stepped into the room, dressed in his suit and a brown silk tie with a checkerboard pattern that reminded her of a chocolate bar. He was clean-shaven and smiled when he saw her. She returned the smile and let him approach her, his arms opening to take her into a gentle embrace. She hugged him, noticing the smell of garlic. Evelyn cooked with it so much the entire family smelled of it.

"You'll stay?" he asked as he kept her in the embrace.

She looked up into his cold blue eyes that contrasted so sharply with his dark hair. She saw sympathy in his expression, and pain—deep, clouded pain. She opened her mouth to answer. It was always, "Yes, I'll stay," but this time she paused.

"I'm not sure," she replied, her bottom lip trembling.

Eric tensed and pushed her away from him, blood rushing to his face. His eyes narrowed and darkened. "Not sure?"

She felt the space between them widening as she backed farther away. "What you've done is wrong."

"What we've done is care for you when nobody else gave a shit about you. How is that wrong?" He marched forward and took her by the arm. "Answer me."

When she looked up, she saw beads of sweat on his brow and his fist raised, ready to hit her.

"I'll stay," her voice cracked.

The smell of a forest surrounded her. She opened her eyes. Stacy was leaning forward in her chair, her eyes wide. "Something different happened, didn't it?"

Nodding, Naomi clenched her arms around her legs, pressing her knees as close to her body as she could. "I told him I wouldn't stay this time, but then he threatened me and I gave in."

A smile spread across Stacy's lips. "We've made progress. This method seems to be working well for you."

"Yeah, I think so. I wish you'd get the beach wax smell again. I miss California."

Laughing, Stacy glanced at her bookshelf. "They were out last time I ordered. I'll check again if it's that important to you."

"It helps me think of home." Not that she understood why that was the greatest comfort ever.

"I understand." Stacy put her hands together and lowered her voice to her usual calm tone. "Let's move on and talk about the past week. Did your memories impair any of your activities?"

Naomi winced. "My memories aren't the problem. It's Jesse." She noticed a slight crease forming on Stacy's forehead. "Not that I'm blaming him, but I hate school right now, and I've never hated school. I can't concentrate on my homework. If I get bad grades again, I'm screwed. So it's not my kidnapping that's holding me back. It's none of that. It's . . ." Her voice trailed off as she realized she didn't want to tell Stacy about Jesse or Italy.

Stacy waited, the crease in her forehead disappearing.

"I'm worried about what I really want, that's all."

Keeping her hands together in her lap, Stacy nodded once.

Naomi narrowed her eyes and then let her shoulders droop. "I don't know what I want. That's the problem."

"Yes, I can imagine. Let's talk about school and your art."

Naomi's shoulders drooped even more. "I don't like art right now."

"Why?"

"I don't know."

Stacy cocked her head and gave Naomi the, *If you don't try, I can't help you*, look. Naomi sighed and thought about the unfinished projects piled in her room and the countless photographs she had yet to download from her camera card. In her head, everything was a mess and no longer fun. Art had always been an outlet. Now it was nothing but a chore.

"It's like when Jesse convinced me to read all those novels when I was captive," she explained, pushing through the thoughts in her head. "He expected me to read them, just like when Mom expected me to read *The Awakening*. Now I'm expected to be creative here at school. I was fine at first because it was my choice, but now it doesn't feel like my choice anymore."

Stacy nodded. "You told me you were happy you read those books."

"Yeah, I was. It wasn't bad . . . I felt pressured, is all. In the end, I was happy I read them."

"And the book your mother wanted you to read? What of that?"

"She was trying to connect to me in any way she could . . . because I shut her out."

Naomi was surprised how quickly she had answered the question. Her arms relaxed even more as she realized how much she had learned to accept in the past few years. When she had first started seeing counselors, she hadn't been able to say the word *kidnapped*. It was such an ugly word. She could say it now, but there was still a long way to go.

Stacy unclasped her hands. "You feel pressure to do what others expect of you, and you find that difficult to work with."

Naomi stared ahead, her vision blurry. "Yes, so what should I do? Quit?"

"That would be a drastic course of action, but not unheard of. Only you can decide."

Stacy wasn't the type of counselor to give magical nuggets of advice. Naomi nodded and leaned her head on the back of the sofa. She didn't want to decide anything.

"Sometimes I wonder," she said, staring at the ceiling, "if I'm a totally normal person and I'm using my kidnappers as an excuse for all my problems."

A long pause, and then Stacy said, "If you can go through an entire day without feeling impaired by what happened to you, I'd say that's the case, but judging from what we've discussed today, it's clear you're still suffering from something outside of your immediate control. It's going to take more work to get you to a place you feel happy, content, and safe."

She lifted her head and looked at Stacy. "What if I'm fine the way I am? What if I don't want to try to fix myself anymore?"

Looking her straight in the eyes, Stacy asked, "Are you happy right now? Are you functioning the way you'd like? Those are the things that matter."

Naomi sighed. She wasn't going to pretend nothing was wrong, but a part of her wanted everything to stop so she could think. She thought about Finn's secret spot on the train tracks and how everything was so quiet there. If only her life could settle into a space like that. Maybe it could. There was Italy. Then again, she wondered if staying with Jesse meant she would never recover. Or, if she did recover, if that would mean she would lose herself in the process—who she was at the core. Closing her eyes, she imagined herself in the bedroom once again. This time, she walked to the door before Eric could enter. She pulled on the handle, twisting it as hard as she could, but the door wouldn't budge. For a moment, she thought she heard weeping on the other side. Concerned, she tried the handle again, and the door swung open. On the floor, curled into a ball and weeping, was herself.

XIV

November

JESSE WAS SCHEDULED TO FLY INTO CAMBRIDGE A WEEK before Thanksgiving. To distract herself until he arrived, Naomi buried herself in school. She caught up on her art assignments and spent every afternoon in the library reading textbooks. For a brief moment, she felt normal, as if nothing was amiss. It didn't last long. She knew as soon as Jesse arrived her world would turn upside down.

The day before his flight, she went to the Java Lounge and sat in her usual spot. Finn was nowhere to be seen, so she ordered her tea and cake and pulled out her sketchbook. It was the same sketch she had been working on when Finn started talking to her back in April. She hadn't touched it since then. The pencil lines were smudged in a few spots. She held her pencil poised above the woman's head, afraid to make any marks whatsoever. After a full minute, she flipped to a clean page and started sketching a deep valley filled with licking flames and smoke. When that was outlined, she moved to the sky and sketched four dragons, each one monstrous and scaly with magnificent wings. They circled the valley, as if waiting for something to appear. It was the first time she had ever drawn something from her dreams. At the house, she had never asked for sketch paper, but she hadn't drawn a lot back then—only doodles like her mother did at the foundation office. A class here at Harvard was what had awakened the new art form in her, and as the terrible image from her dreams blossomed across the paper, she regretted not drawing more often. Maybe her art didn't suck as badly as she thought.

She had sipped most of her iced tea by the time she finished, but her almond cake sat untouched. Setting down her pencil, she pushed the sketchpad back a few inches and stared at the drawing. Those dreams had been so vivid during her captivity. The dragons represented her kidnappers, and in the end, she had hopped onto the scaly back of one and flew away into the distance. She wondered now if that dragon was Jesse.

"No more women walking into the ocean?" Finn asked.

Naomi looked up to see him standing over her, a smile on his lips. She hadn't seen him in over two weeks, not since she had shown him how to make the pasta dish. Warmth spread through her when she met his eyes.

"I guess not," she said, motioning for him to join her. He sat in the chair across the table and picked up her fork by the almond cake.

"Not in the mood for this, either?"

She laughed. "I was too busy drawing. Go ahead and eat some if you want."

"Great, thanks." She watched him take a bite and set the fork back down. Then he ran his finger along the plate, sweeping up some powdered sugar.

"So," he asked, putting his sugar-coated finger in his mouth, "have you decided about Italy? I've never been there."

"That's a sin, since you're Italian," she said with a mock gasp. "No, I haven't decided. Jesse flies in tomorrow."

Finn paused, pulling his finger out of his mouth and wiping it on his jeans. "Are you excited?"

"Yes, though I keep trying to forget he's coming." She looked at her sketch again and her palms began to sweat.

"There's something I need to tell you, Naomi."

She looked up and spotted a smudge of powdered sugar on his bottom lip. "What is it?"

Picking up the fork again, he tapped it gently on the plate. "I've been meaning to tell you for a week now, but I keep worrying you'll get upset." He dropped the fork, and it clattered across the table. He didn't bother picking it up. "Not that you'll get upset. You have Jesse. I don't know."

"Just say it, Finn." Her heart was beating fast now as she anticipated what he could possibly have to tell her.

He met her eyes. "I've started dating someone. I was excited to tell you, but then, I don't know, it seemed weird to tell you."

"Oh." She remembered watching Finn through the window as he talked with the cashier. Glancing behind her shoulder, Naomi saw her helping someone at the counter, her hair streaked with lime-green now instead of blue. "Her?" she asked, turning back to Finn.

Finn's eyes widened. "Yeah, you don't miss a beat, do you?"

"I guess not."

He picked up the fork again. "Her name's Carly. She likes drawing stuff, like you do. She's an art major. Sorry if that's weird."

Naomi laughed, but it came out weak. She knew everything would fall back into place when she saw Jesse tomorrow, but for now, knowing Finn was dating a girl with colored stripes in her hair was a stab in the chest. Maybe it never would have worked between her and Finn, though. Now they could both have someone they loved and still be friends. Maybe. Then again, that just seemed strange. She looked at the dragons circling the valley. Maybe none of it mattered anymore, if she was going to Italy. The whole idea was suddenly more appealing.

"So, I guess Carly is cool with you hanging around me?" she asked as Finn took another bite of cake.

"Yeah, she is. We're honest with each other. She knows I'm telling you about her right now."

"Does she know about me and Jesse?"

Finn stopped chewing. "Yes," he said through his mouthful of food.

"And you told her about my kidnapping? Who Jesse really is?"

Swallowing, Finn nodded and set down the fork so softly it didn't make a sound. "Only about your kidnapping, but that's something anyone could figure out."

Naomi felt her jaw tightening. She remembered her professor's words. *It's not classified information.* He was right. It wasn't—but she wanted it to be. She didn't like Carly knowing. It felt like an invasion.

"Please don't tell anyone else," she whispered, leaning forward after a quick glance behind her shoulder. "I'm not comfortable with people knowing unless I want them to know." She rolled her eyes. "Apparently, the whole art department at Harvard knows."

Finn stared at the table. "I'm sorry for telling Carly. She kept asking me questions about you. She was jealous because I was acting all secretive about who you are."

"And now that she knows, I'm not a threat. Got it. Listen, if I'm going to be a problem, you can stop talking to me."

He lifted his attention from the table. "No, that's not what I meant. She understands we're friends." He let out a heavy sigh. "I was afraid we'd argue about this. I was hoping once you were back with Jesse, we could hang out together, the four of us. I'd like to meet Jesse, if you're okay with that."

Naomi wasn't sure if she should be flattered or annoyed, but as she stared at her drawing with the dragons and thought about all the times she was weak enough to give in, annoyance won. She picked up the fork and stabbed it into the almond cake. "We sure do have a strange relationship," she said, gathering up her sketchpad and pencil and shoving them into her bag. She took the last sip of her iced tea and stood up.

Finn stayed in his chair and watched her. "Why are you upset? I told you, I'm sorry."

"I don't understand what you want, Finn. We can't stay friends like this. It's awkward and stupid. I don't see how it can possibly work."

"Sure, it can work." Finn glanced at Carly, who was eyeing them as she counted back a customer's change.

Naomi watched her for a moment and then looked at Finn. Panic spread across his face.

"Are you serious?" he asked. "You don't want to be friends anymore? What if things don't work out with Jesse? The whole thing with him getting off parole so fast and then wanting to move to Italy right away feels wrong to me. I want to make sure you're okay." He hesitated for a moment. "You don't have anyone else who really understands you."

Everything clicked into place. "So that's it? I can't possibly make things work with an ex-con, right? The whole idea is ludicrous and I'll end up alone and crazier than I am already."

He looked away, unable to meet her eyes.

"I knew it. You don't want to feel responsible because you've found someone else now and I could end up alone."

Her face was hot and she took a long breath to calm herself down. Her shoulders drooped.

"I'm sorry, Finn. I'm sorry I'm such a crazy, freaking mess. See you around." She dropped two dollars onto the table for the waitress and marched to the other end of the café. Carly closed the till and looked up. She was pretty, with a heart-shaped mouth and a dainty chin. For the first time, Naomi noticed a swirl of tattoos snaking up her left arm. She was probably a real artist, not some hack like Naomi.

"The usual?" Carly asked. Naomi nodded as she dug through her purse for the exact amount. The faster she could leave the better.

Carly punched a few buttons on the register and Naomi handed her the money and left. When she looked back, Finn was gone.

✶ ✶ ✶

Waiting by the baggage claims, Naomi twisted her hands together as she watched the escalators leading to and from the terminals on the second floor. She was sure she would be able to spot Jesse in a heartbeat with his red hair. It wasn't bright, but it was unique enough to stand out. As she waited, she let her mind wander to yesterday and her argument with Finn—if it could be called an argument. Forcing her friendship with Finn around undefined boundaries would lead nowhere except to trouble.

Her heart jumped when she saw Jesse. He looked tired but excited, especially when he spotted her. There were people in front of him, so he waited until he was off the escalator and could walk quickly to her. He dropped his carry-on bag and took her into his arms. He smelled faintly of cologne, the same spicy scent she remembered he used to wear at the house.

"Finally," he whispered into her ear.

Naomi snuggled her face into his neck. She wanted to absorb everything at once. The feel of his skin, the smell of him, the way he held her as if he would never let go. Of course, he had to let go. Pulling away, he kept hold of her arms and looked at her, studying her face. Naomi wanted to kiss him, but held back.

"Want to get out of here?" he asked, smiling.

"Yes. Do you have luggage?"

"Yeah, on number four."

Once they had his bags, they headed out to the parking lot and found Naomi's car. She turned off the alarm and opened the trunk. "Toss your stuff back there," she said, and got in the driver's seat. She fastened her seatbelt and wrapped her hands around the steering wheel. She had to breathe. She felt warm and weak, like she needed to eat something. He was here. With her. As if they had always been together and were going to drive home and live a normal life. But Becca would be there. She would see him and judge him. Naomi hoped she wouldn't have an issue with him staying there. She had never asked if that would be okay. She hadn't thought through a lot of things.

Jesse closed the trunk and came around to the passenger side. Once he was settled in, Naomi started the car and drove out of the parking lot as she took long, deep breaths.

"Are you all right?" Jesse asked once they were on the freeway.

"No," she answered, determined to be truthful with Jesse every step of the way in their relationship. "I'm having a hard time believing you're here."

"Well, I'm here." He reached over and set his hand on top of her thigh. She glanced down and smiled.

"So, how was it? You went to Rome?"

"Yeah." He rested his head on the seat and sighed. "It's beautiful, Naomi. You'll love it. I sorted out a lot of the paperwork I've been having problems with, so now I have to wait and see if I get the position. They told me I should know in a few days."

Naomi's heart was beating fast now that she was going to have to decide soon. Eager to change the subject, she said, "I planned our favorite pasta dish for dinner. Do you want to help me make it?"

His shoulders relaxed as he looked away. "Of course. Why don't we pick up some wine to go with it?"

"Okay."

* * *

Dinner felt rushed. Naomi wanted to take Jesse up to her room as soon as they stepped through the front door, but he had mentioned in the car how hungry he was, so cooking seemed like the sensible thing to do before anything else. She didn't want to be sensible, but at the same time, she was more nervous then she thought she would be. So, dinner it was.

With her mind on a million things, she undercooked the pasta and overcooked the mushrooms. When she cut her finger slicing bread, Jesse went to find a Band-Aid in the bathroom.

"Top shelf in the medicine cabinet!" she yelled after him as she pressed a damp paper towel to the cut.

A moment later, the front door opened. Becca walked in with her backpack slung over one shoulder and her laptop case over another. She dropped both bags on the couch and wandered into the kitchen. Dark circles rimmed her eyes.

Leaning against the sink, Naomi watched her trudge to the refrigerator.

"I need caffeine," she mumbled in a deflated voice. "Or alcohol. This semester is going to kill me." She pulled open the refrigerator door and peered inside, then glanced at Naomi. "I hate Professor Davis. If he gives me less than an A in his class, I'll find a pack of rabid dogs to hunt him down next time he's walking out to his car."

Naomi smirked, watching as Becca grabbed the bottle of wine Jesse had put on the top shelf.

"Um, that's ours," Naomi said, stepping forward.

Becca looked up, the bottle gripped tightly in her hand. It had cost Jesse a small fortune. He had refused to let Naomi buy it.

"Ours?" Becca asked. "You mean mine and yours? Great."

"No, mine and Jesse's. For dinner. We put it in there to chill for a few minutes."

Becca blinked. "He's here?"

"Yeah, he flew in today."

"How the hell does he have permission to fly here and see you?"

"He's off parole."

Leaning forward, Becca asked, "Already? That was pretty damn fast for the crime he committed." Her focus hardened on Naomi's face. "And it seems like they still wouldn't let him see you right after parole, especially if it's that short of a time."

Naomi glowered. "He's done everything they asked him to. It doesn't surprise me." She pressed the balls of her feet hard into the floor, trying to move past her annoyance. "You can join us for dinner if you want. There's plenty."

Becca put the wine back in the fridge and closed the door. "I guess so."

Looking down at the paper towel pressed around her cut, Naomi noticed blood was starting to seep through. "So, you're all right with him staying here for a while, right?" she asked, stealing a glance up at Becca's widened eyes.

"Um . . ." She looked away.

"He's not going to murder us in our sleep."

Becca stiffened. "Did I say that?"

"No, but—"

Jesse came into the kitchen, stopping in his tracks when he saw Becca. "Hello," he said, his expression cautious.

Naomi motioned to Becca. "Jesse, this is Becca, my housemate."

He stepped forward, his hand extended. In his other hand, he held a Band-Aid and a tube of antibiotic cream. "It's nice to meet you."

Becca glanced at Naomi as if making sure Jesse wasn't going to pull a gun on her. Naomi supposed it might be unnerving meeting an ex-con for the first time. But he was Jesse. He didn't look scary. It wasn't as if he had killed anyone. She glared at Becca, who stepped forward and quickly shook Jesse's hand.

"Nice to meet you," she said in a fake sweet voice as she pulled her hand away.

"Becca's eating dinner with us," Naomi said, reaching for the Band-Aid. Jesse held it away from her.

"I'll do it." He looked at Becca, still smiling. "We'd love to have you join us. You live here too. I don't want to intrude. Did Naomi ask if it's okay for me to stay?"

"She did," Becca answered, and swallowed as if a lump had formed in her throat and she couldn't get it down. This was ridiculous. Naomi held out her hand for Jesse, who unpeeled the paper towel.

"Nasty cut," he mumbled. "You need to be more careful, love."

It was the first time he had ever called her *love*. She looked up at Becca as Jesse cleaned the cut.

"It's okay if you stay," Becca said, her voice hesitant. She watched Jesse with a wary expression.

Naomi straightened. "Since Derek stays here all the time," she growled, her anger mounting. "Right, Becca? Just because you know Jesse was in prison doesn't mean you need to be afraid of him."

"It's not that," Becca snapped. "It's that he kidnapped—" She glanced at Jesse and snapped her mouth closed.

Finished with the Band-Aid, Jesse let go of Naomi's hand and looked back and forth between her and Becca. He folded his arms and a steely expression settled across his face. Naomi knew that look all too well. He had made up his mind about something and he wasn't going to budge.

"I'm not staying if it makes either of you uncomfortable," he said, focusing mostly on Becca. "It's obvious Naomi has told you about me."

"A little, yes." A tiny spark of fear flashed across her face. It was the first time Naomi had ever seen her so uncomfortable.

Jesse nodded. "Would you like me to leave?"

Naomi stepped forward, her muscles tense. "Jesse, no, you don't have to leave just because she—"

Becca put up her hands. "No! I'm fine, I promise. You seem like a nice guy, okay? It's a weird situation, that's all. I wasn't expecting you here." She threw Naomi a sharp look. "So chill the hell out. I'll leave you two alone." With that, she walked out of the kitchen and disappeared upstairs.

"Well," Jesse said, staring at the space Becca had occupied. "That's one example to back up my point."

"What point?" Naomi cradled her finger in her other hand. The cut throbbed now that a Band-Aid was wrapped around it.

Jesse turned to her, his expression softening as he said, "I don't think Becca meant any offense—"

"What point?" she interrupted.

Jesse shrugged and walked to the fridge, taking out the wine and setting it on the table. Then he went to the counter where Naomi had been cutting the bread earlier. He picked up a clean knife and began slicing the crusty loaf. Dinner was ready whenever they decided to sit down. Finishing a slice, Jesse began another. "Like I said, I don't think Becca meant any offense. Her behavior was a natural reaction if she's not accustomed to . . . people like me. She seems like a nice girl, so I doubt she's been around many criminals."

"You aren't a criminal. Not anymore." She folded her arms and watched the knife sawing through the bread. It seemed to go in rhythm with the throbbing in her finger.

"Your reaction is what I expected," Jesse said, looking up at her without moving his head. "You seem bent on defending me."

"Of course I'm going to defend you." She leaned over to look him in the eyes as he kept cutting. Her jaw was tight before relaxing to speak again. "It's not a crime for us to be together. Becca has no right to—"

"To what, Naomi?" He stopped cutting. "Be afraid of me? She can't help that." He set down the knife and pulled Naomi into his arms, rubbing her back as she relaxed against him. "This is exactly what I was trying to tell you earlier. It's not everyone's reactions I'm worried about. It's yours. You're too sensitive to deal with this. What's going to happen when newspapers start printing stories about us? How are you going to feel? And when reporters start knocking on the door? What then?"

She was crying now, her cheek pressed against his shoulder as he continued to rub her back. "You always make me cry," she muttered through her sobs.

"I don't mean to," he said, chuckling. "I'm sorry."

"No, you're right. I get so angry whenever anyone mentions you at all. Nobody . . . not *one* person wants us to be together, except for us. It's not fair. For the longest time, I didn't think it would matter what other people thought, but it does, and I hate that it does. My mom doesn't even know you're here."

Jesse pushed her away from him so he could look into her face. "You haven't said anything to her. That's good."

"Of course I haven't." She looked at the dishes on the table. The pasta was getting cold. "Can we eat?"

"Yes, of course." He kissed her forehead and went to open the wine. When he had poured her a glass, she sat down and took a few sips of the deep red liquid, realizing she was sitting in the same spot she always sat whenever Finn came over for dinner. Now it was Jesse in Finn's place, eating from the same bowl with the same silverware.

"This is excellent," Jesse said, already eating with as much gusto as Finn.

"Not as good as Evelyn's. I've made it better before."

Jesse swallowed and took another bite. "It's perfect," he mumbled.

Smiling, Naomi took a bite and decided the pasta was nothing special. Nobody would ever make it as well as Evelyn, but it didn't matter now. Jesse was here. She didn't want it any other way, mediocre pasta and all.

* * *

"So, your parents pay for this house?" Jesse asked as he unpacked his bag in Naomi's room.

"Yeah, they do."

"It's a nice place." He threw a pair of jeans into the drawer. He had told her he had a few days off because of the Thanksgiving holiday, and he planned to spend all of it with her. She wanted it to be longer, no matter how awkward it might be with Becca around.

"Jesse, I—"

He walked to his bag beside her on the bed, and with a sweep of his arm pushed it to the floor. "I'm tired of waiting," he said, embracing her. "You've fed me and played proper hostess long enough."

She giggled and wrapped her arms around him. The glass of wine she'd had with dinner had made her warm already, but now she felt on fire. It was a good feeling. It was more than she had felt in a long time. "What are you saying?" she asked, her words a little slurred.

"I want you. Now." He started undressing her and she didn't stop him. She pulled his shirt over his head, kissing him every moment he came in contact with her. He tasted so good. He smelled of garlic and thyme from dinner. "I love you," he whispered, pressing her onto the bed. She rested her head on the pillows. When she closed her eyes, she remembered her first time with him at the house, how gentle he had been, and how he was still gentle, but forceful too. She didn't know how he managed to combine the two and not mess it up.

Holding her wrists together, he secured her hands above her head. Her knuckles grazed the wall behind her. Jesse smiled and she smiled too . . . and then she remembered kissing Finn. Crap. If she didn't tell Jesse about Finn now, she would regret it forever. She wanted to be honest with him. No secrets ever again.

"Jesse," she said with a crack in her voice, "I need to tell you something."

"Yes?" He kissed her neck and then her bare collarbone.

"Um, please don't hate me. Please, please don't hate me, but being here with you like this, I have to tell you in case it's an issue. I think you'll understand." She closed her eyes, keenly aware of how Jesse was pinning her down by holding her hands above her head. In a way, the submissive feeling was comfortable and put her at ease. Jesse was in control. She wanted it that way and he knew it. It was how it had been at the house.

"Go on," he urged, putting his full attention on listening to her.

"There's a guy I met before I found out you were on parole."

"Uh-huh."

She couldn't do this. She couldn't. She loved Jesse. Opening her eyes, she looked at him and knew she would do anything to keep from hurting him. She had to tell him. So, taking a deep breath, she delved into telling him about Finn. He listened, his expression calm and understanding.

"That's it?" he asked, laughing. "If that's all you've done since I've been away, I'm relieved. I expected you to be long gone by the time I was out. I never said you had to wait for me. Did I give you that impression?"

"No."

"And you care for Finn as a friend, but it's me you love." His hands tightened around her wrists.

"Yes," she said, leaning up to kiss him. "Yes."

XV

NAOMI WOKE TO THE SOUND OF HER PHONE RINGING. Ignoring it, she rolled over in bed, hoping to feel Jesse next to her, but his side was empty and cold. She opened her eyes and sat up, relieved to see his luggage still on the floor and his shoes by her desk. He was probably in the shower. She lay back down, smiling. Everything felt perfect, and then her phone rang again. Annoyed, she reached over and grabbed it off her desk.

Karen Jensen.

Swallowing a lump in her throat, she answered. "Hi, Mom."

"Hi, sweetheart. I hope I'm not calling during your classes. You told me Thursdays are free in the morning."

Naomi glanced at her clock. It was ten-thirty. "Yeah, I have class in an hour."

"Oh, good."

A long pause. Naomi stared at the ceiling and wondered when Jesse would get back.

"So, how are you doing?" her mother asked.

"Fine."

"That's it? Fine? How are your classes?"

"Fine." Naomi stared at Jesse's luggage on the floor. It bothered her that she couldn't tell her mother about him, but he was right—it wouldn't go over well. Her throat felt scratchy when she swallowed. She threw off her blankets as the room seemed to shrink.

"So," her mother said, drawing out the word as long as possible, "I'll see you in a week, then?"

Naomi slid out of bed, her body sweating as she stood in the middle of her room. "I'm not coming for Thanksgiving," she said, her voice so weak it sounded like a twig about to break. "I'm sorry, but I have to . . . I have to . . ." She squeezed the phone and gulped. "There's a guy here I want to spend some time with."

"The one you were texting over the summer break?"

"Yeah."

"That's . . . that's great, Naomi." Her mother's voice wavered. "But are you sure? You always come home for Thanksgiving."

"I know." Walking across the room, she opened her door and peered down the hallway. The bathroom door was open, the room dark, so Jesse wasn't in there.

Becca's bedroom door was cracked open, but it looked dark inside. That was expected since she left at seven every morning.

"It's okay if you stay there for the holiday," her mother replied, as if she had final say over Naomi's decision, "but maybe you can drive up to Elizabeth's for dinner on Thanksgiving Day. It's only two hours away. Or does this boy have family in Cambridge you'll be eating dinner with?"

Elizabeth lived in Maine. The last thing Naomi wanted to do was drive up the coast and spend time with an aunt she barely knew. She decided to stay away from that topic. "He's not a 'boy', Mom. He's twenty-nine."

Silence. Naomi stood at the top of the stairs, waiting. She wanted to hear her mother's reaction to little facts dropped here and there about a man she had no idea was Jesse. If Naomi's instincts were right, her mother would urge her to pursue any relationship outside of Jesse, even with an older man. That started an angry fire inside her gut.

"Twenty-nine is a good age," her mother finally said, her voice slow and even. "I'm assuming he's through school and has a career."

"Yes." Starting down the stairs, Naomi peeked into the living room and saw Jesse sitting on the couch, his back to her as he spoke quietly into his phone. In front of him on the coffee table was his laptop. He bent forward and scrolled down a page.

"Mom, I need to go," Naomi said, trying to suppress the heat boiling inside her. Of course her mother would be okay with her dating a nice, upstanding twenty-nine-year-old with an established career.

"All right, sweetheart, but are you sure about Thanksgiving? Elizabeth would love to have you up there."

"Yes, I'm sure."

"Or maybe we can fly out there to be with you. Then we can meet this man."

Naomi tensed. "No, Mom, please. It's not that serious."

"Can you at least tell me his name?"

Wincing, Naomi took a few more steps down the stairs. By now, Jesse had heard her talking and looked up from his computer. He closed the lid and said something into the phone before lowering it from his ear.

"Good morning," he mouthed, smiling warmly.

She returned the smile, even though she felt like puking. She wasn't lying to her mother, but she wasn't telling the whole truth, either. It made her uneasy, as if she was trying to keep a handful of threads connected to everything in her life, and they were all unraveling and snapping at a tremendous rate. She kept trying to tie knots in them, but it wasn't working. Finn was gone. School was nearly gone. And the thread to her mother had fifty knots, each one twisting away until Naomi stood staring at it, waiting for the final break.

When she looked up, she saw Jesse. He was stability and strength, a hand held out to her, thicker than any thread. He wanted to take care of her, simple as that. He wanted to make her happy. He didn't make her feel obligated to finish school. He didn't make her feel upset about her unresolved emotions over the kidnapping. He wanted her just the way she was. If she asked for help, he would give it without judgment. That was more than her mother was trying to do. It was more than anyone could ever do.

"His name is Finn," Naomi lied, feeling like crap.

"That's a nice name."

Naomi couldn't tell if she was being sarcastic or not. "I'll keep you posted," she mumbled.

"All right, I love you, sweetheart."

"Love you too, Mom." She hung up and walked the rest of the way down the stairs.

"What was that about?" Jesse asked, standing to pull her into his arms as she reached him. Hugging him, she trembled with a mixture of fear and sadness and anger. It was a wicked concoction. Bitter.

"My mom will never understand," she said. "She won't be happy until I've graduated with honors and married some perfect man who can make me forget about you."

Jesse pulled her away and looked her squarely in the face. "Do you want to forget about me?"

"Never," she answered, meaning it with every ounce of passion left inside her. "Sometimes I think you're the only person left in the world who understands every single part of me. I'm tired of everyone manipulating me. I see it happening, but I'm too scared to do anything about it. I'm tired of avoiding choices and situations and people. I want to live. I want to move on."

He brushed some hair away from her forehead. "And Italy is the perfect place for all of that," he said, leaning in to kiss her.

She breathed him in until she felt drunk on his words and his mouth and everything he did to hold her together in one piece.

"Italy," she whispered. "It's my only option now."

* * *

Thanksgiving Day, Naomi packed her last bag and stood at the open front door to wait for her and Jesse's taxi to the airport. Becca had left a few days ago to be with her family, so the house was quiet and felt empty with all of Naomi's belongings boxed up and sent to a storage shed in Cambridge. She had paid in advance for a year of storage and figured after that she could deal with getting rid of everything or paying for a longer period of time.

"You're sure about this?" Jesse asked, coming down the stairs with the last of his things. He approached her from behind and wrapped his arms around her waist. She snuggled into him and glanced down at the two bags she had packed.

"We've paid for the tickets," she said calmly. "I've sold my car, paid out my lease, cashed out my bank account, and told the school I'm not coming back. You've accepted the job. There's no way I can change my mind now. Everything is settled."

Jesse slid a hand down her side and took hold of her fingers. "You're white as a sheet and your skin is cold."

Swallowing a bitter taste in her mouth, she looked out the window as cars drove down the street. "I'm excited, I promise. It's *Italy*."

"Uh-huh."

She tensed and let out a sigh. "I'm nervous, okay? Scared out of my freaking mind."

Squeezing his hand, she focused on a maple tree in the front yard. Most of its branches were bare by now. The yard service had long since bagged up the leaves and taken them away. "In fact," she whispered, "I've never been so scared in my whole life, even when I woke up in that motel room with you watching me. You had that poetry book, remember? I thought that was the weirdest thing I'd ever seen—a kidnapper reading poetry."

Jesse let out a grunt. "I guess that would seem odd. I'm sorry, Naomi."

"For what? Reading poetry?"

"No, for the motel room. That day. When you woke up, I wasn't sure what to do. You'd been unconscious for two days. You'd woken a bunch of times, but only for a few seconds, then you were out again. Seriously, it freaked me the hell out. I thought for sure you were going to die from internal injuries or something. I didn't want to be responsible for your death."

"I don't remember that. Maybe a tiny bit. Maybe." She shook her head, trying as hard as she could to reach the memory, but it was all so dark, like puzzle pieces made of shadow.

"Eric was out selling what we'd stolen," he continued, "so I was trying to pass the time reading poetry since it always relaxes me. Then you woke up, this time a lot more alert than before. You kept asking where you were. You wouldn't shut up, so I told you flat-out you were kidnapped and we weren't going to let you go—not that you seemed to hear me, but maybe you did."

She tensed in Jesse's embrace as something clicked in her mind. For years she had tried to piece together the first few days she had been captive. There were only a few snippets—pictures in the fog, telling Brad she could walk home on her own, the parking lot, the headlights coming at her. Then blackness, the smell of leather, and finally Jesse.

"I must have heard you," she whispered, "even though I don't remember it. All I remember is opening my eyes and seeing you there. Everything was fuzzy in my head, but somehow I knew you had kidnapped me and you weren't alone. There was something about you—the poetry—it was all I could hold on to."

His hand tightened around hers. "You didn't come out of it completely until I started asking you to remember things. Eric and I wanted to feel justified in taking you. That's why I kept asking what you'd seen that night."

Outside the courtroom, Jesse had never spoken so frankly about kidnapping her. It sent a strange feeling down her spine, as if her muscles were tying themselves into complicated knots. She kept her focus on the bare branches outside.

"That's all over," she whispered. "It's over and this is my choice now—to be with you. You aren't forcing me to do anything. Eric is in prison. I'm not . . . I'm not kidnapped anymore."

Jesse let go of her hand and turned her around to face him. He almost looked angry, the way he lowered his eyebrows and clenched his jaw. "Of course you're not kidnapped," he said, emphasizing each word. "Why would you say that?"

She looked down at her luggage. "I don't know."

"Naomi, answer me." He took her face in his hands and forced her to look at him. "Tell me why you'd say that. I need to know if there's any way I can help."

His eyes were so green, so intense. She thought of every counselor she had ever spoken to, every lie she had told herself about feeling free, every disappointed look her mother had given her. She thought of every time she had imagined the bedroom and the locked door and Eric asking her if she would stay—and how she could never tell him no.

"Because," she said, her voice cracking, "I've never felt free since that day you took me. I've felt lighter, more in control, but never free."

His hands dropped from her face, confusion and disappointment filling his expression.

"It's not you," she cried, "it's not you. It's something deeper I can't shake, no matter how many counselors I talk to, no matter how many times my mother tells me I should be over it . . . I can't do it." Her body shook with her sobs now, each one so strong she thought it might bring her to her knees. Jesse wrapped her in his embrace, not squeezing, and she sensed he knew she might break into pieces if he did.

"Italy," she said, calming herself down enough to speak again. "That's where I can start over."

Jesse kissed the side of her head. "I hope so," he said as Naomi heard the taxi pull up. "I hope so."

XVI

"Do you want the window seat?" Jesse asked after he closed the overhead bin with their carryon luggage safely stowed inside.

Naomi looked at the oval window and shrugged. "No, you can take it," she answered, smiling. "If I want to see out, it'll give me an excuse to lean over you."

Laughing, Jesse sat down and she took the middle seat beside him. Nobody had taken the aisle seat yet.

"So," Jesse said, slipping his hand into hers and squeezing, "is this your first international flight?"

Naomi nodded and looked around. The plane was two decks high, and instead of the normal two rows of seats and one aisle, there were two aisles and three rows, the middle row four seats wide. "I've never seen such a big plane before," she said, a little awed. "It's amazing it can get off the ground."

Jesse leaned over and touched his nose to hers. "Big engines," he whispered, and then pulled away. "But I'm surprised you haven't flown overseas before. Doesn't your father's company have a division over in Germany?"

"Yeah, in Berlin," Naomi answered as her hand grew limp in Jesse's. It was strange that her parents were not a part of her first trip out of the country. She had always thought they would be since they were the ones who made sure she had a passport. "He's never taken me over there, though," she continued. "My mom goes sometimes. I've never really wanted to."

Jesse nodded and leaned his head against his headrest. "So this is a huge deal for you," he said, keeping his eyes focused ahead. "No wonder you're nervous."

Naomi slid her hand out of Jesse's and stretched her legs as much as she could in the cramped space. "I'm feeling better," she declared, mostly to herself. "I think this will be a good thing. It's important for me to make my own decisions now. I need to stop trying to please everybody else."

Jesse's eyes widened as he turned to look at her. His hair was sticking up near his left ear, but instead of fixing it, Naomi stared at it and decided she loved everything about him, every blemish, every shortcoming. The mistakes he had made in his life made him who he was. They made him stronger, and they proved to her that it was never too late to change and fix things that were wrong. She could fix things that were wrong with her, too. She could go to Italy and prove her independence and start her life over in a new, exciting place.

"I'm happy you're feeling better," Jesse said, his eyes brightening with relief. "As much as I want you with me right now, I never want to make you feel obligated or forced." He gently touched her elbow. "I hope you know that."

Looking into Jesse's eyes, Naomi understood how serious he was about what he was saying. After her whole speech earlier about not feeling free, he was probably terrified she was going to freak out at some point. Maybe that was a possibility, but at the moment she felt confident and excited.

Setting her hand on top of Jesse's, she made her expression as serious as she could. "I promise you I don't feel obligated or forced," she said firmly. "I love you, Jesse. I never want to be without you."

Jesse's eyes softened as he leaned over to kiss her gently on the lips. "Then let's make the most of this," he whispered.

She kissed him back, her heart pounding with hope and fear and excitement. Things could only get better from here on out.

* * *

"Trastevere is the heart of Rome," Jesse explained to Naomi as she stepped out of the Italian taxi. "It's one of the untouched cities, they say."

She looked up at a towering apartment building covered in limp ivy. Across the narrow street a similar building stood. Everything seemed old here, almost crumbling. A few shiny bicycles leaning against the buildings were the only things that made her believe she hadn't been transported back in time.

Blinking from the light drizzle of rain, Naomi wrapped her arms around herself and shivered. This was not how she had imagined Italy—cold and ancient.

"Heart of Rome, huh? Well, it's beautiful," she said, giving Jesse the warmest smile she could despite the cold. It was at least fifty degrees, but the rain and thick, humid air made everything seem colder. Despite all of that, she liked that Jesse had rented out a place in a part of Rome almost untouched by modern architecture and changes. It almost felt medieval.

"I already love it here," Jesse said, sweeping her into his arms and kissing her. She laughed and let him twirl her around until the taxi driver cleared his throat and opened the trunk. He said something in Italian and Jesse let go of Naomi to help unload the bags. When everything was unloaded and Jesse had paid the taxi driver, Naomi grabbed what she could and followed Jesse to the door, where he pressed a buzzer and said his name. The door clicked and he opened it wide for her to walk inside.

"Everything smells wet," she whispered, scrunching her nose as Jesse led her to a front desk. An older woman with a sun-weathered, wrinkly face looked up. Her thick white hair was pulled into a loose bun. She smiled when she spotted Jesse, a string of Italian flowing from her mouth as she looked at Naomi and clapped her hands together.

"What is she saying?" Naomi asked through her teeth, not wanting to appear rude. She would have to learn the language here if she was going to survive.

Jesse nodded at the woman and answered her in Italian. His words came out carefully. The woman nodded, motioning to Naomi.

"I speak English, for her sake, your lovely wife."

Naomi almost choked. "Oh, we're not married. We're—"

"Nonsense!" the woman interrupted. "Your Jesse here tell me much about you when he lease apartment. You lovely girl. You love Trastevere!" She opened her arms and raised them high, as if embracing the entire city. Then she lowered them and clasped her soft-looking hands below her chest. "If you not married in two months, I be a'surprised. Come now, let us sign final paperwork so I give you keys." She tapped the top of the desk and sat down.

Naomi waited beside Jesse as he signed some papers and paid the rest of his deposit to the old woman, who told Naomi to call her Lalia.

"Laa-li-a," Naomi pronounced, trying to place her accents in the right place.

"That is correct." The old woman smiled and handed over the apartment keys to Jesse. She wished them both well as they gathered their luggage and trudged up the concrete stairwell to the third floor.

"There's . . . no elevator?" Naomi panted as she dragged her bags up the final set of steps.

"Um, yeah, sorry. It was the most affordable place I could find when I was looking." He glanced back at her, grinning. "At least every time you come up the stairs you won't be hauling eighty pounds of luggage."

"Right," she gasped. "Well, it's charming." They walked down a short hallway to apartment number fifteen. Something inside of Naomi was sparking to life. Everything might have smelled old and ancient, but in her mind it was turning into a good thing—a solid thing so foreign it was almost comforting. Here, away from everything she had ever known, she might be able to truly live for the first time in her life.

Jesse unlocked the door and they both stepped inside. Naomi dropped her luggage. "It's a lot smaller than in the pictures you showed me."

He laughed. "I expected that. It's cozy." He turned to her, frowning. "If you hate it, I've only signed it for three months."

Naomi slid her gaze over the worn but clean furniture. The couch was upholstered in a yellow-orange color that made her almost giggle it was so hideous. There was a desk near a set of rickety-looking doors leading out to a balcony big enough for one person to stand and hang laundry on the wire strung up between buildings. The kitchen looked manageable, at least, with lots of cupboard space and a refrigerator. There was no dishwasher, no television in the living room, hardly anything modern at all.

"I remember seeing a washer and dryer in the pictures?" she asked, raising an eyebrow at Jesse.

"I'm sure we can find them," he answered, taking her hand and leading her through the front room and down a hallway. He opened a closet door to a tiny room stuffed with a newer-looking washer and dryer. Naomi let out a sigh.

"As long as I don't have to wash our clothes by hand, I'll be happy."

Jesse grunted. "You've never lived in anything less than finery. This will take some getting used to, I suppose."

"Are you saying I'm spoiled?"

"Possibly." He smiled and twirled her around once again, bumping her against the wall. "Whoops, sorry."

"I don't mind." When she looked into his eyes, she saw life and love and excitement. It seeped into her like a ray of sunshine. With him, everything was possible. She would live in a cave with him if she had to, even if she had to scrub clothes by hand.

"Where's the bedroom?" she asked in a sultry voice, tracing her finger down his strong, firm chest. She wanted him so much her knees were starting to tremble. "I feel like I'm going to die from jet lag, but I think I need something before I sleep."

Looking eager, Jesse led her down the hallway. "Can't be far."

* * *

All Naomi did for the next two days was eat at odd hours and sleep. Every time she woke, there was sun peeking through the thin bedroom curtains. Groaning, she threw the blankets back over her head and closed her eyes. Finally, Jesse rolled her out of bed, undressed her, and made her get in the bath.

"There," he said, looking down at her as she soaked in some hot water scented with salts, "now you can start waking up at the right time." He looked at his watch. "It's nine a.m. You're not allowed to go back to sleep until ten tonight."

She rolled her eyes and grabbed a round jar of bath salts that had appeared in the bathroom the day before. Jesse must have bought them while she was sleeping. For some reason, that made her smile. It was one of the reasons she loved him—the little things he did for her. She lifted the jar to her nose and sniffed. The crystal-like salts smelled rich and mysterious, like a combination of flowers she couldn't identify.

"I'm sorry!" she laughed, returning the bath salts to the edge of the tub. "I'm not used to this kind of thing. My body thinks it's been tipped upside down."

"It's okay," he answered, getting on his knees by the tub. He rolled up his sleeves and traced a finger through the water as he studied her nakedness. She blushed a little and touched his fingers.

"So everything is going to work out?" she asked, every nerve in her body awakening as Jesse moved his hand up her arm.

"Of course," he said, laughing. "Why wouldn't it work out?"

"I mean, I haven't told anyone I've come here, except Finn—and even then, I never told him for sure

I was leaving. I told the school I was moving, but I didn't say where. Becca thinks I moved back home. Somebody's going to catch on."

Jesse winced. "I wish you hadn't told Finn, even indirectly, but it's all right. When we're more settled, you can tell your parents you've decided to move here."

She sat up, bathwater sliding down her shoulders. "Why can't I tell them now? It's all over. You're free. There's nothing they can do."

His hand stopped near her elbow. "Let's wait," he whispered, leaning down to kiss her bare shoulders. She closed her eyes. "Thanksgiving break is barely over and they won't know anything is wrong for a while."

"Wrong?"

"Not wrong," he said, lifting his lips from her skin. "Changed, I guess, is the right word. They'll need to accept you're independent now. Let's give it some time, okay?"

"Okay." She leaned her head back and Jesse moved his kisses to her neck. "I like the way independent sounds," she said, her breaths coming faster as she turned her head to give him better access to nibble on her ear. She stared at the bath salts and lifted her hand to scoop some out of the jar. They were rough and smooth at the same time. Jesse moved his way to her cheek and then to her lips. She dropped the salts in her hand. They plunked into the water and sifted down around her legs.

"Free," Jesse said, his lips caressing hers. "Free."

* * *

Later that morning, she and Jesse walked around Trastevere, buying essentials for the kitchen and the bathroom, more blankets and sheets for the bed, and a few books from a shop Jesse didn't want to leave. With their arms full of bags, they meandered up and down narrow alleys overgrown with vines and low-hanging trees. All the plants seemed limp, as if the humidity in the air made them heavier. The buildings were the colors of the sunset—terracotta browns, deep wines, and honey-yellows. Even on a cloudy day the city seemed alive with color. Tourists were roaming the more popular areas, creating a constant buzz of activity. In the dead of winter the buzz felt almost lazy. Naomi guessed in the summer it would swell and pick up momentum, but she didn't want that to come. She wanted to wander Rome forever, just as it was, losing herself in quaint restaurants and shops with Jesse by her side. She knew it couldn't last.

Two days later, Jesse began leaving every morning for work, and Naomi found herself sitting on the couch for hours at a time, staring at the front door. It was painted a soft eggshell blue and had a brown coffee-colored stain along the bottom, shaped like a turtle. She stared at that shape forever, thinking about turtles gliding through a perfect sea of blue. Calm. It was a place in her head where she didn't have to worry about anything.

Finally, she realized Italy itself was not going to spark her to life. She was going to have to beat down the wall of fear she had built around herself. She would have to begin by leaving the apartment.

Gathering her courage, she walked to the entryway and put out her hand to open the door. There was talking down the hall, the muffled sounds of a couple arguing. She undid the chain, her fingers trembling, and then turned the handle and opened the door. The hallway smelled damp and musty. Whitewashed walls. Weathered wood floor. The man and woman arguing one stairwell down were speaking in Italian, their words like bullets firing at each other in the otherwise quiet atmosphere.

Naomi stepped into the hallway, her pulse pounding in her head. Then she looked down and realized she hadn't put her shoes on. She needed her purse too. Swallowing, she backed into the apartment and closed the door. She didn't want to go outside. She didn't want to walk down the stairs and risk having to see the arguing couple. She fastened the chain and rushed to the couch, grabbing her purse from a nearby end table. Her phone was at the bottom. She wasn't sure she dared turn it on. It had been off since before she and Jesse had flown here to Italy. The problem was he didn't know she had a new phone. He had told her he would buy her one here so she could call him once he started working every day, but he had yet to get her one. He didn't know she had gone behind his back and upgraded to a global plan so she wouldn't feel cut off from everything she was leaving behind. It was the one secret she had kept from him. It made her feel dirty, as if she was cheating on him. With a phone. How stupid was that? Even keeping Finn's kiss a secret for so long hadn't made her feel so terrible. Maybe if she never used the phone, that would make it all better.

Or maybe not.

Glaring at the phone, she almost dropped it back into her purse, then changed her mind and pressed the power button with her thumb. She could at least check to see if anyone had tried to call her from home. She scrolled through the voicemail message list.

Three voicemail messages from Karen Jensen.

One voicemail message from Jason Jensen.

Her heart sank. They knew something was going on. Her father had never left her a voicemail message in his entire life.

Next, she scrolled through her text message list.

Four text messages from Karen Jensen.

That was surprising. She didn't know her mother even knew how to text. Her finger trembling above the screen, she selected the first message.

Hi, sweetheart, I'm texting because you haven't answered your phone and I'm a little worried. Please give me a call when you can.

Naomi selected the next message and then the next and the next. They were all similar, each one sounding a little more worried than the other. When she finished, she went back to the voicemail list and dialed the number to listen to the first message.

"Hi, Naomi," her mother's voice chirped, "I hope your Thanksgiving went well with—Finn, I think?— but I hope everything was great. Give me a call when you can."

Naomi saved the message and listened to the next.

"Hi, sweetheart, it's Mom. Give me a call when you can."

And the next.

"Give me a call, sweetheart." She paused. "Did your phone break? Maybe I'll try texting you."

Naomi paused before listening to her father's message. She noticed it had come yesterday, after all the worried-sounding texts from her mother.

"Hi, Naomi, it's Dad. I'm not sure what's going on, but we're a little concerned about you not answering your phone. You understand why we might worry, right? You told Mom you were spending time with someone over Thanksgiving and we haven't heard back from you, that's all. I hate to be one of those pushy parents, but give us a call when you can, all right?" His voice got a little muffled, as if he was covering half his mouth with his hand. "If you're mad at Mom or something, you can call my office . . . all right? Don't let us worry like this."

Naomi saved the message and lowered the phone to her lap. It had been ten days since she had last talked to her mother. That didn't seem like too long to go without talking to her. She had gone much longer before, but her father did have a point about her not following up with them after the holiday. They were paranoid because of her past. She sighed and opened up her text-messaging program. Jesse's voice echoed in her mind. *When we're more settled, you can tell your parents you've decided to move here.*

He was right. Telling her parents where she was would not go over well, but she could at least let them know she was alive. She typed to her mother, *I'm fine.*

Just super-busy right now, so I'll call you back when I've got some time. Love you!

Not a complete lie, at least. She hit send and quickly turned off the phone.

XVII

THE NEXT DAY, AFTER READING BOOKS UNTIL SHE thought she would go mad, she walked to the door again. She heard no arguing this time, but when she reached for the handle she broke into a sweat and turned around.

Not today.

This was what had stopped her from trying to escape the house—a deep-seated fear of the unknown, of wondering what might happen if things didn't go right, a precarious feeling her universe might implode if she couldn't plan everything down to the last detail and know how it would end. So, instead of trying, she held back. It was what had kept her from leaving Brad before her kidnapping. More than Jesse's plea, it was what kept her from calling her mother.

She curled into a ball on the bed and cried herself to sleep until Jesse came home and woke her up. He started rubbing her back.

"This is how it's going to be," he explained, leaning down to her ear. "I'm sorry, but I have to work if we want to live here. Your money won't last very long and we've spent most of mine now."

"You want to work," she said, burying her face in the pillows. "I know you love the job you have. It's everything you ever wanted."

"Everything I ever wanted is right here." He scooped her into his arms and held her close. "You're scared, I know, but you'll get used to everything. It'll get easier. This is a new start, remember?"

"I don't know what I was thinking," she said, feeling like an idiot. "Why can't I be strong?"

Turning her to look up at him, he lifted a hand and traced her lips with his fingers. "You're stronger than you think, just not in ways most people expect."

"What do you mean?"

He continued tracing her lips as a warm smile lit up his face. "Do you think you'd be alive right now if you weren't strong? Eric would have killed you in the first three weeks if you hadn't kept your cool like you did."

"I was too scared to try anything," she whispered. "I wasn't being strong."

He lifted his fingers from her lips as his smile melted into a straight line. "Strength doesn't always mean fighting back. Sometimes it means enduring to the end—quietly. Not everybody could have handled your situation the way you did. Most would've tried to get away because they would've been too impatient to evaluate the kinds of people they were dealing with. They would have pissed Eric off so much he would have shot them in the head the first chance he had. You saw past that. I don't care if you call it cowardice or fear. To me, it was smart and brave."

Naomi didn't know how to respond. She hadn't thought of herself as handling her captivity very well, but maybe Jesse had a point. He watched her for a moment, admiration sparkling in his eyes. It made her want to hug him and never let go.

He leaned down and kissed her forehead. "How about we get some dinner and then read for a while?"

She nodded, embracing him before he sat up. "That sounds good. Maybe that little soup shop we keep passing by when we're out?"

He laughed. "That's exactly what I was thinking."

The soup they decided to get was white and creamy, thick with dark red kidney beans and wilted spinach. Naomi ate so much her stomach felt like it might burst, then Jesse read to her from *The Great Gatsby*—the one book he had brought with him from home. He sat cross-legged on the bed, resting on the pillows as Naomi lay in his lap, her arms folded over her full belly as she scanned the words on the yellowed pages in front of her. Jesse's voice spread through her like a comforting mist. Hours later, when her stomach felt normal again and she was starting to get sleepy, Jesse paused on the last passage of the book, his words faltering until they caught and held strong.

"'So we beat on,'" he read, his knuckles turning white as he squeezed the edges of the book, "boats against the current, borne back ceaselessly into the past.'"

He closed the book and let out a sigh so loud it was like longing and awe and heartache all wrapped into a single vibration. It made Naomi wonder what he thought of that last sentence—if he meant something by reading it with such passion. The past, it seemed, was something he wanted to escape forever, but perhaps he believed it was impossible. Maybe it was.

* * *

In the morning, she woke with her head full of Jesse's voice. He was already gone to work, so she wandered into the kitchen, her stomach rumbling. So far, she and Jesse had eaten out for every meal except breakfast, which was always bread and fruit Jesse picked up the night before. She was tired of the same things over and over. She wanted to cook. Her fingers were itching to do something productive. If she sat around long enough, she would start to feel like she was back in the house again. Kidnapped.

Forcing herself to bathe and dress, she grabbed some money and stuffed it into her back pocket, then stared at her purse and wondered if she should take her phone. Perhaps it was silly to freak out over going to the market, but having her phone would make her feel a little bit safer. She snatched it out of the purse and turned it on. No new texts or phone calls. Yet. Once it was in her pocket with the money, she made it as far as the stairwell before stopping to second-guess herself. She held tightly to the handrail.

"No," she hissed to herself. "You can do this."

One step down the stairs. Then another and another. Jesse had taught her how to count euros and read prices. She knew her way to the market. There was nothing stopping her.

Fifteen minutes later, she was wandering aisles made up of vegetable stands overflowing with onions, turnips, and tomatoes. She picked some of each, and then stopped in front of a stand stuffed with artichokes.

"Very good to try," the market owner said in English.

Naomi looked up and smiled. The woman was middle-aged but pretty, with skin so smooth it looked polished. It reminded her of Finn's skin—that sweet caramel color.

Naomi blinked. "I've never cooked with artichokes before," she said, picking one up. It was heavier than she expected, and such a beautiful green, like a faded emerald.

"Oh, it easy!" the woman said, picking up two and placing them in Naomi's basket. She picked up another artichoke and held it up for Naomi to see. "You slice off thick leaves, see?" She bent back one of the leathery outer leaves. "Then put whole artichoke in water with lemon."

She turned the artichoke upside down and then spun to her left and snatched two lemons from a nearby stand. She put them in Naomi's basket.

"When soaked, you take two out." She lifted two artichokes and pretended she was beating them against each other. Her eyes grew big and round. "You hit together to open up!" she said with a loud laugh. Some of the other shoppers looked over, smiling. "Then salt and pepper and fry in olive oil upside down. Push down so look like flowers, see?"

She set down the artichokes and spread her fingers wide. "Like sunflowers! Put water on leaves when frying to make crunchy." She kissed her closed fingers and grinned. "The best! You buy?"

Naomi looked down at the artichokes and lemons in her basket. "Of course," she answered, remembering the sunflowers Evelyn had told her about when she first described Italy and how wonderful it would be to come here. "I hope I can remember what you told me."

"You remember. I tell you again when you pay, yes?"

Nodding, Naomi grabbed two more artichokes and put them in her basket. Maybe this going out thing wouldn't be so hard, after all. Next, she found the bakery and bought a crusty loaf of bread. She would worry about finding a butcher later. It seemed there was no large supermarket nearby, but Jesse had said they were awful, anyway.

"Thank you very much," the man at the bakery said in thickly accented English as he dropped change into her open hand. He seemed accustomed to foreign-speaking customers. He had been able to spot Naomi as one even though she hadn't said a word to him yet.

"Thank you," she answered, smiling as she left the shop with her arms full. The sun was shining and the sky was the exact color of blue she had always imagined it would be. For a moment, she stopped in her tracks and stared at it. Sapphires. She had dreamed about coming here for so long. Italy had been a simple idea when her kidnappers were deciding everything for her, but now she was making her own choices and she was choosing to live in a place that scared her so much she couldn't walk down the street without trembling. It was all so new. It smelled different. It looked different. She didn't know the customs or traditions, no matter how many things Jesse had told her. It was all new to him, as well. She could do this. She could be strong and push beyond her ugly past as she embraced something new. Even if it was frightening at first. People didn't know about her past here.

Taking a step forward, she continued up the road and around the corner to her and Jesse's apartment. Her phone beeped in her back pocket as she pressed the buzzer for the door. She said her name into the intercom and the door clicked open. Lalia rushed across the room and helped her.

"You go shopping today!" she said with a big grin, holding the door open. "What you make tonight?"

"I'm not sure. What do you call artichokes shaped like sunflowers?" she asked, laughing.

"Beautiful, beautiful!" Lalia cried, clapping her hands together. "You make *carciofi alla guidia!*"

Naomi loved the way she spoke, how every syllable was pronounced so succinctly. "Yes, I guess so," she laughed, and set her bags on a little bench near the door. "Phone," she explained to Lalia, and pulled it out of her back pocket. For a moment her heart seemed to freeze in her chest.

Incoming text from Finn Giachetti.

Crap. Not now. She pushed the button to receive the text.

Hey, did you move to Italy with Jesse? I haven't seen you at Java. Is everything going okay? Please, please let me know if you're okay.

She stared at the words, her heartbeat rapid. Her parents were constantly in her thoughts, but she could handle that. Finn, however, was another story. Knowing he had reached out to her was like watching a bridge form across two continents—and it wasn't a bridge she was ready to cross. She didn't want to remember Finn's caramel skin and that moment on the dance floor when she had felt free and open and more herself than at any other time in her life.

"Naomi," Lalia said, "you look hurt."

She looked up, forcing a smile. "Oh, it's nothing. Thanks again for your help." Gathering her bags, she rushed up the stairs and into the apartment. Her heart was still pounding, but she was sure it was from the climb up three flights of stairs instead of Finn's text. She wouldn't let it get to her. That part of her life was over. She would cook an Italian meal in her Italian kitchen with her Italian produce. She would forget Finn and Stacy and the smell of the beach.

As she started slicing the leaves off the artichokes, she thought about her and Jesse's plans for the weekend. They would go see the Colosseum and she would try her first gelato. For a moment, nothing felt real. She looked out the balcony doors to the apartment building across the street. It was unseasonably warm today. An older woman was hanging laundry on her part of the line, moving lazily. Naomi remembered the bedroom once again. There was the soft quilt on the bed, the clean smell of the sheets, and the shiny deadbolt on the door. And then Eric was undoing the lock and stepping inside. When she fell into his embrace, she breathed in the smell of him and held tightly to everything he represented. He was guilt and pain and suffering. He was loss and grief and the abuse she had never left behind.

"You'll stay?" he asked.

She pulled away a fraction of an inch, her focus moving to the door behind him. He had closed it, but she knew what was on the other side—herself, set free, curled into a ball, helpless and alone. It was what she had always been, she realized. Even after she had escaped, she had moved from one prison to another, and it was all her own doing.

Looking into Eric's eyes, she knew there was no escape as long as she could remember what she had done to him and the others, and what they had done to her. The cuts ran too deep.

"I'll stay," she said.

* * *

When Jesse came home, Naomi was on the couch facing the balcony doors. The lady's laundry hanging on the line was swaying back and forth in a gentle breeze, reminding Naomi of seagulls on the horizon. She was aware Jesse had returned, but couldn't tear her focus away from the laundry. Jesse would see dinner unfinished on the counter, half-prepared artichokes and sliced lemons, noodles draining in a colander in the sink. They were probably sticky and ruined by now.

"You went shopping," Jesse said, standing in the middle of the living room. She could feel him looking at her.

"I did," she whispered. "I made it out the door. I didn't get lost."

"That's great." He came closer and knelt beside the couch. His head obstructed her view of the swaying clothes. She moved her attention to his face. He gently touched her shoulder. "What's the matter? Are you still upset about me having to leave you every day? I thought you would be okay with this."

"I am," she answered, the words coming out in a croak. "I'm . . . this is all so new and I feel so alone."

"Alone? I'm here with you, even if I leave for a few hours. If you need me, you can call me on the landline

223

down in the lobby. I wrote down my number for you. We'll get you a cell phone soon, okay?"

"Okay." She closed her mouth and then opened it again to tell him about the phone she already had, but couldn't force the words out. Instead, she moved her attention to the buttons on Jesse's shirt. He dressed so nicely in clean, pressed clothes. She had ironed a few of his shirts already. She guessed she would be doing it a lot more, but it didn't bother her. For a moment, she compared the way Jesse dressed to the rip in Finn's jeans. She would see her parents again—someday, somehow—but what about Finn? And why did she care? He had Carly now, and she had Jesse. She wasn't in love with Finn like she was with Jesse, but there was something about Finn, so casual and carefree and open, a splinter twisting into her heart.

XVIII

December

NAOMI MADE HERSELF GO OUTSIDE AT LEAST ONCE A day. On the weekend, she and Jesse went to see the sights, but when the workweek rolled around again she wandered Trastevere, exploring everything deeper, finding shops she could lose herself in for hours. When she felt inspired enough by the medieval feel of the town and its rustic buildings and maze-like streets, she pulled out her camera and started taking pictures and video. She was surprised how many Italians she met spoke English. Many of the local men watched her. They had sun-browned skin and eyes swimming with passion as they strolled the streets or sat at their tables with their mochas and lattes and espressos. Some of them followed her with a lazy stride, their eyes focused on her body in ways she wasn't used to. As long as she stayed where there were people and tourists wandering about, they eventually fell away and she could keep walking without falling apart.

She found a shop selling art supplies and began filling the apartment with pencils and oil pastels and stacks of paper. She loved the way the supplies smelled earthy, different from her supplies back home, as if they were more real.

When she was back at the apartment, she spread out paper on the desk near the balcony doors and then lined up her pastels along one edge. They were so pretty, with ivory wrappers covered in Italian words she couldn't read. She sketched the sky and the laundry line, and then the old woman who had hung up her clothes the other day. For hours, she lost herself in drawing and coloring. She tried to push back any uneasiness she felt about Jesse and the words he had said when she was in the bathtub—*Thanksgiving break is barely over and they won't know anything is wrong for a while.*

Wrong.

So many things could be wrong, like the anger she had seen on Jesse's face when he had looked at his father, or the fact that she had snuck around Jesse to buy a phone, or how dark she felt inside whenever she thought about all those texts and phone calls from her parents.

There was nothing to do about any of it now. She picked up an oil pastel the color of the artichokes from the market. She rubbed her thumb along the soft, slick surface before setting the tip of the pastel to paper, coloring in her sketch until she lost herself in a sort of stupor, a desperate attempt to force out everything unpleasant. Mostly, she wanted to get rid of her constant memories of the house and Eric and the bedroom. So often when she closed her eyes, she saw him. Whenever she heard a deep male voice speaking Italian it morphed into Eric's voice. Every time she chopped garlic, she thought of him. She realized that without a counselor to guide her through all her disturbing thoughts and memories, they were getting the best of her. They were like the mazes of Trastevere. Her counselor-free summers had never turned as dark as this. It was Italy. It was the realization she was living here, where Eric and the others wanted to live, that was killing her inside. They were stuck in prison and she was living their dream. Evelyn's dream. Eric's plans. Her life now. Every night, she fell asleep in Jesse's arms, knowing he loved her and would take care of her forever. But no matter how hard she tried to make herself believe everything was how it should be, she knew she was deluding herself.

The calls and texts from her mother kept coming. *Naomi, please call me. Please. Did you go stay with that man you were talking about? Hasn't the semester started again already?*

And then Finn sent another text. *Please let me know you're okay. I went to see Becca, but she hasn't heard from you, either. She said you moved back home? What happened with Jesse? Oh, and I have something great to tell you about my mom.*

That night, a few hours after she read Finn's text, Naomi buried her face in her hands. She couldn't keep lying to Jesse. It felt so wrong. Everything was stacking up around her, forcing her emotions into a space so small she knew she would burst any moment.

"I got a phone," she said into her hands during dinner.

Jesse was quite for a moment. "You . . . what?"

She lifted her head from her hands and stood from her chair. Walking into the living room, she found her phone in her purse and returned to the table.

"It's a global phone," she said, her voice trembling as she watched confusion sweep across Jesse's face. "I got it before we came here because I was afraid of feeling cut off . . . or something. I was afraid you would see it in airport security, but you didn't seem to notice with all my other crap I had to put through the scanners."

Jesse's confused expression melted into disappointment. Naomi could see he was trying to control his emotions. He swept away the negative expression and looked up at her with a calm, sweet smile.

"I'm so sorry for making you feel like you might be cut off," he said, reaching for the phone. "You don't have to apologize."

Breathing a sigh of relief, she sat in her chair and leaned back. "I need to tell my parents what's going on. Everyone's going to think I've been kidnapped again, and I can't deal with that. I have to tell them."

Jesse nodded, his face still calm. "I think we should block certain numbers," he said. "Namely, your mother's . . . until you're ready to deal with this. She'll be all right until then."

Naomi watched him take the phone and then navigate through some screens. A crease formed between his eyes. "Finn is texting you?" he asked, lowering the phone.

"Y-yes." She didn't like the way he looked at her all of a sudden—that steely glaze over his eyes. He wouldn't make her block Finn. He wouldn't. Shakily, she said, "He's concerned, that's all."

He softened his expression, gazing at her with what almost looked like pity. "I think you might be able to handle things easier if you don't talk to him for a while."

She reached for the phone. "I'm not talking to him. I haven't even texted him back. I haven't talked to *anyone*."

"Naomi," Jesse said firmly, "don't lie, please. There's a text here to your mother. I asked you not to talk to her."

Folding her arms, she grunted. "Telling her I'm fine is hardly talking to her. And that's all I've texted." She glared at Jesse as he stood and walked into the living room. He was doing something to her phone— punching buttons, scrolling through screens. "What are you doing?" she demanded, standing up from her chair. She put her hands on her hips.

"I'm making things easier for you." His back was to her, and suddenly she hated the way he hunched his shoulders forward, the way his muscles in his forearms slid under his skin as he moved his fingers wildly across the phone. She wasn't sure what to do or say. He had never acted so rashly before—at least not toward her— not since that night he rushed her out of the house to help her escape. She hadn't wanted to leave, she remembered. There had been a gaping hole in her chest as she had walked away, but Jesse had kept pulling on her, and then when he drove her to the police station and ordered her out of the car, she had thought her shattered heart would never heal. And it hadn't. Not yet.

"Jesse," she said in as calm a voice as she could. Her throat was tightening with a surge of fear. "I want my phone back. I don't want people blocked on there. I promise I won't talk to them until you think I'm ready." She reached out a hand even though he couldn't see her. "Please?"

Finally, he turned around. "Your password for your online phone account is *Jesse128*, isn't it?"

How the hell did he know that? Her jaw dropped open. "Yeah."

He smiled. "I thought so." Turning around again, he kept working on the phone.

It shouldn't have surprised her that he had guessed her password. It was his name and birthday, after all. It was her own fault for choosing something so obvious.

He finished whatever he was doing and turned around to face her. "I've changed your password on your account so you can't make any changes. I've deleted everyone on here but me, and I've blocked your parents and Finn from being able to text or call you. It's for your own good, Naomi. Trust me."

She lowered her arm and it flopped back to her side. "Can I still access the Internet? What if I want to check my e-mail?" Not that she received a lot of e-mail. She checked it maybe once every week, but at the moment it seemed like her last lifeline to home.

"No, I've disabled that too."

"Why?" she whispered. "Why would you do that? It's been almost two weeks. People are going to know something is wrong by now."

Jesse's eyebrows knit together. "Do you think coming here with me was wrong? Are you regretting your decision?"

It was then that she felt the age difference between her and Jesse. He would turn thirty next month. He was an adult and she was barely old enough to legally drink. She hadn't even finished college. Maybe he knew what was best, but as she let her focus drift from his face to the phone in his hand, something inside her twisted into knots.

"I don't know," she squeaked, her knees giving out from under her. She sat back down in her chair. "I have nothing back home, do I?"

"You have your parents," he said, his voice gentle. "I know they mean a lot to you, so I promise you can see them later when everything is settled." He walked to the table and set her phone near her plate. "I'm not upset with you for getting a phone, but for now, just be happy with how things are. Okay?" He touched her shoulder, sliding his finger down her arm.

She picked up her phone. It felt different. Empty. She couldn't call her mother now, even if she wanted to. She couldn't answer Finn's desperate text messages. She couldn't find out what he wanted to tell her about his mother. There were Internet cafés in town, or she could call her phone service and set things back to normal, but she didn't want to be dishonest with Jesse again.

"I don't know how to feel," she said, dropping the phone onto the table. "All you had to do was ask me not to talk to anyone."

"That *is* what I asked you to do."

She looked up at him. "Are you not going to trust me now because I got the phone behind your back?"

His finger paused on her arm. "No, I understand why you got it, and of course I still trust you. I think this will make it easier for you not to be tempted, that's all. I can't stop you from calling your parents if that's what you want, but ask yourself . . . is it what you want right now?"

She looked away as a sigh escaped her lips. "No."

XIX

THE NEXT EVENING, JESSE CAME HOME FROM WORK with a thin brown box tucked under his arm. He steered Naomi out of the kitchen and into the bedroom, where he set the box on the bed and told her to open it.

"You don't have to buy me things," she said as she tucked her fingers under the lid and pulled it off. Inside was something flat wrapped in white and gold striped tissue paper.

"I want to buy you things," Jesse answered, wrapping his arms around her from behind. He watched over her shoulder as she picked up the tissue paper. It was limp, clothing of some kind. Once she had it unwrapped, she ran her hands over the smooth black material and then pulled it out of the box. Holding it up, she watched it fall into shape. It was a dress with a plunging neckline and a knee-length skirt. When she turned it around, she saw the back was cut to reveal her shoulder blades. She blushed. She definitely wouldn't be wearing a bra with this outfit.

"This is sexier than any dress I've ever worn," she said, turning around in Jesse's arms. "Where the heck am I going to wear it outside of this bedroom?"

Jesse smiled and leaned close enough for his forehead to touch hers. He smelled of cigarette smoke, which seemed odd. He didn't smoke. He must work with people who did. Everybody smoked here. "To a nightclub," he answered. "It's about time we went out at night and did something fun. I've found the perfect place."

"A nightclub?" she asked, her mouth going dry. She remembered her night with Finn, the sweat on his neck, the way he smelled, his body moving in time with hers.

"Yeah, don't you like to dance?" Jesse touched her cheek. His expression was sweet and endearing. His eyes pleaded.

"I do like to dance," she answered, wondering what it would be like to move with Jesse on a hot, dark dance floor with music pounding through her. She hoped it would be even better than her time with Finn. In fact, she was counting on it.

"All right, then. Do you have shoes you can wear that'll match?"

She nodded and pushed him out of the room. "Let me try it on. You go finish dinner."

He grinned on his way out. "All right."

When the door was shut, she turned to the dress on the bed. The idea of loud music and lots of people wouldn't normally appeal to her, but right now it did. She wanted to lose herself and all the emotions welling up inside her. Jesse had told her she was independent now, but what had he meant? Independent from her parents, yes, but from him, no. That would never have bothered her before. She wanted to be a part of him, to depend on him, but now there was the phone incident yesterday. She looked at it lying on the desk by the window. Had he planned to restrict her access to home all along? The very thought made her turn cold inside, but it also seemed ridiculous. He had only done it because he could see how much the texts and unanswered phone calls were affecting her. He wanted her settled and happy with her decision before talking to anyone back home. He knew as well as she did how someone might convince her to come back if she already doubted her decision. He saw her afraid to go outside on her own. He heard the panic in her voice whenever she spoke of her mother. All he wanted was for her to stand strong before anything else could move forward. That was all. It had to be all.

Stripping off her clothes, she pulled on the dress and looked at herself in the full-length mirror by the closet. The word that came to mind was *wow*. She looked hot, and surprisingly, it didn't make her uncomfortable to wear such a thing. The only place she would wear it was a nightclub, but it would fit there. Unlike the jeans and T-shirt she had worn to go out with Finn, this outfit did scream '*sleep with me*!' That wasn't an issue with Jesse. She was already his. Smiling, she ran her hands down her hips. She would try to have fun and forget about the phone and the disappointment in Jesse's eyes. She needed to let him protect her.

* * *

The nightclub was packed with people. Naomi forced her mind to a place where she could let herself enjoy the constant feel of bodies surrounding her instead of wanting to escape. This was a place where she could be herself without anyone caring. With Jesse next to her, keeping her safe, she could dissolve. The music was loud and different from what she was used to, more techno and less pop and metal.

"You want to get on the floor right away?" Jesse asked close to her ear once they had paid at the entrance and were let in. He kept an arm tight around her waist.

"Sure," she answered, but her quiet voice was lost in the noise. Jesse smiled, reading her lips, and led her into the throbbing crowd where they found a space next to several other couples. Some of the men looked her up and down, but as soon as their eyes met Jesse's, they looked away. His face was bathed in alternating blue and red light. Naomi saw his tightened jaw and an expression so territorial she was sure no man would even consider touching her.

For a moment, she worried Jesse wouldn't be a great dancer. He looked around the room while she stood stupidly in front of him. She wasn't sure how he wanted her to dance, but she guessed he would want it a little dirty, just like Finn had. She cringed. She couldn't start thinking about Finn. Not now.

Finally, Jesse turned to her and began to dance. He had worn a black T-shirt tight enough to show off his muscles, and his jeans fit him just right. She wished he would dress like that all the time. And damn, he could dance. Watching him, she matched his moves and inched closer. For the first time in days, she felt a spark she hadn't realized was missing. She wanted him. Here, in a public place where nobody cared who he was or what he had done, she felt like she could sort through her feelings. There was no judging, no expectations from anyone, no silence giving her space to second-guess anything. It was freedom.

Jesse looked over every inch of her. He wet his lips. "I knew that dress would look great on you."

"It feels great on me too," she answered, her breaths coming heavier when he ran a hand up the back of her thigh, squeezing as he went along. They finished one dance and began another, and then another. Naomi's body felt pliant and eager. She kissed Jesse whenever he leaned into her close enough. She loved the way he felt against her.

He put his lips to her ear. "I had no idea you could dance like this. You're gorgeous."

"And you're hot. You need to wear black more often."

Then she paused for a moment, remembering how she had always envisioned him in head-to-toe black as he robbed jewelry stores. Eric had worn black T-shirts all the time. She closed her eyes, trying to push Eric out. He had to leave. But she was back in the bedroom and he was holding her, and when she looked up his brown eyes pierced through her like arrows. *Not now. Not now.* She pressed her fingers to her temples. The music around her faded and the next thing she knew she was resting against a strong chest and the smell of Jesse surrounded her. She held on to him as tightly as she could.

"Naomi!"

She looked up into his face. His green eyes were almost black.

"I'm sorry," she whispered, sure he couldn't hear her.

"Come on." Still holding her, he led her through the crowd and to the bar. As she sat on a stool, Jesse spoke to the bartender in Italian and then leaned down to look her in the eyes. "Naomi?" He waved a hand in front of her. "Look at me."

"I'm trying," she mumbled. "I'm sorry." He was blurry. She should have known better than to go somewhere so public so soon. She was too much of a mess. Too weak. She wished for Stacy's couch and the smell of the beach as Stacy listened to every stupid thing she could say about her captivity.

"Naomi, drink," Jesse said, pressing a glass to her lips. She felt lukewarm liquid and took a sip. Club soda. The carbonation in her mouth brought her vision more into focus. Jesse's face was clear now and she reached up to hold the glass, taking several gulps.

"Just . . . dehydrated," she said with a nervous laugh. "That's all."

Jesse's expression turned skeptical. "Yeah, okay. What was that, Naomi? You looked terrified and then you almost passed out."

"I did?"

"Yes. Were you feeling too crowded?"

"I guess so." She gripped the glass, savoring the feel of it against her fingers. Jesse opened his mouth to say something else, but then reached into his back pocket and pulled out his phone. It was vibrating. He pushed a button to read an incoming message. Curious, Naomi tried to read the screen, but Jesse moved it out of her line of sight. His eyes narrowed before he shut off the phone and slipped it back into his pocket.

"What's the matter?" she asked, annoyed he would hide something from her.

"Nothing." He looked past her, searching the room. His face glistened with a thin sheen of sweat. "Listen, I'm going to leave you here for a minute, all right? I'll be right back."

She turned around, but nothing seemed amiss. "Jesse, I—"

He was already handing the bartender several bills and talking to him in Italian. She guessed he was paying the guy to keep an eye on her. The bartender, a thin, olive-skinned man with a ponytail, looked her up and down. A soft smile spread across his lips.

"I speak English if she need," he said to Jesse, taking the bills and shoving them into his back pocket. He winked at her and she turned away.

"Don't leave," Jesse ordered, leaning down to kiss her cheek. "Five minutes, okay? Get a drink and try to relax."

She folded her arms and glared at him. "I almost pass out and now you're leaving me?"

The muscles in his arms flexed. "Please, Naomi. Don't argue."

"Fine."

She watched him disappear into the crowd. When she turned back, the bartender was looking at her chest. The dress's wide, plunging neckline pretty much invited anyone to look, but it still annoyed her. She gave the bartender the dirtiest expression she could manage and then ordered a drink as Jesse had suggested. When she had it in her hands, she was sure she wouldn't get through half of it before Jesse returned. She was wrong. She finished the drink and ordered another one. She finished it faster than she should, and ordered a third. It wasn't a good idea, but she was caring less and less. The alcohol calmed her nerves, but she hoped she wasn't dead drunk by the time she saw Jesse again. This would be her last drink, for sure.

The lights for the music changed to neon green and the room lit up brighter than before. Then she saw him leaning against a far wall half-hidden in the shadows. His back was to her, but she recognized his hair and the shape of his shoulders. He faced two men taller than him. They wore black suits, of all things, and Naomi felt something dark sink into her stomach. She finished her drink in three more gulps and sat stone-still on the stool, waiting. Her mind spun in circles.

"That your boyfriend?" the bartender asked, leaning forward. She could feel his gaze wrapping around her, studying every inch of her exposed skin now flushed from the alcohol.

"Yes," she said, keeping her eyes on Jesse as he talked to the two men. She wanted to know what he was discussing and if it was something illegal. Whatever it was, she knew deep in her gut it was nothing good.

The bartender made a swishy sound like a low whistle, and Naomi tore her attention from Jesse. The bartender's eyes were still on her.

"What?" she asked, her words slurring. "What do you mean by that?"

He shrugged. "Nobody ask questions. If you ask questions, you die." He slid a finger across his neck and gave her a wicked smile. "You be careful with boyfriend."

Naomi thought she might be sick. Pushing some hair away from her face, she stood up.

"You stay here," the bartender said with a growl in his voice. "Boyfriend pay me to keep you here. You owe for drinks."

She let out a heavy sigh and sat back down on the stool. Now a bartender was controlling her. All she wanted to do was go home. A headache began throbbing behind her eyes—the same rhythm as the music. She leaned forward and buried her face in her arms. The counter smelled like bourbon.

"You need more drink?" the bartender asked, a laugh in his voice.

"No, just leave me alone, please." She allowed a nagging question to blossom in her mind. Had Jesse brought her here so he could talk to those men? She wondered why he hadn't left her home and invented work as an excuse to go out by himself. Mostly, she kept thinking about the bartender's finger sliding across his throat.

* * *

When Jesse returned, Naomi was half-asleep with her face still buried in her arms. Jesse ran a finger up her left shoulder blade and leaned close to her ear.

"I'm so sorry."

"How long were you gone?" she asked, keeping her face buried.

"Forty minutes."

"That's a lot longer than five minutes."

"I know."

Lifting her head, she glared at him. The sweat on his face had dried. He looked worn out, just like she felt.

"I want to go home," she said, taking his offered hand to help her off the stool. The bartender approached with a curious expression. He said something in Italian and Jesse answered in cold, clipped words. He handed over some more bills to pay for Naomi's drinks.

"We'll go now," he said, and pulled her close as they made their way out of the building. They stopped to pick up their jackets and were soon on the street. The moon was a sliver in the sky.

Naomi sucked in the crisp air as Jesse helped her into her jacket. She pulled it close around her middle, not bothering to zip it up. There were so many things she wanted to say, so many things to ask, but she couldn't open her mouth for any words at all. Instead, she let Jesse wrap an arm around her shoulders as they started the walk home. Christmas lights twinkled everywhere, reflecting in countless rain puddles along the street. Everything blurred.

"Isn't it pretty out here?" Jesse asked, his words pushing little white puffs into the air.

She shrugged and answered in a monotone voice, "Sure." She didn't know if Jesse knew she had seen him talking to the two men in suits, but she was certain that if he knew what the bartender had implied to her, he wouldn't be so relaxed. She was quiet the rest of the way home. As soon as they were inside the apartment, Jesse closed the door and took her into his arms.

"I want you," he whispered. "I keep thinking about you on the dance floor—the way you moved." He kissed her on the lips, but she didn't kiss him back. Instead, she pushed away.

"I, uh, gotta get out of my jacket," she said, stuttering as she yanked at the material over her arms.

Jesse smiled and helped her. "Mmm, that's better," he said once she was standing in front of him in nothing but the dress. He dropped the jacket onto the floor and slipped out of his too.

At any other time, Naomi would have laughed and pulled him into the bedroom, but now she simply stared at him, feeling naked as he looked her up and down. She remembered how frightened she had been the first time he kissed her. He had wanted her then too. He had always wanted her.

He cocked his head, a concerned expression spreading across his face. "What's the matter? Aren't you feeling better?"

She knew her voice was going to tremble and the alcohol in her system would slur her words. There was no way Jesse was going to take her seriously tonight. "I have a headache," she answered, turning away. "I want to sleep." She walked down the hall and into the bedroom, Jesse right behind her.

"Drink too much?" he asked. "Or are you still not well from what happened on the dance floor? Do you want to talk about it?"

She put a hand to her head as she stopped in front of the closet. "Too many questions," she muttered, ripping off her boots and then slipping out of the dress. She stood in nothing but her panties, knowing it would take all of Jesse's willpower not to touch her. She wondered why he wanted her, why he had urged her to come to Italy with him, why he had chosen to spend the rest of his life with her. Or if she was assuming he wanted to spend the rest of his life with her. It was those two men in suits, she realized. They were messing up her head. They made her question everything more than she had before. Anger boiled up inside her, forming words she shouldn't say. So instead of letting them free, she pushed them down, pressing as hard as she could. She turned away from Jesse and started rummaging through her drawer for a pair of sweats and a shirt.

"I'm sorry," he said. She could hear him undressing behind her.

"For what?" she muttered, still digging in her drawer. She looked up for a moment, staring at her oil pastel sketch of an artichoke. She had set the drawing on the dresser, leaning it upright against the wall. The paper was thick enough to stand up on its own, but if she slammed a drawer shut, it would fall.

"For leaving you," Jesse said as Naomi tried to soak in the rich greens of the artichoke and remember all the good things about Italy and why she was here. "You weren't feeling well and it was an unfamiliar place for you. I'm sorry."

She spun around with a pair of sweats clenched in her hand. "Who were they?"

"They?"

"The two men in suits."

Jesse was looking at her naked breasts, and she threw the pair of sweats at him. They hit him in the face and then fell to the floor, but he didn't move.

"Answer me!"

Now he was looking at her face. "They're helping me with paperwork," he said, each word coming out precise. He had taken off his shirt and unbuttoned his jeans, but she refused to want him right now, no matter how hot he looked.

Her voice came out in a hiss. "Paperwork?"

"Yes. Italy's government requires certain permits and visas for non-citizens living here past a short period of time."

"So you take care of that in a *nightclub*?" She folded her arms.

"It's because of my parole. I'm not exactly . . . it's illegal . . . without these men's help, I could be extradited back to the US."

Her jaw dropped. "I thought you came here legally. How did you get a job if you're not supposed to live here? How did this not come up in customs when we flew here?"

He kept his attention on her face. She could see in his eyes he was telling the truth, but the truth was almost too much. Her heart was racing now. She felt like she was standing on hot coals and should start running away.

"It's complicated," he said, keeping his words controlled. "I know the right people who are handling everything as quietly as possible."

Her face turned hot. The headache pounding behind her eyes was beginning to feel like a sledgehammer trying to split her wide open. "You always know the right people, don't you?" she spit at him. "You stole millions of dollars' worth of jewelry without ever getting caught in the act. You hid from the FBI for three months after you let me go. Now you're here making deals with some sort of underground network, and I don't even know—I don't—I can't make sense of—"

"Naomi, explaining all of this would take hours. You aren't feeling well. You're tipsy and you're tired. I'm going to put you to bed and we'll talk about everything tomorrow."

She watched the rise and fall of his shoulders. He was right that she was tipsy. Her body couldn't handle much alcohol, and what she had drunk at the club was doing a number on her. She was beyond tipsy and Jesse didn't want to tick her off by saying so. He was too late for that, though. She already wanted to throw something a lot harder than a pair of sweats at his head.

"Fine," she muttered, and walked to the bed without putting on any more clothes. She yanked back the covers and climbed in. "But I want to be alone."

"That's fine. I'll see you in the morning."

The last thing she thought about as she drifted into a hazy sleep was the yin and yang tattoo on Finn's arm. The deeper she got into her screwed-up life, the more she realized there couldn't be a balance of black and white. Not for her. It had to be one or the other.

XX

WHEN SHE WOKE, THE ROOM WAS FLOODED WITH light. It wasn't happy sunshine, she realized. It was a gray, dismal sort of glow from clouds covering the city. All the same, any light at all made her headache worse. She groaned and covered her face with the blankets. Last night. The club. Jesse.

She sat up. His side of the bed was empty. She remembered the men in suits and the neon green light and the bartender. Another groan. Throwing back the covers, she shivered and rushed to the dresser to find some clothes. Those three drinks last night had been a terrible, stupid idea, but she wondered how much worse things could have gone if she hadn't been so tired and drunk. She might have reacted worse. Or better. She sucked in a quick breath. She had no idea about anything.

"Love?" There was a soft knock before Jesse cracked open the door and looked inside. She finished pulling on her shirt and turned to face him.

"Morning," she mumbled, hardly able to meet his eyes.

He opened the door wide. "I have lunch ready. Are you hungry?"

"Lunch?" She glanced at the clock on the wall. Twelve-thirty. "Oy," she moaned, putting a hand to her forehead.

"Oy is right." Walking to her, he gave her a hug and then steered her out of the room and into the kitchen. He had made some grilled sandwiches with fresh mozzarella and prosciutto. Naomi sank into her chair. The room was spinning

"I'm not hungry," she said. "I'm sorry."

"You don't have to eat any, but at least drink some water." He went to the cupboard and pulled out a bottle of water. He put it in front of her as she picked up her sandwich and took a small bite. It was good, but her stomach twisted as she chewed. She forced herself to swallow.

"No good?" Jesse asked, watching her with a frown as he sat in his chair across from her.

"I feel like crap," she sighed. "Otherwise it would be amazing." She picked up the water and took three swigs. Setting it back down, she pushed her plate away

252

so the smell wouldn't make her stomach turn any more than it already was. "So, tell me about those men."

Jesse leaned back in his chair. He needed to shave. Naomi noticed he had put on a dirty shirt from the laundry room, probably because he hadn't wanted to wake her earlier. "What do you want me to tell you?"

"Everything."

He sighed. "I didn't want to tell you any of this until later, but I guess it'll have to be now. Those men you saw last night are helping me. They forge legal documents, and they're damn good at it. They take care of everything, right down to encrypted online files and fingerprinting, if needed. I was going to use them for your paperwork when Eric and the others wanted to bring you here. That's how I first found them."

"Okay." She kept seeing the bartender's finger slice across his throat and wondered if forged legal documents were a bad enough crime to involve such violence. "So you were going to give me a new identity, then?"

"Yes."

She took another drink of water. "So why do you have to do all of this? Why is it illegal for you to live here?"

Lifting his sandwich, he took a few bites, chewing slowly as he prepared to answer. "There are a lot of things I can't do now that I've been in prison," he said in a bitter voice after swallowing. "That's one of the reasons I wanted to come here. It's a fresh start."

"I thought it was because of the job."

"That too." He leaned forward. "Listen, Naomi, the less you know about any of this, the better. Trust me on that, okay?"

She watched him reach across the table for her hands, but she pulled away, disgusted by how much he had lied to her. "And what about my parents? When can I talk to them? When my mom finds out you're here, she'll know it's illegal and she'll shove 'I told you so' in my face. She'll do whatever it takes to get me away from you."

Jesse returned his hands to his side of the table. "Now you understand why I don't want you to talk to her. Maybe sometime in the future I'll arrange a way for you to tell them you came here on your own. You can tell them you have no idea where I am. Years from now, you can fly back and see them, but not with me."

"But there's—"

He stood up so fast his chair tipped over. The clatter made Naomi wince.

"Jesse, I—"

"Hear me out," he said, walking around to her side of the table and bending his knees so she could look down at him. She turned to face him.

"This is crazy," she whispered as he took her hand. "You knew I wouldn't come here if you told me about any of this. You knew . . ."

He nodded. "I know, but you waited for me for over two years. You've given up everything to come here with me. I knew there was a good chance this would all work out."

She thought about a conversation she'd had with his father after her escape. *Jesse doesn't have a mean bone in his body*, he had said. She believed him even now as she looked into Jesse's eyes filling with frustration. Beyond all of that, she saw fear. He didn't want to lose her. He would do anything to keep from losing her. She wasn't afraid he would hit her, as Brad had, and she wasn't afraid he would yell at her. But she was afraid of being manipulated and lied to. Deep down, she knew she had to ask herself if *she* would do anything to keep from losing *him*—if she could accept some of his darkness and move on. She tried to push away the thought of Finn's yin and yang tattoo.

"Why didn't you trust me enough to tell me?" she asked, trying to ignore how good it felt when he held her hand, even when she was so upset with him. Her frustration boiled even more. She needed him. He was all she had left. "I told you the truth about Finn and my phone. I thought secrets and lies were over between us. You could have told me."

His grip on her hand loosened. "I was afraid," he answered. "If you knew the truth, you would be too confused to make the right decision, no matter what it ended up being. There's . . . something else." He kept his eyes on hers. "Not that it makes any difference now since I'm taking care of everything, but you need to know."

"Okay." She braced herself as best she could.

"I told you it's illegal for me to come here, but it's not because I was convicted of a federal crime. It's because I broke my parole."

"You *what*?" She ripped away from his hand and stood up, knocking her chair over just as he had. He stood and caught her before she tripped over it.

"Let go of me," she growled, gaining her footing as she broke free of him again. He folded his arms and watched her seethe at him.

"I knew that would set you off."

"Set me off? Jesse, they'll put you back in prison *forever*!"

"Not if they can't find me. And they won't. I've made sure of it."

"Even with me? They'll know you're with me. They'll track it somehow—see that I traveled with someone here, and they'll know it's you."

His jaw flexed. "They can't find me. Trust me on that."

"But this apartment is in your name. You signed paperwork. You—"

"Lalia and this building belong to some important organizations and families," he said, glancing at the floor as if he could see through three apartments to the front desk where Lalia sat. "I didn't pick this apartment just because it was cheap."

Naomi looked down at the sandwich on her plate. Mozzarella was oozing out of the side, firm and gooey at the same time. She thought she was going to be sick. Sweet little Lalia was part of some underground network, Jesse had broken parole, and she had left behind everything she had ever known to be with him. She had thought she was leaving with someone who had changed—someone nobody had a right to judge anymore. She was wrong. She was always so very, very wrong about everything in her life.

Looking up at Jesse, she realized she knew him intimately on some levels and not at all on others. He probably felt the same way about her.

There was a nasty hiss in her voice when she spoke again. "I thought you had changed. Don't you remember that day on the beach when you told me you were going to turn yourself in? You said we could never be free like this. You wanted to fix what you'd done wrong." Her throat swelled up as she looked at him. He had kidnapped her and she had forgiven him because she thought he could erase all of it. But he couldn't. She was a fool to have ever believed it was possible. "What happened?" she asked, her throat burning with unshed tears. "Why would you do this?"

Jesse kept his eyes on hers. At least he wasn't looking away in shame, although she believed he wanted to. He straightened his shoulders. "I know what I said that day, and I meant every word. I turned myself in. I served my time."

"Not all of it."

He nodded, looking away. "Not all of it, no."

She had to bite her lip to keep the tears in. She wouldn't cry in front of him. Not again. "Why?" she asked. "Tell me."

He flexed his fingers at his sides and kept his shoulders straight as he looked at her again. "Because when I went in for one of my parole hearings, I was told there was a strong chance I would never be allowed to see you again. Not legally. You were a minor when we kidnapped you. Do you have any idea how bad that is in the eyes of the law? A ridiculous amount of time would have to pass before I'd be allowed anywhere near you." She watched his hands ball into fists. The muscles in his forearms tightened. "I should have known I could never undo what I did. I should have known turning myself in would never make it right for me to be with you. I thought you would move on and I'd get over you."

Naomi needed to sit down, but her chair was tipped over. She grabbed the edge of the table. "Then I went to see you," she whispered, remembering the pink and white licorice candies spilled across the floor of the car.

"Yes, and I saw how much you still wanted to be with me. It was too much, Naomi. That's when I started digging to find a way—any way—to be with you again." His lips curled as he leaned forward and said, "To start over and never look back."

She took a long, deep breath. "Even if that meant leaving your father?"

His shoulders drooped. "Yes."

She knew what a sacrifice that was for him. His father was all he had, except for her. As much as she tried to stop them, her tears broke free. Jesse stood still, not moving to comfort her.

"I planned things so they'd work out either way," he said, his fists loosening. "If you decided to come with me, great. If not, I'd either return home to finish out my parole—if my plan worked and nobody noticed I was missing yet—or I'd fly here, knowing I'd probably never see you again. Either way, I figured if you decided not to come with me, you didn't want me badly enough. I could let you go if that's what you needed. I want what's best for you."

But she *had* decided to come. She wondered what that said about her. She focused on breathing as steadily as she could.

"After you picked me up at the airport," Jesse continued, "I noticed how much the kidnapping still affects you—how much I still affect you because of it. Despite how much I wanted you to come with me, *I* was secretly hoping you'd tell me school was too important and you wanted to stay. I was hoping you'd show me you were strong now. But you're still so . . . so—"

"Weak," she spat at him. "That's all I'll ever be. Dependent on other people. Never free. Before I left to come with you, I was still seeing a counselor. It's been almost three years and I'm still pouring my heart out on a couch. I'm still stuck in that bedroom with Eric, and I can't get out." Sinking to her knees, she buried her face in her hands. "I'll never get out."

Finally, Jesse stepped forward and knelt down beside her. Pulling her into his arms, he rubbed her back in long, smooth strokes. "I've told you before," he said, "you're stronger than you think, but you still seem to need me. I'll admit I feel responsible for you in a lot of ways."

"You shouldn't," she said.

"Maybe I shouldn't, but I do. Then there's your mother. She controls you by making you feel dependent, but you don't have to be. You decided to come here. You can break free of her and everyone else judging you for something completely out of your control—something that was my fault. At least I've made it so we can be together, so you have someone there with you every step of the way. I can help you get out of that bedroom you're talking about." He moved her hands away from her face and made her look up at him. "At least let me try," he pleaded. "Can you do that?"

She looked out the balcony doors across the living room. There was no laundry hanging on the line today. "I don't know," she answered. "Maybe."

"Good." He kissed her forehead. "That's a start." He sounded so relieved, and it was then that she realized he still hadn't told her everything. She was so gullible, and Jesse knew it. He had played her from the second he saw her lying in the parking lot all those years ago. The most terrible thing of all was she had known all along how much of a naïve fool he took her for—a fool he loved, but that didn't matter—and she had refused to see it or care. Now, as he held her closely, reality hit her. Hard.

"You don't have a job, do you?" she asked in a voice trembling from fear or anger. She couldn't tell.

His arms tensed around her.

She added, "You never flew here for an interview."

"I have a job," he explained, "but I didn't come here for an interview."

"It's not architecture, is it?"

She heard him swallow. "No."

"Then what is it? Stealing?"

He let out a sigh. "It's illegal, Naomi. Those men the night before last aren't only helping me out with paperwork. I work for them."

"Doing what?" she demanded.

"Planning jobs. I research. Gather information. That's it."

"Jobs for what?"

"I don't ask. It's always something different, but I never know the details. Sometimes it's trafficking, sometimes routes and technical data for espionage. It's bigger stuff than I used to do, but I'm on the quiet end. The safe end."

"Safe?" she shrieked, backing out of his arms. She was surprised how hot her face felt. "It's all illegal!"

His eyes seemed to burn straight through her. "How is that any different from the rest of my life?" he asked. "Face it, Naomi. I'm a lost cause. I tried to do the right thing and couldn't hack it. I wanted to keep all of this from you for as long as possible."

She folded her arms and readjusted her knees on the floor. "Guess I'm not as dumb as you thought."

He leaned forward, pleading in his eyes. "That's not how I think of you."

"Then how do you think of me? How the hell did you think I wouldn't figure any of this out? I might be weak. I might be so blind and brainwashed from the kidnapping that I can't see past my own nose, but I'm not *that* stupid!"

His shoulders drooped. His tense arms relaxed. "I hoped you would accept it once you saw how happy we could be when we got here. I hoped getting you away from your parents would help you see everything they want for you doesn't matter. All of that is still possible." He chewed on his bottom lip and then looked away. "You're a better person than me, Naomi. You've always been better than me. I guess that's why I've never wanted to let you go."

* * *

Later that day, Jesse took her to the Vatican. Her headache finally slipped away as she stared at the magnificent paintings, how they bled from ceiling to wall, the colors so silky and alive they seemed to float against nothing. They were ethereal.

"This . . . this is . . . I don't know," she whispered to Jesse as he took her hand and squeezed. Several tourists around them started speaking loudly. An usher rushed forward and hissed, "*Silencio!*"

"I know," Jesse whispered as the usher left and everyone quieted down. "No words, huh?"

"Yeah."

For a few hours, she forgot about what Jesse had kept from her. She forgot about everything she had left behind. She forgot about herself. But it all came back as soon as they were home. Jesse drew her a bath and then they ate a late-night dinner of bread and cheese and wine from the market.

"I shouldn't drink anymore," she said, her mind fuzzy from the wine as she lay on the couch and rested her head in Jesse's lap. He played with the ends of her hair as she looked out the balcony doors. She could see stars twinkling in the sky.

"Nothing wrong with a little wine to help you relax," he said, smiling down at her. "I hope you're feeling better now. This morning wasn't easy, I'm sorry."

"This morning was necessary," she answered. "I wish you would have told me all of that earlier." She looked away from the stars and found Jesse's eyes instead. "Unless there's more you haven't told me."

He blinked.

"Jesse?"

"Let me get you something," he said, helping her sit up. He stood and walked down the hall, where she heard him rummaging around for something in the bedroom. Putting a hand over her eyes, she groaned. There was more he was keeping from her and a part of her didn't want to know what it was. She wondered if the rest of her life with him would be this way—a web of secrets slowly unraveling.

When she heard him come back into the room, she removed her hand from her eyes and looked up at him holding out a stack of papers.

"What's that?" She reached for the papers, but he held them up high as he looked her in the eyes.

"This is your journal. I made a copy of it before I handed it in to the police. I thought you might want it one day."

She lowered her hand. Her journal. The dragons. The year at the house and all those thoughts and feelings she had recorded day after day. "I'm not sure I want to read that," she said, shrinking. "That's . . . that's everything I'm trying to forget about."

Jesse sat on the couch next to her and gently placed the stack of papers in her lap. It felt heavy, like a brick, although it only weighed a few ounces. "I think you need to read it," he said in his tight, *don't-argue-with-me* voice. "You need to face this, Naomi. I know your counselors have tried to get you to face all of it, but not like this. I want you to read every word in one sitting."

Her tongue seemed to swell inside her dry mouth. She couldn't swallow. "It's ten-thirty," she argued. "I'm tired. I just drank a glass of wine. You can't expect—"

He narrowed his eyes. "Read it, please."

"Okay, okay." She threw him a glare before picking up the first sheet. On each paper, front and back, were two photocopied journal pages. There were probably twenty-five sheets. She cringed as she stared at her handwriting. It was like her mother's handwriting, but more cramped and unsure of itself. She remembered a few of the journal entries had made it into the courtroom during trial. She had cringed then too as her words were read out loud as an example of her state of mind while captive. In the end, the jury decided her written words proved she suffered from Stockholm syndrome and her obvious compassion for her kidnappers did not merit them lighter sentences.

Intent to brainwash was a phrase repeated over and over by the lawyers.

Brainwash.

"They never loved you," her mother had told her when the trial was over. "I hope all of this has made that clear. It was proven in court. Your kidnappers used you. It wasn't love."

No matter what anyone told her or how they tried to prove it, she knew her kidnappers had learned to care for her beyond any desire to use her. She knew Jesse loved her. She knew, looking at the words in front of her, that nobody except her and her kidnappers would understand any of it.

Jesse was watching her, waiting for her to start reading. "You want me to read it out loud?" she asked, terrified.

"No, but I see you staring at the words and not reading them."

"Okay, okay, I'll read it."

"I'll go wash the dishes and then I'm taking a shower."

She nodded as he left. Within ten minutes, she was buried in her past.

XXI

THERE WERE ALWAYS DRAGONS, BUT NEVER AS DARK AS the ones before her now. She stood in a burning valley so hot that ash fell from the sky like slow-drifting snow. The dragons had started the fire, their scales blackened, skin peeling, their eyes hard as diamonds. She watched four of them land in front of her. Thick smoke curled to the darkening sky.

"I want to leave!" she screamed, but their only response was to open their mouths and breathe flames at her. She didn't feel the pain, but when the fire cleared and she held out her arms to see the damage, she saw her skin was like dragon skin—black and peeling in jagged pieces. Falling to her knees, she grabbed a handful of dirt and threw it at the dragons. Their mouths turned up in sneers, showing their pointed, blood-stained teeth.

You read too many fantasy novels, she could hear Jesse's voice in the back of her head.

They don't love you, her mother said.

Remember why you fell in love with him.

She stopped at the memory of that last set of words, trying to remember who had said them to her. The dragons moved closer, and then she remembered it was Finn who had said the words. She saw the saltshaker on the table as he pushed it around in circles.

With a start, she sat up in bed, realizing all the journal entries were still fresh in her mind. She had finished reading them hours ago and then stumbled into the bedroom to find Jesse already asleep. She had crawled in with him and drifted off, but the nightmares made her toss and turn. Jesse stirred beside her now, his toned arms reaching out for her. Morning sunlight fell across the bed.

"You all right?" he asked, pulling her close.

"I think so." Lying back down, she snuggled into him. He smelled like spicy soap from his shower earlier. She took in a deep breath, savoring the feel of him holding her.

Remember why you fell in love with him.

Shut up, Finn!

She wanted to scream the words into the silent bedroom, but couldn't. She loved Jesse because he loved her. It was that simple. He sacrificed things for her. He wanted to make her happy, and she wanted the same for him. She had left everything to be with him.

A knock on the front door made Naomi jump. It frightened her to think of who might knock on their door so early in the morning. Jesse stirred again, mumbling something she couldn't understand.

"You want me to get it?" she asked, almost afraid to wake him.

Groaning, he sat up and blinked. His hair had dried in spikes. "Where the hell is my phone?" he asked. "Why are the curtains wide open?"

He was always cranky when he was woken up too early. "I wanted to look at the stars as I fell asleep."

Turning to her, he blinked again. The sun made his green eyes pale. "How did that go, then? Last night? Did you read it all?"

"Yes."

"And?"

She looked away. "I was so tired I'm not sure how much of it stuck."

"It's all in your head now. You can start sorting through it and face it all."

"Yeah, I guess so."

Another series of knocks. Jesse cursed and got out of bed. He was in his boxer shorts, and pulled on a pair of sweats before grabbing his phone off the dresser. He walked out of the bedroom. Curious, Naomi slipped out of bed and peeked down the hallway as Jesse looked through the peephole. She asked herself if she cared that he had lied to her about his parole, that he was a fugitive. Did it matter? Her stomach clenched.

"What is it?" Jesse asked, opening the door a crack. His body blocked her view of whoever was on the other side. There was an answer. A man's voice. A shudder went down Naomi's spine.

"No," Jesse said, "she's here."

Naomi gripped the door handle to steady herself.

More mumbles. Every muscle in Jesse's back tightened as he hissed, "Damn it," and glanced behind his shoulder. She backed away, catching a glimpse of the man outside the door. Dark hair to his shoulders. Intense, light-colored eyes.

Turning on his phone, Jesse started whispering to the man. Naomi backed away until she couldn't see him anymore. For a terrifying moment, her world turned ice-cold as she wondered if this was the rest of her life.

When she reached the bed, she sat on the edge as her last thread to everyone she had ever cared about twisted tighter and tighter, snapping until one fiber remained, and no matter how hard she tried, she wasn't sure it would hold. Jesse was all she had left. Her mother would kill her if she ever tried to go back. It would be exactly like when she had returned home from the kidnapping. Constant awkwardness. Fights. So much therapy and so many reporters wanting stories. She couldn't do it again. She looked around the bedroom at what her life had become—at her phone Jesse had rendered practically useless, at the slinky black dress hanging in the closet, at the stack of Jesse's favorite novels he liked to read to her, at the dozens of drawings she had created of places she had visited—and she asked herself who she was and what she wanted. She knew what Jesse wanted. She knew what her parents wanted. She knew what Finn wanted. Okay, maybe she wasn't sure what Finn wanted. But what about herself? The scariest thing, she realized, was that maybe it wasn't about her at all.

She looked up when Jesse returned to the bedroom, his face red from frustration or anger, she couldn't tell. "We have to leave," he muttered.

"Leave? You mean the apartment?" She straightened.

Jesse's jaw flexed. "Yes. It was the texts and phone calls to and from your phone. The feds are already attempting to track it all. This is why I didn't want you to have a phone, but I didn't think they'd catch on this quickly. They shouldn't have. Nobody should have known I was missing until a few days ago."

Her stomach clenched again. "So now you're going to take my phone away completely? I didn't know you were *hiding*! If you'd told me the truth, I—"

"It's done now," he snapped. "We'll need to pack and leave today, just in case."

All the words from her journal swirled around in her head. Sentences like, '*He'll take care of me forever*' and '*I've never felt more at home than when I'm with him*' stabbed her. Tiny daggers. Jesse was right. Reading her journal had opened her eyes, but probably not the way he wanted.

She looked at the cheery sun shining into the room. It was warm on her face, but she was a cold statue. She imagined what it might be like to stay with Jesse. Her life would be hiding, she realized. Not only hiding from the law, but from herself. At one point she had been willing to accept such a life, but now she remembered the men in the suits and the dread in her stomach when she had seen them. Now there had been some strange man she didn't know knocking on their door at eight in the morning, warning them they had to leave. This was only the beginning. Jesse would never stop. He hadn't changed. He didn't belong to her. He would never be what she needed, no matter how hard she tried to pretend he was.

"Last night," she said in a soft voice, "I dreamed about dragons."

Jesse nodded. "You wrote about those in your journal."

"In my dream, there were four of them—one for each of you who took me. I flew away with one of the dragons. He was you."

He stepped forward. She couldn't back away. "That's one of the reasons I thought this could work," he said, reaching a hand out to her. "When I read your journal, I saw parts of you that made me believe you could deal with this. You're *that* kind of personality."

She scrunched her nose. "What kind of personality?"

Placing his hand on her arm, he inched closer. "Stubborn but submissive. Eric saw that in you. He tested you, and when he was convinced you were wired that way, we all agreed to push you into wanting to stay with us. Eric knew if we could nudge your stubbornness in the right direction, you'd be ours forever. He also knew heavy violence wasn't the way to push you, so he forced himself to be as gentle as possible. We all did."

Naomi let out a deep sigh, knowing everything he said was true. "That was all while I was captive. I'm not kidnapped anymore. I'm trying to break out of that frame of mind. I'm trying to be stronger."

Jesse was close to her now. She felt as if the walls might be falling in on top of her. "This will take time to sort through," he said as he wrapped an arm around her waist. "I love you, Naomi. I'll love you forever."

Looking into his eyes, she felt her heart melt into oblivion. She did love him more than she had loved anyone, but how far could that stretch if he was going to take her into dark places she didn't want to go? How could she be sure he wasn't doing the exact same thing he and the other kidnappers had done before?

And then the thread snapped.

Naomi pulled away from him, sliding along the edge of the bed until she was free of him. "I have to . . . I have to . . ." She swiped a hand across her mouth as her stomach churned. Running to the bathroom, she slammed the door behind her. This wasn't happening. It wasn't. She had made her choice and it was over. She knelt in front of the toilet and let everything come up her throat. There was nowhere to go and nobody to turn to except for Jesse. Always Jesse. He had made sure of it.

XXII

There were two things on her mind as she sat retching over the toilet for the next ten minutes. The first thing was did she want to leave? And the second was did she have the courage to leave? She didn't have an answer for either one. It was like the house all over again. She wasn't technically being held against her will, but she might as well have been. In fact, it was worse because most of it was inside her head—and everyone knows your head can be a worse prison than anywhere else. Like at the house, she had a choice to wait things out and see where they went. Or she could suck it up and leave already. Jesse wouldn't dare stop her. Then again, maybe he would.

There was a knock on the door before he came into the bathroom and looked down at her.

"Go away," she snapped.

"We have to pack and leave," he said, leaning down to take her by the arm.

She yanked away from him. "What if I don't want to go with you?"

He folded his arms, and even though he wasn't touching her, she felt as if he was holding on to her so tightly she couldn't escape. She knew arguing was pointless.

"I'm not letting you leave on your own," he said. "Right now, you're going to pack your bags and get in a taxi with me. When we're settled again, we'll talk things over. You're emotional. Do you want to make such a big choice when you're a complete wreck? Look at yourself."

She glanced at the toilet bowl filled with her vomit, and the fire inside her spluttered to a wet pile of ashes. She *was* a wreck. He had a point she couldn't ignore.

Refusing his help, she got to her feet. Her knees wobbled. "I hate it when you're right," she snarled.

He shrugged and walked out of the bathroom.

* * *

Packing their bags took less than an hour. Naomi bundled up her drawings and managed to stuff all of her art supplies into the corners of one of her suitcases. When she reached for the new sheets on the bed, Jesse told her they'd have to leave them behind along with everything else they had bought for the apartment. As they walked out the door and she looked at the apartment one last time, he assured her where they were going would have everything they would need.

"And where is that?" she asked as they tromped down the stairs with their luggage.

"A safe house just outside of Rome."

Stepping down each stair behind him, she mumbled, "Safe from the good guys, you mean."

Pausing, he set down the suitcases he was carrying in each hand. The sound echoed off the concrete walls as he turned around to face her. "What did you say?"

"Nothing." She was sure he had heard her clear as day.

"The world is not split up into good guys and bad guys," he hissed as she looked down at him. "Is that the category you put me in? 'Bad guy'?"

The luggage in her hands pulled hard on her muscles, making her lean against the wall to support her weight. "I don't know," she whispered. "All I meant was things are upside down from what I expected them to be. I thought you had changed and nobody could tell me you were bad anymore."

He tilted his head. "And all those years ago when you told me you'd rather run away with me than live without me, were you lying? Would you have done it?" He glanced at the luggage she carried. "Or does the fact that you're with me now mean you would have?"

She stumbled a little, but caught herself. "I don't know about back then, but this time I thought I was making a different choice. Now it's too late. I thought I loved you. I mean . . . I do love you . . . but maybe it's not . . . oh, I don't know." She gritted her teeth, angry that nothing she wanted to say would come out right.

He looked into her eyes. "Of course you love me," he answered in his maddeningly calm, level voice.

She stared at a big chip in the concrete stair below her, squeezing the luggage handles in her hands. Yes, of course she loved him.

"Jesse!" Lalia's voice echoed up the stairwell. "Your taxi here! You coming down? I hear you talking."

Jesse cringed. "Yes!" he yelled out. "Be right there." He turned around and lifted his bags. Naomi pursed her lips shut as she followed him, determined not to say another word while she was still so upset. When they reached the lobby, Lalia was holding the door open for them.

"I sad to see you go," she said, looking straight at Naomi. "You such lovely girl."

Naomi saw her differently now, knowing she ran an apartment building to house criminals. Perhaps it was best they were leaving. She hadn't stopped to think about what other kinds of people might be living here. Of course, the place they were going probably wasn't any better.

After giving the old woman a brief hug, Naomi followed Jesse out the door. The taxi driver helped them load the trunk with their luggage. Soon, she was sitting in the back seat watching the heart of Rome slip by in a blur of sunset colors.

* * *

The safe house was more like a safe palace. A wall of ancient rock blanketed with ivy surrounded it. A black wrought-iron gate guarded its entrance. As the taxi driver pulled up to the gate, Naomi caught a glimpse of the house inside the walls. It was at least three stories tall, built of rock and what looked like peach-colored plaster, with columns and white-trimmed windows. The grounds were lush and manicured, even in December, shaded by palm trees and flat-topped pines.

"Who owns this?" Naomi asked as they climbed out of the taxi and began unloading their luggage.

"Lots of people," Jesse said, shrugging. "I don't ask questions."

It seemed there was a lot he didn't know, and even more she didn't know, and there was nothing she could do about it. A man wearing a suit and sunglasses came to the gate and pushed a code on a panel in the rock wall. The gate slid open and the man motioned for Jesse and Naomi to walk through. Jesse paid the taxi driver, and Naomi watched the car drive off before she turned to look at the house. She wondered how many people lived here and what kind of illegal crap they did to make money. Her stomach sank at the realization she was one of those people, even if she didn't directly do anything illegal. She was with Jesse. She was staying with him, and that meant she supported whatever he was doing.

They were escorted into the house through the front door. The inside was as grand as the outside, filled with plants and sunlight and pastel décor. A thick rug woven with images of swans adorned the floor. Naomi looked up as a beautiful woman with slick black hair pulled into a bun on the top of her head greeted them, speaking in Italian. She wore a cream-colored suit, much like Naomi's mother wore.

"English," Jesse said, motioning to Naomi, and then continued in carefully pronounced Italian. He was far from fluent, she realized, but at least he could communicate.

The woman nodded and then smiled at Naomi. "I am Angelica," she said in a thick accent. "We welcome you here while you need protection." She held out a hand, palm-up. "I will need all mobile phones, please. They will be returned to you shortly."

Jesse nodded and handed his over. Naomi pulled hers from her purse and placed it into Angelica's hand.

"Hers you will need to destroy," he said with a nervous glance at Naomi. "It's no longer safe."

"Of course," Angelica said with a nod, and then motioned to a maid standing near a wide staircase leading upstairs. "Sonia will take you to your apartment." She looked at Jesse and spoke in Italian before he nodded and motioned Naomi to follow him. Sonia gathered a few of their bags, and the three of them walked up the stairs.

Once Sonia left them in the apartment and Jesse closed the door, he set his bags on the floor and turned to Naomi. "We'll be safe here. It's nicer than the last place, anyway." He smiled and pointed to a small kitchen to Naomi's left. "And we can still cook if we want."

She grunted and folded her arms. "So how do you know *these* people? Same as the guys in the suits?"

"Same network, yes." He glanced at his watch. "Listen, you can relax here in the room for a while. I have to go meet with some people and get some work done." When he spotted Naomi's vicious glare, he sighed. "I know you have issues with this. I know we need to talk about things, but I have work to do and there's no way out of it. I'll be back in a few hours and we can go out to eat for dinner, okay? There should be food in the kitchen if you get hungry, but don't leave the apartment until I'm back."

She continued to glare at him as he gathered up his computer bag and a few other things and left the apartment. When he was gone, she stared at the door. There was a chain lock and a deadbolt, but both were on the correct side of the door, not the wrong side locking her in, like at the house. The two windows in the lavish living room looking out over the grounds didn't appear as if they were locked from the outside to keep her inside, either. When she walked over to one and pulled the curtain aside, she thought the glass looked thicker than normal. Probably bulletproof. Great. She was living in a bulletproof palace. At least she could leave if she wanted to.

She found the bedroom and an office and then sat down on a leather sofa in the living room. There was a large screen TV on the far wall. She stared at it until her focus blurred. She didn't want this, no matter how nice it might seem to live in luxury with her every need met. Her whole life had been that way so far, but worst of all, it was like being back in the house. As much as her heart sometimes ached to return to that time where she was happy with Jesse and felt safe with her kidnappers, she knew it was ridiculous to want such a thing. It was the Stockholm syndrome. She had read enough about it to know how her mind had been twisted. The worst thing was that much of what she had read made it clear only a certain type of personality responded so deeply to such manipulation. Everybody else, it seemed, would have tried to escape their kidnappers, even if the clear outcome was death. Most would rather die than live in such circumstances, so what was wrong with her? Jesse had called her stubborn and submissive. How could she be both? She was screwed up, that's what it was. Everybody else was normal and she was wired in such a way nobody would ever understand her. Including herself.

She pulled a couch pillow into her lap and hugged it to her chest as she realized Jesse didn't understand her on every single level, no matter how much she had convinced herself he did. He would never have brought her here to Italy if he understood her. He would never have kept so many things from her if he knew how betrayed and frightened it was going to make her feel. Here, in a place where she was alone, she looked into the darkest parts of herself and saw a girl desperately weaving threads into a thick shroud to hide the truth. All those threads she had thought connected her to others were nothing more than excuses to weave into the shroud, one by one. Jesse's was the thickest and ran straight down the center. He loved her, of that she was certain. But he loved her for all the wrong reasons and she loved him for all the wrong reasons. She wanted someone strong to make decisions for her, protect her, and cradle her from the reality she had been running from her entire life. As far as she could see, he still felt guilty for kidnapping her. Prison hadn't erased the guilt, so taking care of her was his next attempt at fixing everything. It was all wrong, wrong, wrong, and she wanted to escape no matter how much it hurt to leave him. Thinking about doing such a thing made her squeeze the pillow even tighter to her chest. She fell sideways onto the couch and curled into a ball, too exhausted to do anything except count her trembling breaths.

* * *

When she woke, the room was a mix of gray and purple light. The sun was beginning to go down. She sat up with a start. Jesse hadn't returned. A clock on the wall showed the time was just past four-thirty. She hadn't expected to fall asleep, but it made sense that her subconscious wanted to escape. In fact, her entire being wanted to escape, but she wasn't sure how to do it without breaking her heart in the process. Leaving Jesse—after all she had sacrificed to be with him—made no sense. She knew it would hurt, but to the logical side of her brain, it made perfect sense. That was the side Stacy tapped into, or at least what she had tried to tap into for so long.

Looking down, Naomi realized she had been hugging the couch pillow so tightly that it was damp with her sweat. She set the pillow aside and went into the kitchen. It was small but clean. There were sleek granite countertops, bone china plates stacked in the cupboards, and shiny black stools set in front of a bar at the far end of the room. Naomi opened the refrigerator door and peeked inside. Cheeses, condiments, some vegetables in the crisper. None of it looked good at the moment. Closing the door, she walked out of the kitchen and stood staring at her and Jesse's luggage they had both left in the entryway.

Money.

That was what she needed to get away. She had cashed out her entire bank account before coming. Jesse had deposited half of it into his bank account, and the rest they carried on travel money cards and in cash. Jesse had told her he didn't like the cash all in one place while traveling, so he split up what they didn't carry in their wallets between several envelopes separated into different luggage bags in case one was stolen or lost— as if that would happen driving across town, but she didn't question him. Some envelopes held euros, some held dollars.

Taking a step forward, she realized how much her heart was pounding. Her hands shook as she knelt and unzipped the first bag. Digging around, she found an envelope. Euros, pretty and colorful. She slid out the stack and set it aside, then moved on to the next bag. Finally, she had all of the money on the floor in front of her. Several stacks of euros, one stack of dollars. Worth thousands all together. Jesse was probably carrying more with him, but that didn't matter. She could pay a taxi, hop on a rail, find her way to the airport, and then buy a plane ticket and fly home.

Gathering the cash and stuffing it into one envelope, she carried it to her purse and buried it at the bottom. She had more than enough now, and under her breath she whispered, "*I can do this. I can do this. I can do this.*" There was a bag already packed by the door, filled with clothes and necessities for a week. Enough people spoke English for her to get around.

Then she remembered the black iron gate guarding the bulletproof palace she was standing in. She remembered Jesse handing Angelica her phone to be destroyed. She remembered Jesse's order not to leave the apartment until he returned. She had no doubt someone would stop her. He had probably told that fancy-dressed man with the glasses to make sure she didn't try to walk out.

Wiping her sweating palms on the front of her pants, she told herself Jesse wanted to protect her. It was all he had ever wanted. He kept Eric from killing her when they hit her with the car. He kept her safe all those months at the house. This was for her own good.

When she looked up and saw herself reflected in one of the windows, she knew it was all a lie. Maybe she didn't need protection anymore. Maybe she didn't want to be protected. Her parents wanted to protect her too. But from what? Pain? Living a *life*?

She set her purse on an end table and went into the kitchen to make a snack. She would force herself to eat something and then wait for Jesse to return. Whatever was going to happen, it wouldn't be here in the palace.

XXIII

Jesse returned by seven and asked her to change quickly into something nice so they could make it on time for a reservation he had made at a restaurant.

With a sigh, Naomi did as she was asked and changed into a skirt. "Which restaurant?" she asked, slipping on a pair of heels.

"They serve whatever the chef decides to make for the day," he answered, smiling as they headed out the door.

The restaurant was small and decorated with indoor plants and wrought iron. The floor was red brick. Naomi stared at it after settling in her chair.

"Do we know what they're serving today?" she asked, making sure her purse sat squarely in her lap. It was heavy with all the cash stuffed in the bottom. She looked up as Jesse shrugged.

"I don't know. We'll have to see. A guy I met with today told me about this place, so I thought we'd come give it a try."

"I hope they're not serving fish," she mumbled. "I hate fish."

"I know you do."

She looked into his eyes and hated how he was ignoring all the obvious issues swirling around them. She hated that he had left her alone in a cage all afternoon. She hated that he didn't see it as a cage.

The waiter approached and told them the dish today was salmon with lemon sauce and capers. Naomi almost stood up to leave, but Jesse put on his warmest smile and talked to the waiter in slow Italian. Naomi felt her purse heavy in her lap. She thought about the money. She thought about taxi drivers and navigating an unfamiliar airport. She thought about what it might be like never to feel Jesse hold her again, his lips on hers, the gentle but firm way he made love to her and knew what she liked.

When he looked back at her, still smiling, she wiped away her terrified expression. "So, will we need to leave?" she asked. "Because I'm not making myself eat salmon, I'm sorry."

He leaned forward. "No, I talked him into convincing the chef to make us something special.

Don't worry." Reaching across the table, he tried to take her hand, but she pulled it away.

"We need to talk," she said, looking him in the eyes.

He leaned back into his chair. "Yes, I know. So, start asking me whatever you want. I'll answer. No more lies. No more secrets, I promise."

"That's not the issue anymore and you know it."

The waiter returned to pour their wine. Naomi waited until he was gone before taking a sip. She wanted Jesse to continue the conversation. She wanted to see where he would take it—if he had any idea how close she was to walking away.

"All right, Naomi," he said, folding his arms. "Let's look at this from the ground up. I kidnapped you and we fell in love. It was that simple."

"It was not *that simple*," she snapped.

He unfolded his arms and lifted his hands in defense. "Okay, okay, it wasn't that simple. A lot of crap happened. I understand that, but what do you want to happen now? The way I see it, there are only a few options. I can't change who I am as a person, so that's out, and I can't go back to the US or I'll risk getting caught and thrown into prison again. If that happens, I can guarantee you we will never be together, so what's the point?"

"Aren't you missing another option?" she asked, squeezing her purse.

"The other option," he said, leaning forward, "is you learn to accept me the way I am and what I have chosen for us. This can be a beautiful life for us if you'll relax and trust me. Let some time pass and we can get back into our own place and go wherever we want. I don't have to do what I'm doing forever. It's a transition, that's all."

For a moment, she almost believed him. She looked into his gorgeous green eyes and saw her life with him stretching out like a magical fairy tale. Then she tore her attention from him and looked around the room at several couples eating their meals. Some of them leaned across their tables, their fingers touching as they laughed and smiled. Some of them talked seriously, like her and Jesse, but she doubted their conversations involved talk of kidnapping and other crimes. One couple in particular, an older man and woman, simply looked at each other as they ate. Their expressions were content and calm, soft smiles playing on their lips, as if their relationship together was a blanket they had wrapped themselves in and nothing could touch them. The woman had a calico scarf wrapped loosely around her neck. The man was clean-shaven and had a sparkle in his eye that reminded her of her father. It was then that she remembered her parents and how much they loved each other. Their careers hadn't driven them away from each other. They accepted the best and worst of each other, just as Jesse wanted her to do with him. Every couple in the restaurant had problems, she realized. Only, they worked through it all. They dealt with crap and moved on.

With Jesse, however, it didn't feel like there would be a period of 'moving on'. With him, everything felt wrong. He would always be the dragon burning her world to pieces and then trying to put it back together again.

"I can't do this," she said, looking at him once more. Tears filled her eyes and she fought them as hard as she could before several escaped down her cheeks. "I will never trust you like you want me to, and you will never measure up to the kind of man I need. I know that sounds terrible, but it's how I feel. It's what I know. I can't live in this life, just like I was starting to see I couldn't stay at Harvard in the life I was trying to live for my mother. I need something else. I don't know what it is, but I'll figure it out—alone."

Just then, the waiter arrived with their meals. He placed two identical dishes of pasta on the table. Naomi looked down at her plate, her breath catching in her throat as she recognized Evelyn's mushroom pasta dish.

"You didn't—" she said, looking up at Jesse.

"I know how much you love it," he said with a nervous smile. "I thought it might make you feel better, so I explained to the waiter what we wanted. He said the chef should be able to do it. I doubt it's as good as yours."

Naomi picked up her fork and stabbed a campanelle noodle and a mushroom. The noodle was shaped like a little bellflower and was covered in the thick, creamy sauce. When Naomi put the food into her mouth, she closed her eyes. It tasted just like Evelyn's. Everything rushed at her in a whirlwind. The house. The bedroom. Eric's arms around her.

You'll stay? His voice echoed in her mind, over and over.

No! she hissed inside her head. *I won't.*

"It's just like Evelyn's," she whispered, almost choking on the food as she pushed Eric out of her head. "Why can some random chef in Rome get it right and I can't?"

Jesse hadn't touched his food yet. He watched Naomi and smiled, but his apprehension was a dark cloud surrounding him. "So, you still want to do everything alone? Were you trying to say you want to leave?"

Swallowing, Naomi set down her fork. "Yes." She steeled herself against more tears and drama and stood from her chair. She gripped her purse handle, knowing she had to leave now or she would never be able to do it. There was no time to get her luggage at the palace, so she would have to leave it there. She would walk away from Jesse right now. She would—

He was looking up at her, surprise and disbelief spreading across his face. "Naomi, what are you doing?"

"Leaving," she said, lifting her chin. It took every ounce of her willpower to keep looking at him. "Evelyn once told me it takes a long time to understand love. I thought when I fell in love with you that it had finally happened for me, that I understood it all . . . but I was lying to myself. I have no idea what love is. All I know is my heart hurts when I look at you, and when I think about leaving you, it feels like I'm dying inside."

Jesse's surprised expression melted into a controlled sort of panic. "Then don't leave," he said. A few people were looking over at their table now. He motioned for her to sit down.

Standing her ground, she wiped away a few tears. "I don't know what else to do. I can't live the way you want me to live. I can't live inside a cage, always waiting for you, never knowing where you are or what you're doing. I can't—"

"I told you," Jesse interrupted in a stern voice low enough not to draw attention, "it doesn't have to be that way. This is a transition. Give it a little while and you can go to a university here in Rome. There are two American ones you can think about. Or art schools—

whatever you want, we'll find it. We don't have to be apart."

She fisted a hand at her side. "Stop making this so hard. Please."

"It's hard because you're making a mistake." He half-stood from his chair and reached out to grab her arm. Gently, he pressed her back down into her chair. She hated that she hadn't walked away right then and there. She stared at the food in front of her and pressed her purse back into her lap. Jesse's eyes were burning a hole into her head, but she didn't dare look up.

"I think it's best for me to go," she said. "If I had known—"

"Life is full of the unknown," he interrupted. "I want you to stay with me, Naomi. This can work if you'll trust me to make it work."

She looked up as she wiped her damp hands on her skirt. She remembered a few months ago thinking she would know if she landed in another abusive relationship. Her counselors had made sure she knew the cycle and understood why her kidnappers were abusive and controlling and not loving and kind. The problem was she understood all the mechanics, but that didn't mean she wasn't stupid enough to get sucked back into it all over again. She wondered now if that was what had happened. Her warning bells were going off so loudly she thought she might go deaf any moment. A voice in her head kept screaming, *You're in control!*

Gathering her courage, she stood up once again and hung her purse on her shoulder. "I know you've meant well," she said in a sagging voice, "but I don't think any of this is going to fix me or make it all better. You feel guilty for everything you've done to me, but keeping me around isn't going to make it go away. If I leave—if I'm strong and take control on my own—then you can move on. We can both move on."

Jesse didn't look like he was going to try to stop her this time. He looked up with a hurt expression that sliced Naomi's sense of resolve to ribbons. "I love you," he whispered, "but I guess it's not enough."

She shook her head and took a few steps away from the table. Each movement was like slogging through mud. "Not this time," she whispered, and before she could second-guess her decision, she turned and walked out of the restaurant.

* * *

It was cold outside. Naomi wrapped her arms around herself, realizing she had forgotten to pick up her coat on the rack in the front of the restaurant. Determined not to go back in case she changed her mind, she kept walking. Jesse wouldn't dare follow her. She had made it clear she wanted to leave. It wasn't that she thought he was abusive like Brad—not by a long shot—but he was controlling in a way she could see now was the biggest problem of all. His intentions were good, but his actions weren't.

Tears slipped down her face as she realized she had done the same thing in her own life. She wanted to please her parents and live up to their expectations, but she was going about it in all the wrong ways. Now she had to return to them yet again and watch their expressions melt into disappointment. The thought almost made her turn around, but she held on to her courage and kept walking. Christmas lights twinkled in the darkness, blurring in her teary vision. She gasped when a pair of hands grabbed her from behind and spun her around.

Jesse. Of course.

She tried to rip away. "Let me go, Jesse. It's over. It has to be over."

He held on to her, but she noticed he didn't look angry or upset. "You forgot your coat," he said, meeting her eyes.

She looked down to see it in the crook of his arm. "So what? Give it to me and I'll leave."

His eyes narrowed. "How do you plan on getting anywhere? You don't have enough money to—"

Squirming in his arms, she tried to point to her purse. "I took the rest of the cash. It's mine, anyway. Now let me go. I'll be fine."

"Naomi, you don't speak a word of Italian. You don't have a cell phone or any of your things. You're not thinking this through."

"I *have* thought it through, and I'm leaving. I don't need any of that crap." His restricting hold was starting to make her panic. That was what had happened, she realized—with every passing day she was with him, her sense of panic had risen. This was the culmination, the inevitable point she had to reach in order to leave. Or submit. But she wouldn't submit. Not this time.

"Naomi, please calm down," Jesse said into her ear. "I'm not kidnapping you. I'm not the bad guy. I'm not going to make you stay with me. Let me help you. I'll get you sent off, okay? Safely."

His words flowed over her like silk and she relaxed in his arms as her heavy breaths made white clouds in the air.

"You're right about everything," he said, rubbing her back. "I do feel guilty for what I've done to you, and that's a big reason why I want you with me. Knowing you love me eases that ache. It almost makes me feel like it was worth it, but now I realize it wasn't. I'm sorry I've made decisions you don't agree with, and I'm sorry for digging you even deeper than you were before. I'm sorry." Pulling away a little so he could look into her face, he brushed away the tears on her cheeks. "Let me help you this one last time. Please?"

She clenched her jaw for a moment and then relaxed. "Fine."

He hailed a cab, and as they rode back to the palace, Naomi hugged her purse and tried to suppress the desire to snuggle into Jesse's arms and ignore how wrong she knew it was and how bad things would get with him. She couldn't ignore any of it anymore. Her panic would never ease. She would always remember why she was with him, why she fell in love, and why he felt so obligated to take care of her. She looked out the window at the beautiful city. She had thought coming to Italy was the answer, but it wasn't going to fix her problems. Nothing was going to fix her problems.

"Going home will be hell," she said, still looking out the window.

Jesse grunted. "Yeah, I can imagine. Will you visit my dad if you can? Tell him I'm sorry."

"I'll try, but it might take a while."

"That's all right. You're not going to tell the feds where I am, are you? You wouldn't—"

She turned to look him in the eyes. "If you think I'd tell them where you are, you don't know me at all."

He looked away and rested his arm near the window. "I didn't think you would. I'm sorry, Naomi. I'm sorry for everything."

"I'm sorry too," she answered. "Not everything has been your fault."

He blinked as understanding crossed his face. "Whatever you choose to believe, Naomi, I hope you don't make the same mistakes I've made. I tried to keep my old life and my new life separate, and that landed me right back where I always was. I don't think there's a way out for me now."

Naomi looked down at her hands. "Don't ever give up."

Jesse reached for her hand and then pulled away. Naomi forced herself to look out the window. She wanted to find beauty in the ancient city sliding past, but all she saw was a broken dream.

XXIV

THAT NIGHT, JESSE SLEPT ON THE COUCH WHILE Naomi slept fitfully in the king-sized bed. Jesse had booked her ticket and then told her he would be leaving also.

"Not for the US?" she had asked.

"No, and don't ask me where I'm going, please. The less you know the better."

"But why do you have to leave?"

"Because it needs to look like we're leaving together. If the network finds out I'm letting you go, they'll want to make sure you don't give the authorities information about this safe house. They've set this place up so that any investigations won't lead back to them, but they don't appreciate guests who can't keep their mouths shut. The reason we were allowed here in the first place is because of who I know. I can't screw that up, so I'm trusting you won't breathe a word. You already told me you won't, and I believe you."

Naomi tossed and turned in bed, upset with herself for compromising Jesse as well as breaking his heart. What kind of person was she, anyway? At this point, her parents were probably going mad trying to find her, and who knew what Finn was doing? Perhaps he didn't care. He had Carly. All the same, she had hurt people by leaving the way she did. She felt terrible that none of it had bothered her until now. The shroud she had woven for so many years was finally slipping away.

When she woke, Jesse had made her a small breakfast of toast and scrambled eggs. She had never tried his eggs before. They didn't disappoint. For some reason, that made looking at him even harder. He had dark circles under his eyes.

"Looks like you slept about as well as I did," she said, adding some pepper to the eggs. They were good, but they certainly weren't like Eric's.

"I didn't sleep at all," he answered. Morning sun from the kitchen window fell across the table. It sparkled through Naomi's juice glass.

"Jesse," she said, lifting the glass but not taking a drink. She stared at the rim. "Do you think any of this could have worked?" She looked up to see him watching her. His plate was untouched.

"I think it might have if I wasn't such an idiot," he grumbled. "The truth is I've made too many mistakes. I can design entire buildings from scratch. I can break

303

parole and move to another country just fine, and I have no doubt I can hide for the rest of my life without ever getting caught. I'm sure I can even arrange it so I'll see my father again. But when it comes to you, Naomi, I'm a fool. I make mistakes I can't fix."

She set down her glass and pushed some toast crumbs around the table. Her stomach was rumbling for more food, but she didn't want to eat anymore. "Maybe I'm the bigger fool," she said in a faraway voice. "Sometimes the only way out is to take a stand and fight."

Jesse blinked. "And that's what you're doing?"

She looked out the window at the sunny gardens and blue sky. "It's not you I'm fighting," she answered in the same faraway tone. "It's me. I feel like I'm taking the first step. I'm sorry I've hurt so many people, including you." When she looked at Jesse again, he was gazing at the floor. His lips were closed tightly and his silence made it clear there was nothing more to say.

* * *

There were no kisses goodbye. Not even a hug. They took a cab into the city, where Jesse unloaded her luggage and hailed another cab. He paid the driver and instructed him to take her to the airport. Then he nodded goodbye to her as he got back into his cab and she slid into hers.

Just like that. Clean break. No matter what happened from here on out, things were over with Jesse. After breakfast, he had promised he would never try to contact her again. He didn't seem upset, but she felt coldness in his voice that had never been there before. She watched his cab drive away.

When she arrived at the airport, three suited men appeared as soon as she stepped out of the car. One began questioning the cab driver. Another retrieved her luggage from the trunk. They were American, she noticed as they zeroed in on her like hawks to a flopping fish on land. They flashed badges at her—what the badges said, she wasn't sure—and told her they were from the US embassy. They spoke to her in English and explained she was to follow them.

Knowing she had no choice, she walked with them through the airport until they reached a conference room where she was instructed to sit at a table. One left the room and the other two sat across from her. She groaned inside, irritated with herself for not spotting something like this from a million miles away. Of course the Italian airlines were being watched, probably ever since her phone text had been traced back to Italy. As soon as her name popped up on a flight, they would find her. Jesse had known it too. She guessed that was another reason why he had left so quickly. He was probably out of Rome by now.

"What do you want with me?" she asked, determined not to play into their hands, whatever they were planning. "I haven't done anything wrong."

They looked at each other, their frowns deepening. "We aren't sure what you've been up to," the smaller man with pockmarks on his cheeks said. "But you've been reported missing."

"So what? I'm an adult. I can leave whenever and wherever I want." Her throat was swelling up. She needed a drink of water.

"We're concerned you've been aiding and harboring a United States fugitive," the bigger man said, interlacing his fingers on the table.

Naomi swallowed. Was allowing Jesse to use her money aiding him? Well, of course it was, but she hadn't known he was a fugitive, and he hadn't used much of her money. Some of it was his. Of course, if she had taken three seconds to think through things with a clear head before leaving for Italy, she might have figured it out. She swallowed again, keeping her mouth shut.

"Did Jesse hurt you?" the pockmarked man asked, concern knitting his brow. "Did he take you against your will?"

Her mouth dropped open, but before she could give Jesse away, she clamped it shut again.

The bigger man leaned forward and studied Naomi's face, as if staring at her hard enough would make her lies unravel. She glared at him in response. "As you may already know, Mr. Sullivan likes to use different names. Did you happen to notice what alias he's using right now?"

Her cheeks started to burn. She wondered if they were bright red, and tried to calm down. Jesse hadn't told her about any aliases, but she hadn't bothered asking. She hadn't even bothered looking at his luggage tags. She shook her head and tried to look stupid. She didn't have to try very hard—she *was* stupid. Very stupid. Despite all of that, she denied ever coming to Italy with Jesse. It was one point she knew she must lie about. She had come to get away, she told the men over and over, but her story began falling apart when they started asking her for proof of where she had stayed.

"In hotels," she said, keeping her eyes on the biggest man's face. He had thick sideburns and eyes the color of dishwater. "I paid with cash. I don't have receipts or anything, I'm sorry. I don't even remember the names of most of the places."

She could see they didn't believe her. Far from it. They tried to dig deeper, but she had years of practice answering stupid questions. After an hour, they gave up. At the moment, they had no proof of anything.

"I'm going to miss my flight," she grumbled with a glance at her luggage piled in the corner.

"We've contacted your parents," they responded. "Your father was in Germany, and he's on his way here to pick you up."

That was convenient. He was either there on business or her mother had sent him over with some desperate hope he would come searching for her. For some reason, this irritated the hell out of her. What if she *had* decided to come to Italy on her own? She was an adult. Nobody could stop her. She didn't have to wait here for her father like she was some scolded child. The only reason any of this was an issue was because Jesse had broken parole and fled at the same time she disappeared. She gripped the edge of the table with both hands, her jaw tight as she looked at the men and considered telling them everything.

Then she looked down and relaxed. Telling them would get them nothing except dead ends. Jesse was long gone. The more she thought about it, the more she asked herself what information she really had. She wasn't even sure she could find the safe house again. She could describe it, but Jesse had said that wouldn't get anyone very far. She could tell them about the apartment in Trastevere. She could find that easily. She could tell them Lalia was part of some illegal underground network. She could tell them about the dance club and how the same network owned that too. None of it would matter. She knew nothing of importance. She realized how much Jesse had kept from her and convinced herself it was all to protect her so that when she looked at men like the ones in front of her, she could easily tell them she didn't know a damned thing. Because, in reality, she didn't.

* * *

When she saw her father, she realized how much she loved him. He was dressed in a sharp gray suit and a teal-colored silk tie that reminded her of fish scales shimmering under water. He wrapped her in his arms, holding her so tightly she thought he might break her in half.

"We thought we'd lost you again," he said, releasing a breath so heavy Naomi guessed he had held it in the entire flight to Italy. She folded into him and wrapped her arms around his solidness. He smelled like mints and ink, like an office. It was comforting and familiar, even though she had never realized he was so familiar to her. He had always been in the background, waiting patiently. She stiffened a little as she realized he reminded her of Finn—that same sort of even-tempered strength. She had missed both of them, Finn and her father. She squeezed tighter, knowing it was doubtful she would ever see Finn again. At least on good terms.

Her father pushed her away so he could look into her face. His expression was stern. He was clean-shaven, his hair styled like some suave GQ model. "Now, explain yourself," he demanded, his hands on her shoulders a reminder that she had no way out of explaining things to him. The two men had left the room earlier.

"I'll tell you everything later," she promised, looking into his eyes. "I'd like to go home now. Please?"

His eyes narrowed. "Later, huh?" He searched her face and then relaxed. "I've booked us a flight home. It leaves tomorrow morning, so we'll have to stay in a hotel tonight. I'll get that taken care of." He glanced at his watch. "You're probably starving."

"A little," she said, shrugging. "I'm tired."

He glanced up from his watch. "I'll bet you are." He paused, scratching his jaw as a hundred emotions played across his face. He was confused and frustrated and she didn't know how to fix it.

"Naomi, I . . . I don't know what to say to you, honey. I know you can run off and do whatever you want—you're your own person, and I've always believed in you—but with your past and this whole thing with Jesse, you understand why it wasn't exactly appropriate to—"

"I know, Dad." She looked away, ashamed. She would forever be ashamed.

"Honey, it will be okay." He touched her face and she returned her attention to him. "I'm going to speak with the men who brought you here and sort some things out, and then we can go get something to eat." He raised his eyebrows. "Okay?"

"Yes, fine, Dad. Everything's fine." She slumped back down into her chair and folded her arms. She had been a fool to think she could handle anything on her own.

XXV

THERE WERE TWO LAYOVERS ON THE WAY HOME. BY the time they stumbled off the last flight and made it to the parking garage where her father had parked his BMW, Naomi thought she was going to die. Her father's car had heated seats. She turned on her heater in an attempt to coax out the tension in her lower back.

"How do you survive that flight three times a year?" she asked, rubbing her shoulders. She didn't remember feeling so sore from the flight over to Italy, but at that moment in time Jesse's presence had kept her from caring about anything else.

He father laughed. "First-class, honey. Sorry I couldn't get that for this flight. I booked the first one I could. Only coach was available." He lifted a hand to his neck. "But I hear you—not fun. I'm tired of sitting and waiting. Maybe we should go for a walk on the beach when we get home. I'm sure your mother would love that."

Still feeling sulky over having to be rescued, Naomi kept her mouth shut and slumped in her seat. She wanted her iPod, but it was buried in her luggage in the back. Ignoring her father wouldn't be a smart decision, anyway. He had been nothing but kind and understanding over everything, even when she was sure he knew she was lying about leaving for Italy on her own. At least he wasn't forcing anything out of her.

When they pulled into the garage, Naomi slid out of her seat and shut the door. She wasn't very excited to face her mother's wrath. Her father motioned for her to follow him into the house.

"She won't bite," he whispered behind his shoulder, and then winked. "Not too hard, anyway."

Naomi smirked and nudged his shoulder. If only her mother could be so laid-back. The garage house entrance led into a small sitting room where Naomi took off her shoes and dropped her purse. Her mother was standing at the far end of the room, her arms folded. Naomi could tell she was fighting back tears.

"How *dare* you," she said in a trembling voice, her eyes like knives boring into Naomi's skull.

Her father approached her with both his palms up, as if trying to sooth a rabid dog. Her mother refused to look at him. She kept her glare on Naomi, who stood frozen at the other end of the room.

"I'm sorry, Mom. I didn't do it to hurt you. I texted you. You knew I was okay."

"No, I didn't know you were okay," she retorted. "That text could have come from anyone—from Jesse—anyone who could have taken you again. How was I to know? And you wouldn't return my calls. We worried, Naomi . . . so much. When I heard Jesse broke parole and went missing, I ran to the police. I hired an investigator. I couldn't handle you disappearing again. I couldn't—"

When she burst into tears, Naomi rushed to her and embraced her. Her father stood to the side, a soft smile on his lips. Surprisingly, Naomi didn't feel emotional at all. She wanted her mother to know how sorry she was, but she wasn't about to cry. She was too tired from the journey home, and too sick of thinking about the irreversible decision she had made to leave Jesse. She wanted to collapse and sleep for five days straight.

Her mother backed away and started wiping the palms of her hands across her wet cheeks. Naomi watched her, not knowing what to say

"Naomi is tired," her father said, reaching out a hand to rub her mother's back. "Let's all get some rest and talk about everything tomorrow, okay? She's healthy and safe. That's all that matters right now."

314

Sniffing, her mother nodded. "I'm happy you're back," she said to Naomi, touching her hand.

Naomi tried to smile, but it was difficult. She knew what was coming next. There would be investigators and drama and more counselors. She had brought it all on herself, so she couldn't complain. All she could do was drag herself upstairs to her room. For a moment, she stared at her bed and wanted to fall into its depths and sleep for eternity. Then she turned her attention to a desk in the corner of her room. On top of it sat a computer she hadn't touched in ages. Her laptop was in storage back in Massachusetts. Sitting down at the desk, she buried her face in her hands while she waited for the computer to boot up.

* * *

The next day, Naomi rolled out of bed and took a long, hot shower. She stared at the clean, white tiles and noticed the new shampoo bottles—tea and mint, like she always used—the unused bar of lemon-scented soap, a shiny razor just taken out of its package. She knew her mother had told the housekeeper to go to the store to buy all these things. The housekeeper would pick up clothes left on the floor. She would make Naomi's bed. She would cook dinner. Naomi realized how much she had enjoyed living in her house at

Harvard, making her own stupid meals, cleaning up her own stupid messes and picking up her own stupid clothes.

Leaning her forehead against the tiled wall, she let her tears come fast and hard. Sobs made her chest heave. She remembered all those hours she had spent crying in the shower when she was captive. It had been such a haven, then, but now it was an old ritual she wanted to throw away. She was so *tired* of feeling sorry for herself. She lifted a fist and hit the wall over and over until her tears stopped.

Showered and dressed, she went downstairs. She didn't even know what day it was. Had her parents gone to work? She remembered her father's words from the night before—*Let's get some rest and talk about everything tomorrow, okay?*

And just as he had said, there they were at the breakfast table, waiting for her. Scrambled eggs— please, oh, please no more scrambled eggs to remind her of Eric!—toast and jam, sausage links, and pancakes. There was also a pitcher of fresh-squeezed orange juice. A seed was floating on the top near some frothy bubbles.

Naomi stopped in the doorway of the dining room. She wanted to turn around and run, or keep walking past the table and out the French doors leading to the deck and trails down to the beach. She didn't want to face her mother looking at her with a warm, concentrated smile. It was almost too forced.

"We made breakfast for you," she said, sweeping her arm in front of the food. "Me and your father. Mindy has the day off. I know it's late in the day, but we waited until you were up."

Naomi looked at the fluffy pancakes. "You made all of this yourself?"

Her father looked up, his smile more genuine than his wife's. "Of course we did. You know we've been trying to cook more since your . . . escape."

He meant the *kidnapping* or *captivity*, but Naomi knew how strange it was to say those things. She walked to a chair across the table from both of them and spread her napkin over her lap. Tension hung in the air, mostly from her mother. Naomi started piling up her plate with more food than she could eat. She cut a piece of sausage and stuffed it into her mouth. Maybe if she kept eating, she wouldn't have to say much.

Her mother set down her fork. She gave her husband a nervous look.

"Are you feeling rested?" he asked Naomi.

She swallowed and stabbed the other piece of sausage with her fork. "I'm all right," she mumbled. "Listen, I know you guys want to talk about Jesse. I know you think I ran off with him."

Her mother cleared her throat and folded her arms. "Well, didn't you?"

Stuffing the other piece of sausage in her mouth, Naomi shrugged. "I might have," she said through her chewing. She watched the emotions play across her mother's face. Confusion, anger, a hint of desperation.

"Either way," her father said firmly, "we'd like it if you saw another counselor. Running off to Italy, with or without Jesse, was a drastic thing to do. We both feel you need more guidance right now."

Naomi opened her mouth to object, but her father continued.

"Now, I have no idea why you left without trying to get a visa, but to me, that makes it all the more clear Jesse had a hand in this. In fact, we know he did. When the investigator your mother hired started digging into your phone records, he found a text from Jesse asking you about a passport."

Naomi pushed another sausage around her plate as she recalled the text. Crap.

"Jesse's father has told us what he's capable of doing. I doubt he'll ever be caught."

"No," Naomi said, setting her fork down, "he won't." She looked from her father to her mother and then down at her plate. The scrambled eggs were untouched and probably cold by now. Her stomach flipped over.

318

"Right now, it doesn't matter," her mother said in a calm voice. Naomi looked up at her, noticing she was dressed in her usual whites and creams. "We want you to know we're here for you no matter what happens." She paused and then put on the stupid forced smile again. "It would be nice if you could communicate with us more from now on. You can't possibly imagine what you've put us through. You—"

Naomi lifted a hand and her mother stopped talking. "You should be happy Jesse is gone for good. You don't have to worry about him anymore."

"That's . . . that's good," her mother said. Naomi could practically see the weight lifting from her shoulders.

"Glad you think so." Naomi put her napkin on the table and stood. "I'll see whatever counselors you want me to see. I'll do whatever you want as long as I'm living here, but please don't ask me about Italy. Ever."

Her mother nodded as Naomi left the room. She wasn't sure if she should feel guilty or good for standing up for herself, but part of her knew it didn't matter. She had hurt her parents deeply by running off to Italy after everything that had happened. Nothing was going to fix it.

* * *

The definition of a prison is a place or condition of confinement or forcible restraint. Naomi knew her parents weren't restraining her inside their home, but in many ways, she felt as if they were since she had no car and nowhere else to go. She still had the money she had brought from Italy, but she didn't dare spend it. She wanted to save it for when she finally did get on her own two feet. Her bedroom was a prison. Their house was a prison. Her entire life was a prison, she realized, and it was her own fault. It would be a long time before she could live completely on her own. She typed all this to Finn over a chat program and waited for him to respond. A little bubble with ellipses popped up in the window, indicating he was typing a response.

This was the third time she had chatted with Finn and the third time she felt a breath of fresh air amid all the stuffiness of her mother's overbearing control and the several investigators she had been forced to talk to. Tomorrow, another one was coming by. She already dreaded her mother insisting she brush her hair and put on decent clothes. If only she could scream at them to go away and leave her alone. She wouldn't admit knowing where Jesse was . . . because she didn't know where he was. She wouldn't admit she had spent two weeks with him in Italy. She didn't care that they had found her and Jesse's text correspondence. It wasn't proof that she had left with him. There was no proof, and she wouldn't admit to anyone what had really happened, even Finn.

I'm sorry you're feeling so trapped, he typed. *I'm sorry I can't help you very much.*

She stared at his words, not feeling very comforted by them. He had admitted earlier he was still with Carly, but that hadn't stopped her from asking if they could still be friends. She needed someone. He was nice enough at least to tell her he was happy to still be friends.

You're helping by talking to me, she typed in return. *I just don't know what to do. I've been here for three weeks and I feel like I'm drowning.*

She imagined him shaking his head and thinking, "I told you so."

He responded, *Do you want to come back to Harvard?*

No, I can't.

Why?

She paused with her fingers curled over the keys. Finally, she typed, *I just can't.*

Okay, fair enough. Can you go to another school? What about USC?

She looked up at the ceiling and swallowed. She wasn't sure she was ready for anything that big yet. She had unpacked all of her art supplies from Italy, but they were piled in her closet, untouched. One day she would touch them again, when drawing wouldn't remind her of five billion bad things.

I can't go to USC. Not yet.

Okay, but I'll bet you'd be happier if you moved out to be on your own again. I know you can't right now, but eventually.

She laughed out loud. Again? *I was never on my own. Ever. Not really. Not like you.*

Like me?

Yeah, you have a job. You provide for yourself.

Two minutes passed before he typed, *Heh, barely, and my mom helps out some, but at least I got accepted to Harvard, right? At least I've told her the truth now.*

She warmed up inside, reading those words. He had already told her once that he had been accepted and told his mother about his big lie, but every time she thought about him overcoming such a hurdle, her admiration for him expanded. He had wanted to tell her while she was in Italy, she realized. That was what his text had been about.

I'm proud of you, she typed, thinking carefully about what she wanted to say. *I wish I could make such big changes in my life, but every time I try, I fail.*

A minute passed as the typing bubble popped up. Naomi went over to her closet and pulled out a folder she had brought from Italy. She sat back down and flipped through it. Inside were sketches of Trastevere and the winding streets. In one, she had drawn Jesse sitting at an outdoor café. It had been chilly that day, but there was no more room inside, so they zipped up their jackets and ate outside. The smile she had drawn on his face was calm and peaceful. A part of her wanted to crumple up the page and toss it into the trashcan. The other part of her wanted to cradle it to her chest as she stared at the little ellipses on the screen. Finally, Finn's words appeared.

So I guess I'll go into counseling mode again, the message read. *Remember when I told you to make sure you knew what you wanted before taking off with Jesse?*

She stopped reading for a moment, realizing how positive he was that she had left with Jesse. He knew her better than she wanted to admit. Shaking off the thought, she kept reading the message.

Well, I remember thinking you had no idea what you wanted. You kept saying you wanted to be with Jesse. That was your main goal. I think more than that, what you have always wanted was something a lot deeper. I guess my question for you is did you find that 'something' when you went to Italy?

Sitting back in her chair, she folded her arms and stared at the screen. She didn't know how to answer the question. Had she found something deeper? She had at least realized she wanted to live an honest life. She had realized how dependent she was and how much she hated that feeling. She hated that her father had flown home with her. She hated that she was stuck back in her old bedroom with nothing in her future. She hated that the only person she felt she could lean on now was a guy she couldn't have.

She put her hands on the keys and started typing as her mind reeled in circles.

I want to be independent, she wrote. *I want to be my own person and earn my own way. I've always been the 'rich girl' or 'Brad's girl' or 'that girl who fell in love with her kidnapper'. I don't want to be that anymore. I want to be just plain old Naomi. Boring. With a job in a café or something.* She paused for a long while, waiting for him to respond, and then she typed, *Like you.*

Are you saying I'm boring?

She laughed. *Yeah, kinda . . . but I like that. A lot.*

A little smiley face popped up and she typed one in return.

I should get a job, she wrote.

Another smiley face from Finn. *How come? Because you want to support yourself or because you really want to work?*

Another minute passed and Naomi looked at the open folder of sketches. The top one was of dragons. She didn't break into a sweat when she looked at them anymore.

Maybe a little of both, she typed. *I feel bad for wasting my parents' money.*

Understandable. He paused for a minute before typing, *but I think you should let them keep helping you while you need it.*

Yeah.

I gotta go, Naomi. I'm late for meeting Carly somewhere.

She cursed under her breath.

No problem. Thanks for talking, Finn.

Good luck!

Naomi stared at the screen after he was logged off. Then she opened a web browser to a search engine and typed in the word *chef*.

XXVI

January

CHRISTMAS CAME AND WENT. NAOMI CONVINCED HER mother not to hire someone to put up a tree, and instead went with her into town to buy a fresh-cut pine. With a lot of grunting and cursing, she helped her mother stuff a small tree into the back of the SUV. She could smell pine sap on her fingers for two days after that. Her father bought lights and helped string them up. For the first time in weeks, Naomi smiled as she and her parents stood back and looked at the tree.

"It's lopsided," her mother said as she pressed two fingers to her lips and tilted her head. "It's not nearly as pretty as it would be if I'd hired—"

"It's perfect, Karen," her father interrupted with a glance at Naomi. "Enjoy it."

PIECES

Now, the second week into January, Naomi passed by the sitting room where the tree had been and frowned at the empty space. No more falling needles. No more spicy pine smell. It had reminded her of Stacy's office, but that wasn't why she liked it. The smell had been something foreign to the house. Something new. Smiling at the memory, she rounded the corner in search of her mother. There was a workout room at the end of the hallway. It was the only room she hadn't checked yet.

Stopping in the doorway, she stared open-mouthed at her mother holding a perfect tree pose—one foot held flat against the opposite upper thigh, her arms stretched high above her head with her palms pressed together. Her eyes were closed as she listened to soothing nature sounds playing in the background. Naomi didn't say anything. Instead, she grabbed hold of the doorframe and remembered all the yoga she had done with Evelyn at the house. It had become a ritual— one Naomi missed. Watching her mother now made her want to stretch and reach and bend her body in ways she knew would hurt now that she was so out of practice.

"Naomi!"

Naomi brought her attention back to her mother. She had lowered her foot to the floor and stood rigid, her eyes wide open.

"Mom, I didn't know . . . sorry, I was just trying to find you to ask if I can borrow the car."

"Of course you can borrow the car." Pink crept across her cheeks, as if she had been caught red-handed at a crime scene. Her exercise clothes were bright purple and teal. That was odd, considering all she ever wore was white and cream.

"Okay, thanks."

"May I ask what for?"

Naomi paused, halfway turned to leave. She returned the doorway. "Nothing," she said, and swallowed a lump in her throat.

"Oh." The blush on her mother's cheeks disappeared. "I was going to tell you about a phone call I received yesterday. It was from your advisor at Harvard."

Naomi blanched. She didn't want to think about Harvard. "Kate?" she asked, the lump in her throat returning. "She must hate me. She always told me I had so much potential. Then I dropped out."

Her mother shrugged as she approached Naomi. "I suppose she thinks you still have potential because she said you have a chance to accept your scholarship again. I had to explain your situation and talk to the right people, but your appeal went through."

Naomi looked down at her hands and shifted her feet. A moment ago she was excited to go to her first interview. Now she faced something that would render a job unnecessary. Unless, of course, she decided not to look at it in terms of money. It was more than that. It was about working outside of a school setting. It was about figuring out what she truly wanted. Squaring her shoulders, she looked her mother in the eyes and said, "I don't want to go back to Harvard."

It was as if a grenade had landed in the middle of the room and they were both waiting for it to explode. Her mother's expression fell and then twisted into confusion. She opened her mouth, but nothing came out.

Letting out a heavy sigh, Naomi thought about all the time she had wasted, all the money spent on tuition and living expenses, all the stress over homework and grades—and for what? Maybe it *was* about money, in a way, at least for her parents. She said, "I'll pay you and Dad back, somehow. You paid for the last semester I didn't even finish. I'll—"

"No," her mother interrupted, swiping a hand over her face as if to brush away her confusion. "It's about our trust in you, not what you think you owe us. We want to help you, and letting you live here with us until you're on your own two feet is a part of that." She narrowed her eyes. "So don't ever feel like you have to pay us back."

Naomi watched the confusion on her face melt away. "Then I hope you'll understand why I've applied for a job. It's not for money. It's for me."

Her mother shook her head as her mouth dropped open. "A job? Where?"

"A little café in town. They were advertising for a kitchen assistant. It's just cleaning, mostly, but I can work my way up. I want to . . . I want to be a chef. Maybe when I'm feeling more on my own, I can go to school for it." She glanced at the clock on the wall. "I need to leave soon to get to my interview."

Her mother opened her mouth again. Her shoulders dropped.

"Mom?"

"I thought you wanted to do art."

"Cooking *is* art. At least it is to me. Don't worry, I'll keep helping out at the foundation."

She turned and left before she was sucked into an argument about how cooking might not be a wise career choice. Her mind was still reeling from discovering her mother did yoga.

✳ ✳ ✳

Working was not what Naomi had thought it would be, but she kept at it. Sometimes, if she was helping out at the foundation on a day she worked at the café, she would wake up at seven in the morning and not get home until eleven at night. The foundation was emotionally exhausting, while her café job was physically exhausting, but she wanted it that way. She welcomed it. She thought about how hard Finn worked, and her parents too. She wanted to be a part of that world, even if it meant scraping food off plates and burning her hands in scalding, soapy water.

Another assistant in the kitchen recognized her name and started asking her about Jesse and the kidnapping. Her name was Alyssa. She had colored streaks in her hair just like Carly. Naomi hated her from the start.

"I'd rather not talk about it," she said as she scrubbed a dish clean.

Alyssa was scrubbing a pan. She had bubbles all the way up to her knobby elbows. "Well, all right, but I think it's funny how you work here at the bottom of the employment chain when your daddy is CEO of a huge company and your mommy's a lawyer. Can't they afford to send you to school? Did they make you get a job?" She grunted as a nasty smile spread across her lips.

Fighting the urge to throw hot water in Alyssa's face, Naomi pursed her lips shut. The longer she scrubbed and stared at the bubbles skimming across the top of the water, the more she remembered Stacy's comment that she needed to let both pieces of her life come together. Jesse had tried to separate it all and ended up sliding back into his old habits. The whole point of her getting a job and learning how to work and stand on her own two feet was to move forward and create something new out of who she already was. The point was *not* to run away and ignore things.

She let go of the dish and watched it sink to the bottom of the huge stainless steel tub. Turning to Alyssa, she pulled her arms out of the water and dried them on a towel tucked into the front pocket of her apron.

"You know, it's people like you I've been hiding from my whole life," she said in a calm, even voice. "You judge me and push me around and you don't even know me . . . and the worst part is I let you do it."

Alyssa looked up, her lips twitching as if she couldn't decide if Naomi was serious or not.

"Yes, I was kidnapped," she continued, "and yes, I'm a 'rich girl', but that's not who I am. I'm working here because I've never had a job before and this was all I could get. I want to work in a kitchen and learn how it all functions. Someday I'm going to be a chef, and you'll still be standing here scrubbing dishes and feeling sorry for yourself."

Alyssa opened her mouth, but Naomi wasn't about to let her get a word in edgewise, and kept going.

"As for me, I'm sick and tired of feeling sorry for myself, so if you have questions about my past, ask them and I'll answer, but don't expect me to stand here and take it while you make fun of me." She leaned forward. "Got it?"

Alyssa closed her mouth as she searched Naomi's face. The stupid colored streaks in her hair didn't make Naomi angry anymore. She didn't care if they reminded her of Carly. She had no right to hate Carly, anyway. If she was what Finn wanted, so be it. She would move on and do whatever would make her happy. Period. And right now, as strange as it seemed, that was washing dishes.

Smiling to herself, she dipped her hands back into the water and started scrubbing the dish again.

* * *

That night, when she arrived home from work, she passed her mother's office. She was at her desk, her eyes drowsy as she sat back in her chair with her phone to her ear.

"Hm-mm," she said about eight times before looking up to see Naomi in the doorway. When she motioned for her to come in, Naomi walked across the room and sank into the comfy leather armchair across from the desk. She could tell her mother didn't want to be on the phone. It was eight-thirty and Naomi doubted she had eaten dinner yet.

"No, like I said, we can settle all of that tomorrow at the office," her mother said into the phone. "Yes, yes, goodbye." She set her phone on the desk and turned to Naomi. "So, how was the kitchen?"

Naomi smiled. "Dirty, as usual."

"And you cleaned it?"

"Yep."

"And you . . . like that?"

"Yep."

A deep sigh. "Well, Naomi, you keep surprising me, I'll give you that. Are you ready for a counselor yet?"

"I guess so." She folded her arms, sure her tone of voice made it clear she wanted nothing to do with counselors anymore, but she wasn't going to argue. She was so tired of arguing.

Her mother cradled her forehead in her hands as she stared at her desk. She began massaging her temples with her fingers. "I've been thinking about a lot of things," she said, her words sagging in their middles like wet rags.

"You're always thinking about a lot of things, Mom. I'm sure I give you plenty to think about."

Her mother didn't look up. She kept moving her fingers in circles against her temples. Slow. Calm. "Sure, you do—you're my daughter, and I will always worry about you. But I've been thinking about Jesse and if you'll ever see him again. I'm hoping you'll—"

"I already told you I'll never see him again," Naomi interrupted. She felt her pulse quicken as she realized how important it was to tell her mother the truth. Finn had told his mother the truth. He wasn't living a lie anymore, and she couldn't either, no matter what it would bring on in her life. She was safe now. She had chosen an honest life and she had to keep it that way.

Her mother looked up. "You say that as if you mean it. You're not just saying it to make me feel better?"

Nodding, Naomi shifted in the chair. The leather groaned beneath her weight. "I did go to Italy with him, but I didn't know he'd broken his parole. Some of my friends tried to make me see something was wrong, but I refused to listen. I left with him, and then I found out the truth when I was there." She looked away. "You were right, Mom—about everything. You never told me I couldn't be with Jesse, but that's what I thought you were telling me. You knew things could end up like they did. You knew I was doing everything at the wrong time. I had to face myself there and make my own decisions, alone. I decided to leave him. Forever."

Her mother leaned across the desk, her eyes wide. She looked surprised but sad, and it broke Naomi's heart to think about what she had put her through in the past few years. "I can't be what you want me to be,

Mom," she said, squeezing her hands into fists. "I can't go to Harvard. I can't marry the perfect man. I can't be obsessed with stocks and money. Right now, all I want is to find myself and figure out what to do with the rest of my life."

Her mother shook her head and wiped away a tear falling down her cheek. "That's all I've ever wanted for you."

"Then why have you kept pushing me everywhere else?"

"I haven't pushed you."

Naomi raised her eyebrows and watched her mother's expression melt into horror.

"I mean . . . that's what I've done, isn't it?"

Naomi nodded. "The counselors. Harvard. You told me to choose for myself, but you cleared only certain paths for me. Let me make my own decisions, Mom. Please. Even if it means I'm cleaning dirty kitchens."

"Your own decisions . . .," her mother's voice faded as she scraped her fingernail over a spot on the desk. "I've turned into my mother," she muttered. "I'm exactly what I tried to avoid."

Naomi leaned forward. "What do you mean?"

Looking up, her mother kept scraping at the spot. "She was controlling. She wanted to know everything about my life, right down to what nail polish I was putting on my toes. She drove me away, Naomi. I wanted to avoid that. I wanted to keep everything open for you, but somewhere along the way I swung from one extreme to another." She moved her fingernail from the spot as her eyes grew huge. "I'm so sorry."

Naomi opened her mouth to reply. She wanted to say it was okay. She wanted to say she was sorry too, but as she searched for the right words, her mother's cell phone started ringing on the desk. She looked down at it, sliding her hand forward until she picked it up and turned off the sound. She turned to Naomi, a calm expression replacing the horror on her face.

"I have some things to show you," she said after a deep breath. "It's a box I saved for when you were ready."

"A box?" Naomi's fists started to loosen.

"Yes, it's filled with newspaper clippings and recorded television segments about your kidnapping. There are some journal entries in there too. I put it all in one place for when you were ready to hear my side of the story from when you were captive."

Shocked, Naomi felt herself stiffen. She wasn't sure she was ready for such a thing, but then she remembered Jesse making her read her journal and how it had opened a window inside herself so she could see things more clearly. Maybe this would help her connect to her mother better.

Walking around the desk, her mother held out her hand. "You think you can let me share all of that with you?"

Naomi remembered a crumpled paper cup. She remembered Stacy's couch, curling her knees to her chest as she let her mind enter the bedroom over and over. She remembered the train tracks and the sound of Finn breathing next to her. She remembered a sapphire Italian sky as wide open as a new day. Reaching up, she took her mother's hand.

XXVII

3 Months Later — April

"SO, YOU FOUND ALMOND CAKE THIS FAR FROM JAVA, huh?"

Naomi looked up from her sketchpad, her mouth falling open as she realized Finn was standing next to her table.

"Finn!" she squeaked, remembering her chat with him a week ago on her computer. "You were at Harvard. You were—"

"I know, but I'm here now." His smile was mysterious.

"It's an hour before closing time. How did you know I'd be on my break?"

The café was empty and the bright lights made it seem even emptier. Alyssa, who had moved to a waitressing position a month earlier, gave Finn a lusty look as she passed by, carrying a tray of empty glasses. Great. It was like Carly all over again.

Finn ignored her as a grin spread across his face. For some reason, Naomi wanted to stand up and wipe it off. He looked a little too pleased with himself for surprising her. Leaning down, he peered at her sketch.

"No more dragons?" he asked, brushing over her last question.

She squeezed her pencil. "I don't draw dragons anymore."

"Just women walking into . . . oh, excuse me . . . out of the ocean." His grin settled into a warm smile as he looked her in the eyes. He was holding the edge of the table, leaning his face dangerously close to hers, especially if he was still dating Carly. She inched away from him. "Looks like you found her happy ending after all," he said, standing tall again.

Relaxing, Naomi set down her pencil and motioned for him to sit across from her. When he was settled, she picked up her fork and cut off a piece of almond cake. "It's not as good as Java's," she said, sliding the fork into her mouth, "but you're welcome to share it with me if you'll tell me what the heck you're doing here." She chewed slowly, waiting.

Finn unwrapped a set of silverware from a napkin and pulled out a fork. "Well, it's a long story," he began in a once-upon-a-time tone of voice. He cut off his own piece of cake. "It all started when I met a girl in a café. She was an artist, but she seemed unsure of herself, like me. I liked that, so I kept trying to break down her walls so we could be friends. After a while, when I realized I couldn't break down her walls, I tried climbing over them. It worked, kind of. We got to be friends. I liked her, but then . . ." He slid the bite of cake into his mouth and chewed.

"I should throw this pencil at your head," Naomi laughed, wishing he would finish the story already.

"Good cake," he said through his chewing. "Did you make it?"

She shrugged. "No, but I was the one who suggested they put it on the menu. It's one of their best sellers now. I think in a few months I might apply to move up in the kitchen."

Swallowing, Finn dug his fork into the cake for another bite. "Well, you have to start somewhere."

"Listen, Finn, I'm dying to know what you're doing here. Did you drive? Fly? How did you know when I would be here?"

"I flew, yeah. You already told me where you working, so I called your mom to get your schedule. Once I knew when you had a break, I thought it might be fun to surprise you."

"Why?"

He set down his fork, a smile playing on his lips. "May I finish my story?"

"Of course."

"Then," he continued in the same tone as before, "the girl said someone else wanted to help her over her walls and carry her to a place very far away. I was heartbroken, to say the least, but she'd warned me from the beginning she might leave, so I couldn't complain. I wallowed. It was pathetic. I decided I should try to get over the girl, so I attached myself to another one. I ended up liking her, kind of, but then you—that first girl I could never forget—came back. I was stuck and sad and obligated to someone else. So I waited and decided to tell the truth and break it off with the second girl, no matter what might happen after that. And here I am."

He looked into Naomi's eyes, making her heart thump so hard she looked down at her chest to make sure she was still in one piece.

"I didn't know that's why you hooked up with Carly," she said, breathless. "I thought you wanted to be with her. I thought even if I gave up Jesse you wouldn't want to be with me. I was a wreck. Who wants a wreck for a girlfriend?"

"Did you forget about that kiss on the train tracks? Did you forget how much I wanted you before?"

"No, I just thought—"

"You thought you weren't good enough for anyone just the way you are, and you're wrong. I don't know why you won't admit you went to Italy with Jesse, but I know you did. I know you went over there and realized you were running away from yourself."

She took a deep breath and rolled her pencil across her sketchpad. Finn could open her up like a book, but she didn't mind. "You're right," she said, looking up. "I did leave with him and it was wonderful and terrible at the same time."

Silence stretched between them. It seemed as wide as the Atlantic.

"When are you off work?" Finn asked. He seemed in no hurry to learn everything that had happened, and that was exactly why she liked him so much.

She looked at a clock on the far wall. "Forty-five minutes. My break is almost over, so I need to go."

Finn stood. "I'll wait outside . . . if that's okay?"

"Yes," she said, her heart still thumping, "that would be great."

* * *

He was outside, just as he said he would be. She walked with him to her mother's Mercedes and unlocked the doors. Once Finn was inside, she started the car and drove out to the main road. "So, where are you staying?

I can drop you off if you want. We can see each other tomorrow, right?" When he didn't answer, she looked over to see him blushing. *Blushing.* Her mouth dropped open. "You're staying at my parents' house, aren't you?"

He nodded. "Your mom picked me up at the airport, and then after I dropped my stuff off at the house and picked a room, she drove me to the café. She said she didn't want me to have to pay for cabs."

"I'm going to kill her."

He laughed as he leaned forward to fiddle with the radio. He found a station playing similar music to what they had danced to in the club the night of her birthday. "Don't blame your parents," he said, chuckling. "When I told them I would only be here tonight and tomorrow, they offered to let me stay. Your house has five guest bedrooms." He looked at her and shook his head. "*Five.* You can hardly blame your parents for offering."

Naomi squeezed the steering wheel and glanced at the tattoo on Finn's arm. It was as wicked looking as she remembered, with jagged swirls and dips surrounding it. "My mom didn't have a problem with your, uh—" She pointed to the tattoo.

"She didn't seem to mind. She asked me a lot of questions when I called her before coming. I told her about what happened between us and how I wanted to fly out here to see if you'd be interested in getting back together."

Naomi stopped at a red light. "If I say I'm interested, will you want me to move back to Harvard?" She looked at Finn, studying his strong jawline and the way his chin jutted out a little when he was thinking.

"We could try to keep up a relationship long-distance if you want to stay here. I can't leave Harvard for a while."

The light turned green and it took Naomi a few seconds too long to move forward. The car behind her started honking. Finn laughed.

"Shut up," she teased, smiling. "I know you can't leave Harvard. I wouldn't ask you to do that."

"And I wouldn't ask you to leave your parents and your job if you don't want to."

She drove carefully—too carefully. Cars started passing her until she entered the coastal highway and rolled down her window. Cool air filled the car, whipping through her and Finn's hair. The longer she drove in silence, the more she appreciated Finn's patience with her. He rolled down his window too and rested his arm on the door. He looked out at the ocean glittering in the moonlight, the salty smell of it thick in the air.

"I love it here," she said, unsure if Finn could hear her over the wind.

"I like it too," he answered. "I have some cousins north of here, on my mom's side."

"Oh, yeah, you mentioned that before."

"I won't be at Harvard forever."

"True."

Out of the corner of her eye, she saw him turn to look at her. It was a good feeling to know she didn't have to rely on him for her own emotional stability—a new feeling that made her feel free for the first time. She would be fine without him, but she also knew how much better her life could be with him.

"I want to be with you, Finn," she said as he watched her. "I can't decide right now if I'll go or stay, but I want to be with you, whatever I choose."

"Maybe you could get a job at Java," he suggested with a teasing look in his eye.

"Yeah, maybe. Or maybe I could open my own café," she laughed. "Except I'd have to figure out how to get Eric's scrambled eggs just right."

Finn tapped his fingers on the door. "Sharp cheddar," he said, looking out at the ocean. "Have you tried that?"

"Cheese?" Her breath stopped in her throat for a moment. "You mean in the eggs?"

"Yeah, shredded. You dump it into the eggs when you scramble them up. Gives them a tangy flavor."

That was what she had been missing. "How do you know that?"

"Experimenting. I've been cooking a lot since you were gone. I got tired of ramen noodles and you weren't around to feed me anymore."

She made an exaggerated eye-roll. "Always goes back to food, huh?"

"Well, shouldn't it?"

"It's definitely at the top of my love list." She rounded a bend in the road. There was a pull-off coming up, and when she spotted it, she eased the car off the road and parked. Switching off the engine, she stared out the windshield at the ocean, the sound of the waves a whooshing heartbeat in the otherwise quiet night.

"What's this about?" Finn asked, turning in his seat to face her.

She undid her seatbelt and got out of the car. "There's a trail down to the beach," she said, breathing in the cool, salty air. She remembered all those walks on the beach with Brad, those stupid bonfire parties where everyone would sit around and get drunk. She remembered Jesse reading to her from The *Great Gatsby*, the way her last goodbye to him was nothing more than a glance as she climbed into the cab. She remembered the train tracks and how it would always be difficult to decide which direction to go when there were so many 'ifs' and 'maybes' hanging in the air. But she had the freedom to choose. She knew now that her past had to become a part of her.

When Finn came around to her side of the car, she was already taking off her shoes. "I thought we were going back to your house," he said, a smile playing on his lips.

She moved closer to him, her bare feet crunching over asphalt and sand. She took his hand into hers and squeezed. "I changed my mind."

His playful smile widened. "Then the beach sounds great."

They started down the trails. Once on the beach, they approached wet sand and Finn bent down to pull off his tennis shoes. Tipping one upside down, he laughed as a waterfall of sand fell out. He pulled off his other shoe, rolled his jeans up around his ankles, and left both shoes in the sand as he straightened to face Naomi. "You're pretty in the moonlight."

She blushed, but knew he wouldn't be able to see it. "Thanks."

"Do you want to keep walking?"

"Yeah."

He took her hand and they continued up the beach, inching their way closer to the waves.

"When I was a kid," Naomi said as sand squished between her toes, "I used to jump up and down on the wet sand. It always felt like the top layer was floating over something solid underneath. You know how it sometimes jiggles when you walk on it? Then, if I stood still long enough, I'd start to sink until I couldn't see my feet anymore. I always thought if I stood still long enough, I'd sink to China."

Laughing, Finn squeezed her hand and pulled her to a stop. "Let's see if we can sink to China, then." He faced her so their toes were touching, and then stood motionless, staring down. Naomi did the same, giggling as her toes started to disappear. Cool seawater rushed across their feet, washing away sand, but making it even softer so their feet sank deeper.

Smirking, Finn wrapped his arms around her to hold her close.

"Think you've caught me?" she teased.

Laughing, he leaned down to kiss her on the mouth. He still smelled like the Java Lounge. Cinnamon rolls. Whipped cream. It made her want to melt into him.

"Thanks, Finn," she said, looking up as the kiss ended. His hair hung around his face.

"For kissing you?"

"For being patient with me, for loving who I am and not wanting me to change. I think anyone else would push me to go to USC or something."

He knotted his brow. "Why would they do that?"

"Because art is what I've always loved and wanted. It's my *thing*, you know? So, isn't that what I'm supposed to do?"

He lifted his hand and cupped her face. "Nope, you're supposed to do what feels right for *you*, even if that's working in a café washing dishes."

She smiled. "Even if it meant running off to Italy when everyone else knew it was wrong?"

He nodded. "Everyone else doesn't know what's right for you, including me. When I didn't want you to leave, it was because I was being selfish. I wanted you for myself, but I knew you had to figure things out on your own, even if that meant I never saw you again. So I was a jerk and started dating Carly to get over you. I think the only reason I liked her was because she was an artist, like you. It wasn't fair to her at all. I used her."

"But you broke it off and now you're here."

"Yeah, I couldn't drag it out anymore. She wasn't too upset, but I still feel bad."

Naomi looked down at her feet, now buried. She could feel Finn's toes wiggling against hers. "Probably as bad as I feel about Jesse," she said.

Finn was quiet for a minute as he pulled his feet free of the sand. There was a soft sucking sound, and then a big hole where he had stood. "Want to keep walking?" he asked, nodding to her feet as he held out his hand.

"With you, yes."

Taking his hand to stabilize herself, she yanked one foot out, and then the other. As Finn led her up the beach, she glanced behind her shoulder. There were two sets of footprints being washed away by the ceaseless waves, the moonlight sparkling as it slid across the smooth surface of the sand.

Naomi's journey continues in Unbroken.

Thank you for reading Pieces. *Please consider leaving an honest review on Amazon.com, Goodreads, your blog, or another form of social media. Reviews can dramatically boost visibility for a published book, effectively increasing sales and allowing an author to continue their craft—and you to continue reading!*

ABOUT THE AUTHOR

Michelle lives and writes surrounded by the Rocky Mountains, where she finds every excuse possible to go hiking and be outdoors. Michelle mainly writes contemporary fiction, but occasionally branches into other genres.

Printed in Great Britain
by Amazon